D1522059

ISBN#: 0-9774103-0-7

Cover concept by **Dion Jones, Wylena
Wilkerson, Vonetta Anthony.**
Cover photo by **Dalton Hall, Dizon Productions**
Cover model, Sean Fleming
Cover design by **Sandy Petrie, Zig Zag Design
Studio**

PUBLISHING
Home of the Author

**Penhouse Publishing
P.O. Box 820
Lovejoy, GA 30250**

Penhouse Publishing is a registered trademark.

Printed in the United States of America
April, 2006

DEDICATIONS

*To my mother, Carolyn Easley, this one's for you
mom. You said I do my best work under pressure.*

*To Vonetta & Wylena, you two are wonderful! We
did it! The "A" team.
Thank You.*

They say, life is so harsh that people who can manufacture romance or conjure up fantasy are similar to an oasis in the desert, many will flock to them. It is also said that there's great power in tapping into the fantasies of the masses.

If any of this is at all true, then this is from me to you.

Cum, follow me.

MANDINGO LOVE

CHAPTER LIST

CHAPTERS

1

"THE JOURNEY OVER"

*I*t was the early 80's, and many people were still upset over Nelson Mandela being locked up for trying to help a people who desperately needed it. But not Martzu Demarco Poitier, for he knew there was no fight without casualty. Besides, he knew Mandela had chosen his path and must walk it. Martzu had his mind elsewhere. He had a baby on the way and a beautiful wife, De'shawntu. His thoughts were to move his wife and baby to the free world, North America. He had dreams of moving to the United States and working hard for his family. He wanted to send his child to college so he could become successful.

Martzu only had one small problem. He knew being a direct descendant of the great and well-known Mandingo tribe of the Kongo, he was next in line to be tribal leader. His wife, De'shawntu being an original descendant from the Pygmy tribe (the same tribe as Eve of the bible), was also to be the next leader of her tribe. Yet, this did not stop Martzu's decision to move to the states and seek a new life. If the Americans were anything like he had heard, it would be what he was looking for.

De'shawntu wasn't sure about the move; however, she loved her husband and would never dispute a decision he made. Not to mention, no one ever did. Martzu was 6'7", 245lbs and extremely well built. A giant compared to the small frame of his wife De'shawntu, who was only 5'4", and 120lbs. Martzu was an extremely dark man, with strong features. If you didn't know any better, at first glance, you would have thought he was chiseled from a black marbled stone. De'shawntu spoke with her husband about his decision one more time, for she knew for either of them to leave the tribe, was to go against the laws of both tribes. Many of the laws were inviolable and to leave was one thing, but moving to another country was altogether different. Her being a jurist of both tribes, she made sure her husband was also aware.

De'shawntu was supportive of her husband's decisions for she knew he was judicious when it came to their well-being, for he was sapient. Also, it would give her the chance to have her husband to herself, for he was a well sought after man amongst the Mandingo and other African tribes. You see, the Mandingos were blessed, and every female knew it for they had the purist bloodline, a desire to work hard, and the largest penises in all of Africa. De'shawntu never believed the rumors she heard growing up about the Mandingos. And it was not until she married Martzu that she found out first hand what the Mandingo man was truly equipped with.

After the wedding ceremony, it was truly time for them to go off alone. De'shawntu was afraid to give up her virginity, but happy all the same, for Martzu was a good catch and a wonderful man. She would never forget the night, as they lay there by the fire under the stars. The time had come. As Martzu was about to enter her love mound, De'shawntu looked down and thought to herself, *"My God! It is as a tree branch."*

She remembered telling Martzu, *"Surely, it can't fit inside of me."*

He said nothing, and began working his magic of making love to her. All the while he was in her, it was painful, but she loved him and so she dealt with the pain of pleasure.

De'shawntu said to Martzu, *"This is too much for me."*

All he said was, *"In time you will be able to handle it. And it will be as nothing to you."*

It was the one time Martzu lied to her, or he did not know what he was talking about, because two years later and after many episodes of love making, when he enters her, it feels like the first time, a continuous deliverance of pain and overwhelming pleasure. It hurt her, but he knew what he was doing every time, he had been taught well. De'shawntu loved her mate, and his lovemaking turned her into a sadist because despite the pain, she couldn't get enough.

Soon, they would be in the United States and she would have him to herself, away from the other women who desired him. See, although she didn't like it, their traditions and way of life allowed Martzu to have a wife and concubines. But not in America, she wouldn't have to worry about that. She couldn't wait.

As they sat in the airplane, waiting for their flight to take off, they couldn't help discuss the departure ceremony they attended earlier. Although, many of the members of both tribes were set on being sanctimonious, the Elders were salubrious. And that was most important to both of them. During the ceremony, the Elders of the tribe told Martzu to be ever watchful of the child they were about to bear, for he would be the center of much attention. So much, that it would bring overwhelming recognition amongst those in the States.

Martzu figured there was no need for worry, because the Elders always had visions. Some would warrant attention, others would not. He also felt there was no need to worry De'shawntu with this, because tomorrow this time they will be in the great *U.S. of A*! New life and a new baby!

* * * * * * * * * * * * * * * * * *

The flight to America was 15 hours. They had one layover to switch planes in which they waited about 2 hours to do so. Surprisingly, to De'shawntu, her husband being a man of few words spoke all the way. This let her know not only was he happy with the decision he made, he was also very excited and looking forward to their new life.

3

"So, my king," De'shawntu said with a smile on her face.

"What will we name the baby?" She was rubbing her stomach while waiting patiently for Martzu's answer.

She was so consumed with thoughts of the baby and how happy she was, she hadn't even noticed Martzu staring down at her from the seat his large frame occupied. As he looked over De'shawntu from head to toe, he thought to himself, what a beautiful being she was, a loving, caring, respectable woman. One who devoted her complete self to him. She never once allowed herself to become disobedient to him. He was surely pleased with her, in the couple of years they had been married she had done more than he could ask to make him happy. Yes, with De'shawntu, Martzu was pleased, very pleased.

He thought of how she even put up with the other women from the Mandingo and other neighboring tribes who set out to bed him. Many of them he had his way with and others he refused. He had come to notice De'shawntu's reaction when he would tell her another woman wanted him or he had bedded another woman. He wasn't sure if it angered her or turned her on.

Whichever, it's as if she just wanted to show him he needed no other woman, for when he would tell her, she would literally begin climbing on him, kissing him, sucking him, she would make love to him like an untamed she-lion. Throughout the night or day, which ever one it was, it was at these moments he realized De'shawntu would release her hidden virtuoso on him, it was so pleasing to him he would come home sometimes and just lie concerning his day.

For instance, there was a time when he had been working all day and nothing more had taken place, but, he was desiring to sleep with her but she was still sore from two days earlier. So, when he arrived home, De'shawntu asked him how was his day?

"Fine!" He exclaimed. *"Only when I was leaving work, Amiyna runs out, grabs my arm, and tells me if I bed her she would prepare me a meal fit for a King."*

At the thought of another woman wanting to bed Martzu, De'shawntu dropped what she was doing, forgot her vagina was still sore, and began sexing Martzu. He felt bad for lying to her, but, he could not help it, her sweet, tender pussy was something Martzu could not get enough of, and him being De'shawntu's first and only she fit him like a glove every time.

There were times he felt sorry for her. When he would finish making love to her, on occasion, he would look down at her petite frame and couldn't help but notice how swollen the lips on her vagina would be. It was as if they were turned over inside out, bright pink with a hint of red from the friction of intercourse. And her vaginal hole would be so wide open you would think a ripe melon had sat there for days and then fell out leaving the vagina stretched open. Yes, many a time he had looked down at her sweet pussy gapped open, as if a person's mouth would if they were gawking at something that had surprised the hell out of them. Martzu knew she would never get used to the size of his manhood. He was a Mandingo, and no woman ever did who had a Mandingo man.

His own mother had 9 children from her womb and his father still delivered what she refers to as the "Thunder Rod from the Gods." Many a time, Martzu remembered at dinner his mother would say…, *"We bed early tonight, the 'Thunder Rod' will be upon me,"* as she smiled and winked at his older sister, who apparently got the little joke. She would giggle and wink back. It had never been heard of a woman to get used to a Mandingo.

Well once, Martzu remembered, when he was 15, there had been a woman. At times he heard his father and grandfather speak of this woman. This woman was handling several of the men from the Mandingos to the point that they had brought forth "Kong Mato!" He was said to be the greatest in Mandingo history. It was said he was 14 inches long and 4 inches around. However, even he was easily accepted into her, what had to be a dungeon cunt. Rumor had it, she even took "Kong's" 14 inches in her anus. Afterwards, it was said she had to use a specially made cork to plug it. They say the woman just disappeared into thin air. More than likely, they banned her from coming around.

His grandfather would say, *"She has a demon cunt, sent to bring the Mandingo man down."*

"Ha!" Martzu thought. His father and grandfather could make up what fables they so pleased, as his mother would say, *"The woman is no good. Known in America as a 'Stank Booty Ho!"* Yes, Martzu had remembered hearing this term.

"So Martzu," De'shawntu said, interrupting his long drawn out daydream that had him somewhat aroused.

"What did you say? What is it sweetheart?" Martzu asked. De'shawntu looking up in his eyes, curious of what he may have been thinking. She patted him on his swollen manhood and repeated the question.

"So, what will we name the baby, my King?"

"Ahh! My Queen," Martzu said looking in her eyes with a smile that assured her he was pleased with his mate. *"We shall name him a name that has a combination of both our names. Because he will have us both in him."*

"That is true, and fine with me," De'shawntu said.

"And I know what part of you he'll have," laughing as she reached over and stroked his manhood, one more time they both looked at each other and smiled. De'shawntu quickly snatched her hand away as she caught the stare of an elderly white woman sitting across from them, with who appeared to be her husband sleeping with his mouth opened. The woman stared at Martzu with obvious admiration. Knowing he was a

Mandingo aboriginal, the elderly white woman's eyes gleamed with desire.

"What was she thinking?" De'shawntu thought.

Martzu knew exactly what she was thinking, how could she get a piece of this sweet dark meat of the Mandingo. His father had long since warned him about these women. How they would drive around the village in their expensive safari trucks, offering great amounts of money to any male Mandingo who would even look their way. Young, old, it didn't matter. Once a 12-year-old Mandingo boy was approached. This had the Elders in an uproar! They chased the lady away by hurling huge stones at her expensive truck. However, it didn't stop them from coming and offering money in order to be bedded by a Mandingo.

Martzu's father said, *"To sleep with them, would bring a curse upon whomever did."*

That was enough for Martzu. He needed no such thing in his life, true or not. So, he never thought twice about it.

Again, Martzu's thoughts were interrupted. This time, by the voice over the speaker of the airplane, instructing all passengers to buckle their seatbelts and prepare for landing.

"We are now entering Columbus, Ohio's air strip," the voice said over the intercom. De'shawntu leaned over and looked out the window, as the airplane steadied its decline.

"Wow," De'shawntu thought, *"This is amazing!"* For she had never been on a plane before. Hell, she had never been out the small village she was raised in, for that matter. Her first time out of the village, and not only does she leave on a plane, she's traveling to another country. Altogether, she was overwhelmed and excited about the whole idea of her new life, with her husband and new child. The flight took many hours, but they finally arrived.

"Hey, America!" She thought, as she stared out the window.

Skriiiich!!! Screeech! Was the sound the tires made as the Bowing 747 touched down on the runway, coming in for landing.

"Finally, we are here," Martzu said to himself, *"America. In the Capitol city of Ohio, Columbus."* Martzu initially thought of moving to New York City. Then the thought of L.A., California crossed his mind. However, close friends had informed him of the hustle and bustle and dealing with the fast pace life of both cities. He was assured that was not what he wanted for his new family. So, he settled on Columbus, Ohio, a good place to have a family, and raise a child. Looking over at his beautiful wife he said, *"We are here, my Queen!"*

"Yes, we are," De'shawntu, responded as she returned his glance, with a big Kool-Aid smile. As they strolled hand in hand through the airport, Martzu decided to give his wife the good news.

"My Queen," he said.

"Yes, my King," De'shawntu replied, as she skipped a couple steps to keep up with Martzu, who was walking at a pace that would have made you think he knew where he was going.

"My Queen, you know I have set out to be the best mate I could be to you from the very start," said Martzu.

"Yes, you have," responded De'shawntu, eager to hear what Martzu had to say.

"Well," Martzu paused… *"Along with having a job already waiting for me, I also was able to make the necessary arrangements for us to also have a small house waiting on us. Thanks to my brother, Martum. Good hunh?"* Martzu said excitingly. As he looked over to his wife, hoping to see the same look of excitement upon her face. But, no, De'shawntu did not have a look of excitement in her eyes, nor a look of happiness. No, instead Martzu saw a look of extreme bewilderment in

8

De'shawntu's eyes. Whatever it was, caused De'shawntu to stop dead in her tracks. As she began to squeeze Martzu's hand, his mind started racing.

"What?! What is it?! Speak to me my Queen!" Martzu demanded. Martzu's words were as a muffle of babbling to De'shawntu, as she reached and held her stomach tightly, her eyes looking to Martzu with a look of confusion. People passing by stopped and stared at the two. Martzu looking his wife up and down for an answer, stopped his evaluation when he noticed what appeared to be urine trickling down her legs, and over her ankles. Before Martzu could register what was taking place, a woman yelled, *"Quick! Her water broke! She's about to have the baby!"* Martzu's eyes spread as wide as golf balls.

"Not here," he thought. *"Not in the airport!"*

The woman grabbed De'shawntu's hand and began pulling her through the crowd of curious onlookers. Martzu realized his wife was unable to keep up with the lady who was moving rather quickly.

"Where are you taking my wife!?" Martzu questioned in a puzzled yet demanding tone.

"To a hospital," the lady responded as she looked over her shoulder at Martzu trailing behind his wife. She gave him a kind of wide-eyed look with her nose scrunched up, as if to say, you must be crazy for asking that question. The lady quickly hit the exit door, flinging it open. Still pulling De'shawntu by the hand. Martzu close on his wife's coattail as they rushed outside, the lady threw her hand in the air waving and let out a high-pitched whistle, and yelled, *"Taxi!"* As they climbed into the taxicab the lady told the driver, *"OSU Hospital, quick!"*

She then looked over at Martzu and said sarcastically with a look of disbelief on her face, *"You are aware your wife is about to have a baby, aren't you?"*

Martzu detecting the lady's attempt to slight him responded by saying, *"Yes, I am aware and have been for the last 9 months,"* with a hint of anger in his voice.

"Were you ready for this?" The lady asked.

"Yes, I have been instructed by the elder women of my tribe on how to properly deliver my child."

"And you were going to do this at the airport I take it?" The lady asked again, being sarcastic.

"I was prepared to, if need be." Martzu said.

"At the airport?" The lady repeated.

"Yes," said Martzu.

"Goodness gracious," the lady thought to herself.

The cab driver looked in his rear view mirror and mumbled, *"Get the fuck outta here,"* as he looked at Martzu and De'shawntu. De'shawntu moaned.

"I'm Connie," the young lady offered as she finally took a good look at the foreign couple. It was then she realized how large a man Martzu was, and how petite De'shawntu was. *"How could she handle a man his size?"* Connie wondered. Her thoughts interrupted by Martzu.

"I am Martzu Poitier, and this is my beautiful wife De'shawntu."

"AAAAAAH, OHHHHH!" De'shawntu yelled out as if she was about to have the baby.

Connie yelled at the taxi driver, *"YOU'D BETTER HURRY UP, UNLESS YOU WANT A BABY DELIVERED IN YOUR CAB!"*

She put her hand over her mouth to cover up the smile, after realizing how loud she was.

The thought of a crying newborn baby and blood all over the backseat of his cab made the driver step on it. The cab zoomed through the quiet streets.

Things happened so fast Martzu couldn't help but think about their luggage and other belongings.

"Oh, well," he thought, *"I'll retrieve them later."*

* * * * * * * * * * * * * * * * * *

10

MANDINGO LOVE

Much time had gone by, 17 years to be exact, and Martzu and De'shawntu were pleased to have De'marco. De'shawntu constantly reminded Martzu of how she felt he tricked her when it came to De'marco's name. At the hospital they couldn't come up with a name that was a combination of both their names. At least, not one that sounded right, so Martzu told De'shawntu he had an idea. When he came back in the hospital room after, filling out the papers for the birth certificate he handed them to De'shawntu with eyes wide and an enormous smile on his face and said, *"Well, what do you think, my Queen?"*

De'shawntu's smile turned into a smirk when she realized all Martzu had done was taken his first and middle name and changed them around and gave them to the child, *"De'marco Martzu Poitier."*

De'shawntu said to herself', then out loud, *"If this is what you want my King, so it is,"* appearing somewhat melancholy at the moment but yet accepting.

"I like it," Connie had said at that time, *"A male child having the fathers' name is a great thing!"* She exclaimed.

It was then, Martzu realized he might just like this Connie lady who helped get them to the hospital in time to have the baby. Although there was a little friction in the initial meeting, De'shawntu and Martzu came to like Connie. And to show their thanks, once they got settle in, they invited Connie over on occasion. Martzu was shocked when he found out, at the time Connie was just about to turn nineteen years old.

"She is rather mature for an American female," he thought. Nonetheless, over the years Connie played babysitter to De'marco when De'shawntu and Martzu needed to both be away on business or even a romantic outing. Connie told them places to go, things to do, they learned the city of Columbus by way of her instructions.

At the time Connie was attending hair school, and the money she received from babysitting, though it wasn't much, it helped.

They didn't see much of Connie nowadays, seeing they no longer had a need for a babysitter. De'marco was a senior at St. DeSales High School, a private Catholic School Martzu paid good money for him to attend and receive a well-to-do education. Besides, Connie finished and graduated from hair school and met a young man who helped her open three nice hair parlors around town at one time. Martzu suspected the young man might have been involved in something illegal, because of all the nice things he had, and bought for Connie. His suspicion was found to be true. One evening when De'shawntu had handed him the local paper, the young man had made the front page, *"Local Black Man, Sylvester Fountain a.k.a. Sly, Arrested On Drug Charges,"* is what it read.

"Shame," Martzu thought, although Connie known to be his girlfriend, (along with others), was not involved.

She never spoke of the incident; neither did Martzu and his wife. They had even heard the young man owed some type of gambling debt that Connie made good on for him. How she did it? That was another question they never asked. They figured she could handle it, as she did many circumstances over the years. Besides, she was surviving and doing well, that's all that mattered. Connie seemed to be a young Black American female living her own life, in her own world, and having no quarrels about it.

At times they wondered how she made it through, for she never spoke of her parents. And as with so many other things, she never brought it up. And, neither did they.

After years of anticipation the moment Martzu waited and worked so hard for was drawing near. Demarco's graduation was just months away. You would think Martzu himself was graduating. However, he was just looking forward to being a more proud and happier father. Just as he had been on several other occasions, like when De'marco made the Honor Roll each grading period while he attended St. Augustine Jr. High School, and up until this very day he's had perfect attendance.

It was only spring, and Martzu was thinking of his sons' graduation plans. As he sat in his favorite chair, he looked over to his wife.

"My Queen," he said, *"Have you called your friends for De'marco's' graduation?"*

"Yes, Dear," De'shawntu said, *"And for the thousandths time its really too early to call people for a High School graduation that's months away,"* reminded De'shawntu.

"Yeah, maybe so. But it's always good to plan ahead. By the way, don't forget to call Connie. I'm sure she would love to come. Besides, with the busy schedule she has running those shops, I'm sure she needs advance notice," replied Martzu.

"Okay, baby, I'll call her," De'shawntu said, at the same time turning her nose up. She had often wondered about her husband and Connie. It seems he was always willing to help her. However, she didn't look too deep into it. She figured he was just trying to be kind since she did help at the airport. She picked up the phone and dialed Connie's cell phone.

After the third ring a voice answered, *"House of Beauty, this is cutie!!"*

"Connie is that you?" De'shawntu asked. Immediately, picking up on the accent, *"Yes, it is Darling!"* Connie responded cheerfully. *"And how can I help ya?"* She said.

"Well, Martzu and I wanted to see if you would like to come to Demarco's graduation?"

"Sure!" Connie said excitingly. *"Well, hey, tell me something…"*

"Yes..." De'shawntu said, listening attentively.

"Who's idea was it to call four months in advance?"
She asked in a humorous tone.

"You know," De'shawntu said.

"Big Daaaddy?!?" Connie said in a high pitch squeaky tone. *"No problem, send me an invitation, and I'll make it happen."*

"Okay, we'll send one out to ya. Let me allow you to get back to work." Said De'shawntu.

"Okay De'shawntu," Connie said, *"And thanks for calling. Smooches!"*

The phone hung up and De'shawntu turned around to Martzu who was still sitting in his chair.

"She said she'll make it."

"That's good," Martzu said, *"We don't have many relatives in the states. However, plenty enough friends will be there."*

"Yes, that's true," De'shawntu said, still thinking of how she really didn't care for Connie calling her husband "Big Daddy." Giving Martzu a puzzled stare, as if he were an enigma.

De'shawntu said, *"Well let me get your dinner started, Big Daaaddy!"*

She looked over her shoulder at Martzu for a response as she walked off. Martzu heard the words stumble out her mouth and had wondered where they came from. However, he didn't ponder on it long for he was too consumed in his thoughts, he had come to America to make a way for his family, and to see his son go to college and the day was nearing.

He also remembered what the Elders told him at the departure ceremony. He was wondering if that was drawing near. If so, he welcomed it.

Martzu was happy and proud. He missed his village and the ways of the Mandingo, but America is not bad, not bad at all, he thought to himself.

2

"GROWING UP NAÏVE"

*I*t was Friday and De'marco was glad. He looked forward to this weekend, and was excited. After school he walked hurriedly across the parking lot to catch the city bus. As he reached the bus stop he peeked at his watch and realized he was early. He had a few minutes before the bus came. He began to wander into his thoughts. He was relieved, today was the last day to take the math tutoring class. Although, it was his idea to take the class in the first place, he was happy it was over. He took the class to get more credits although he had the required amount to graduate. De'marco was like this ever since his father had that long talk with him, telling him in life always do more than what's asked of you. So he did every chance he got.

"Because nothing in life is free, my son. Everything has a price. You will pay for things intentionally, or unintentionally. This, my son, is the law of nature and it can not be escaped." De'marco remembered these words clearly, and lived by them. He neither asked nor received anything without paying for it, in some way earning it.

"De'marco!" A voice yelled, snapping him out of his thought. He looked and who did he see walking down Karl Road towards him?!? Jennifer. Jennifer Dyson.

"Yep, it was her," he thought, as she walked towards him. He studied her frame. She had nice shoulders, practically no waist, and hips out of this world!! When she walked she had a stride that was so enticing. At times, when she was in a giddy mood, she walked on her tippy toes and reminded him of a little squirrel.

However, today, she looked like a seductress. And as she got closer, the look in her eyes make De'marco's heart beat faster. Her pretty face and brown skin, those

15

sexy full lips and almond-shaped eyes always did something to him.

"Hi!" Jennifer said as she came close to De'marco, giving him a hug and as she leaned into him, raised her leg, causing her knee to bump the tip of his manhood, as she always did. He wondered about this. Ever since that day, she had been doing this to him.

"Hi, Jennifer!" He said, somewhat nervous, *"How's it going?"* He added.

"Good," she said, *"And you?"*

"Great!" De'marco replied, *"Today was my last day in the math class."*

Jennifer frowned her lips, *"Good for you. Not that you needed it. You have the credits needed to graduate."* De'marco couldn't help but stare at the girl's large hips.

"Yeah, you're right, but it didn't hurt anything," he said.

Jennifer caught him looking. *"Yeah, okay, whatever you say Mr. Over Achiever,"* she said while twisting flirtingly as to give him a quick glimpse of her rear end. De'marco took a deep breath as he blushed; he turned his head so Jennifer wouldn't see. He caught sight of the COTA bus about 3 blocks away.

"Here she comes!" He said out loud.

Jennifer not paying much attention to him, as she was absorbed in her own little fantasy, as she looked De'marco up and down from the back. His 6'2" frame with his broad shoulders that looked as though the muscles from his neck and shoulders had been carved from stone, his large hands at the end of his long, strong arms. She wanted to jump on his back and suck his neck. Every female in school had decided De'marco had the best body of all the guys. He even got voted in the top 3 most attractive guys in the school. And Jennifer was determined to get him. She thought, *"Oh, yeah, fo sho!"*

He had no idea how bad she wanted him, but he would find out one day soon. She always found him to be attractive and rightfully so. She admired his large frame, masculine body, and handsome face, with a hint of his mother in him.

"Oh, yeah, he is fine as all get back!" She thought.

And every since that day, the thought of him made her shake and get chills all over.

So caught up in her little fantasy, she didn't even hear De'marco speaking to her until he touched her on the shoulder. It was at that point; she realized how tight she had been holding her books. Not to mention, how tight she was squeezing her legs together. She looked in his eyes and regained her focus.

"What's up?" He said, *"You going? Here comes the bus. You got change or you want me to pay for you?"* She took too long to answer.

"Don't worry. I got it," De'marco said with a smile as the bus pulled in front of where they were standing. As it stopped, you could hear the hiss from the air brakes as the door opened.

De'marco stepped to the side and with a gesture of his hand smiled at Jennifer, and said, *"Ladies first."* She smiled and stepped on the bus. De'marco was close behind her. He dropped in the change.

"Two transfers, please." He said as the door closed behind him. He made his way to the seat and sat down beside Jennifer. The engine of the bus revved as it pulled away from the curb.

"Here's your transfer," De'marco said, holding out his hand with the transfer in it.

"You know I don't need a transfer," Jennifer said.

"Yeah, that's right. You get off a couple blocks up."

De'marco often wondered why she caught the bus only a few blocks, when she could have walked.

"Lazy," he thought to himself.

As if reading his thoughts, *"I'm not lazy or anything,"* Jennifer said blatantly, *"Just wanted to be next to you,*

Big Daddy," she said rubbing on his thigh, making him uncomfortable.

Although he enjoyed it he didn't know how to respond to this kind of attention from females. Nope, not at all. He was totally naïve to the whole male/female relationship thing. All throughout school since 7th grade, he'd have females do everything from rub on him, blow kisses, and pinch his behind. Yep, sure did and all he ever did was blush or come out the mouth clumsily with a remark that did not even fit. Like, *"Oh, ah, thanks,"* or, *"I'm sorry."*

The girls would laugh at him. And a lot of the females went from Jr. High School to High School right with him. However, the flirting did not stop.

"Ding! Ding!" Was the sound as Jennifer pulled the string for her stop.

"Well, this is my stop," she said, nudging De'marco's leg with hers, so he would move to let her get off. *"So, I'll see you Monday?!?"* She said askingly.

"Yes, at school," De'marco answered, puzzled as to why she'd make such a remark, knowing they both had school on Monday and the two of them never missed a day. The bus stopped and De'marco stood up to let Jennifer by. She stood up quickly, and to his surprise, planted a soft wet kiss right on his lips. At the same time, she was pushing a piece of paper in his front pants pocket. As she pulled away, she allowed her hand to brush across the front of his pants, purposely touching his manhood.

"Call me," she said in a gleeful tone.

As quickly as it all happened, she spun on her heels and exited the bus. De'marco sat back in his seat and peered out the window. Jennifer was waving happily. He waved back, until the bus pulled away. He then reached into his pocket and pulled out the piece of paper. It had her name and number with a heart over the letter "I" where a dot should have been.

"Looks like you have an admirer!" The bus driver yelled back at De'marco. *"And not a bad looking one at that,"* he added. De'marco didn't know what to do or how to take it. The attention was welcomed, and made him feel good inside, however, he wasn't sure where it all was heading. For the rest of the bus ride home De'marco thought deeply on this attention that had started in 7th grade up until now from the females he schooled with, Jennifer included. And thoughts continued on the walk home from the bus stop. Yes, he was a neophyte to all of this. Yet, he wanted to make sure it wasn't him just over thinking things.

As for what he remembered, everything was normal up through Jr. High. The flirting was trivial, a word or two, here and there. Every now and then, a female would call out his name or give a yuppie, *"Hello, De'marco,"* in passing, through the school hallways. Everything was normal, up until about the tenth grade.

From what he could recollect it was the time his father had come up to the school. His mother usually handled all De'marco's school matters, payments, PTA meetings, parent-teacher conferences, etc. His father worked so hard, he rarely had time for such matters. Except for one time in particular. His mother wasn't feeling well and the payment for school was due. So, De'marco's dad said he would take the payment in, as well as give De'marco a ride to school this day. It was a day to remember and one that boosted his popularity amongst the students and teachers alike.

He and his father stepped from the 2001 Navigator SUV, and walked past the front of the school, where other students were getting off of the school buses. Heads were turning from every direction, not that it was anything new. All the kids looked when someone showed up with their parents. Sometimes, someone might even yell, *"Aaaah, you in trouble!"* jokingly.

But for some reason, today was different. Students and teachers not only looked, but also stared! As

19

De'marco and his father walked by the front admissions office, some people even had their mouths hanging open. It wasn't until they approached the front desk that De'marco realized what everyone was gawking at. It never occurred to him, seeing that he lived with his father all his life, and was around him everyday. Besides, his father never had to come to the school before today.

As his father stepped through the office door. He ducked down, so his head would not bump the doorframe. And he slightly turned his body, as not to scrape his extremely broad shoulders on the sides of the door. As he stepped into the office, all the ladies eyes widened from the sight of him. Yes, he was a sight to see. His large 6'7", 248lb chiseled frame of solid natural muscle! Even in his older age, he had practically no waist. He walked self-assured, and had a look of confidence upon his face, that would have led you to believe he was one of the GODS spoken about in "Great Egyptian History." The look in his eyes showed power, and wisdom. He came across as if he could control an army with the wave of his hand.

As he stood at the front desk he looked around at the peering eyes waiting for someone to offer assistance. He looked at one of the two student helpers. She swallowed so hard you could hear it. And when he glanced over to the other for some reason, she raised her shoulders as if guilty of something. Her eyes already wide got wider and out of nowhere said, *"What do I do?"*

Realizing everyone's amazement, De'marco said… *"My father is here to pay on my tuition, who handles that?"*

Just at that moment the principal walked in. Although he too was amazed, he was able to keep his composure.

Noticing De'marco, he said, *"Your father, De'marco?!?"*

"Yes," he replied, *"He's here to pay on my tuition."*

"Ahh, I see," the principal said. He held out his hand to Martzu's and said, *"Good morning, I'm Principal Danmark. Joseph Danmark."*

As Martzu reached to return the greeting, everyone notice his large hand covered Principal Danmark's hand as if he were a baby!

"Good day to you Mr. Danmark. As you can see, I am De'marco's father, Martzu Poitier. I am here to pay for my sons' schooling."

"Right this way," Principal Danmark gestured.

Once they walked off and Principal Denmark's office door closed, everyone started speaking amongst themselves.

Jennifer, who was one of the student aides at the time, looked at De'marco with a big Kool-Aid smile and said... *"So De'marco you're going to be a very laaarge guy. Hhhmmm, how interesting..."* she said.

Although Martzu spent a relatively adequate amount of time in Principal Denmark's office, when he came out, students and surprisingly teachers also, stood around talking and acting like they were busy until Martzu walked out the front office with De'marco trailing behind.

"Pleasant day son. I'm off to work," Martzu said.

"See you at home dad."

Everyone watched Martzu's large frame all the way to the parking lot. As he drove off, everyone quickly turned to De'marco and began asking him who and what his father was, where he came from, and how he became so large?

De'marco wasn't sure how to take their questions. He had been asked where he was from before, but that was simple, 'cause he was born right here in Columbus, OH, at OSU hospital. When they would ask about his parents, he would just say, *"Africa."* But today everyone wanted in-depth information on his background. The day went by fast because of all the questions. There was even a class or two where the teacher stopped the lesson to inquire about De'marco's background. Returning to school the next day was even more of a challenge than the day before. Apparently, Martzu had explained his family background to Principal Denmark, letting him know he was of the "Tribe of the true Mandingo." Principal Denmark told everyone. It was the talk of the school for the whole week. Teachers and student asked continuous questions about the Mandingo ways. However, even that didn't cause what he was referring to as an over dose of female attention. Jennifer began to speak more often and became somewhat more aware of him.

Yet, *"Ah Haaa!"* He thought, *"That dreadful day in gym class..."*

De'marco remembered he was suppose to wear a sports cup under his shorts this day, but was unable to. So, outside of the exercise warm ups, the teacher had De'marco sit through the class and not participate, for not being properly dressing for class.

During class, Jennifer had convinced a couple of the guys to help her get a sneak picture of De'marco once he got dressed after class. She had no idea that De'marco always showered last and by himself, (personal reasons).

So, as some of them came out, they told her to go on in.

"Here he comes..." she thought nothing of it, as the other guys were dressed.

However, the guys had a trick up their sleeves. When she came, they threw the door open and some guys pushed De'marco in the open and pulled his towel off and took off running! He was so embarrassed he froze.

Jennifer's eyes got as big as golf balls and she yelled out, *"Oh, My God! Oh, My God! Oh, My God!"* As if in shock. She didn't even realize she had dropped her camera.

After that day, when he would be sitting in the library, lunchroom, or when he attended the football and basketball games, some girl always wanted to sit on his lap or be up under him. Females, also, began to whisper, and he would catch them sometime referring to him as "G.M.D." What it meant? He didn't know.

"Hey, son!" a voice called. *"You don't live here anymore, or what?"*

De'marco came out of his deep thought, looking up to realize he had been so caught up in his thought he had passed the house. His mother stood there puzzled by her son, who looked up at her, smiled, and shrugged his shoulders.

"Hey, mother," he spoke, as he walked up on the porch where she stood. He kissed her on the cheek and went on inside.

"Dinner will be ready in a minute!" She yelled out behind him.

"Okay, mom," he said, as he walked in the living room where Martzu was sitting in his favorite chair, smiling up at his son.

"Hi, dad!" De'marco greeted his dad.

"How's it going, son?" Martzu was proud and it showed every time he laid eyes on his son.

"Great, dad everything is great. Hey, I was wondering dad, if you had a moment, I could ask you a few questions?"

"Sure son, now is as good time as any. What's on your mind?"

"Well," De'marco paused, trying to choose his words wisely. He wanted to talk to his father about what he'd been experiencing lately with the females. And, he wasn't sure how he would take it, because his father always told him that wasn't important and what he needed to know about that would come soon enough.

Martzu, realizing his son's hesitance, cleared his throat in a gesture to get De'marco's attention.

"Well? Son, I'm listening."

"Well, dad I was wondering if you could give me a complete run down of our history of being Mandingos, and what the legend and mystery is all about?"

Martzu studied his son closely, looking him up and down. Catching a glimpse of his wife as she looked on curiously for Martzu's response to the inquiry on the subject.

"Is dinner ready my Queen?" Martzu asked, not looking in De'shawntu's direction.

De'shawntu was caught off guard thinking, because he didn't look in her direction, she hadn't been seen. She managed to stutter out, *"Y..y..yes my King. Dinner is ready."*

"Well?!?" Martzu said firmly.

Catching Martzu's reaction let her know, this wasn't a conversation she was welcomed to be in on. So, she hurried off into the kitchen.

* * * * * * * * * * * * * * * * * *

As everyone finished up dinner, De'shawntu asked would they care for dessert? They declined. Martzu had told De'marco they would speak more after dinner, and he was very anxious to indulge in the matter.

Martzu continued to study his son. He realized, as well as accepted, an inevitable reality. De'marco was becoming a young man, and one to be desired, as all Mandingo men were. So it was time to pass on to his son the information of the legendary Mandingo, their history, their gifts, their strengths.

"My son, let's have a talk," Martzu said to De'marco.

De'marco stood up from the table, looked excitingly at his father and said, *"After you!"* Martzu smiled and lead the way. De'shawntu looked at the two of them, as she cleaned the table.

"I'll be in the bedroom if either of you need me," she said sarcastically.

Martzu laughed, *"Okay, dear,"* he said, *"If things get rough, we'll call for you."*

You see, not even De'shawntu knew all there was to know about the Mandingo tribe.

"And just think," she said as her thoughts became words spoken out loud, *"I've been married to a Mandingo half my life and do not know all there is to know about the Mandingo man."* However, the part he shared and she did know, she surely enjoyed, *"...And we ain't talking about just the history, more like the gifts and the strengths,"* she said to herself, as she yelled out, *"Yes, Sirrr!"* Martzu and De'marco both looked toward the kitchen at this point.

"You okay in there, my Queen?" Martzu asked.

Realizing how carried away in her thoughts she'd gotten, De'shawntu thought, *"OOPS!"* She covered her hand over her mouth. However, she was still excited over the perverse thoughts she was entertaining about her husband.

She quickly yelled back, *"Think I ain't?!?"* She couldn't help but to laugh at her own antics as she walked down the hall to the bedroom. Telling herself, *"Girl you more than okay, you good to gizzo fo shizzo."* She once again laughed at what she'd said.

* * * * * * * * * * * * * * * * * *

The conversation between De'marco and his proud father carried on late into the evening. Several times Martzu would watch De'marco's actions closely, as he told him certain things. De'marco proved worthy of the knowledge for he sat and listened intently to each and every word his father spoke, and he only spoke when necessary.

"So there you have it. Now, you are aware of what people, especially women, think when they hear Mandingo. You are equally aware of what is expected of you by your family and Elders. Are you not?"

Martzu said to De'marco, as he finished up the conversation. De'marco smiled. He was happy to receive the information from his father.

"Thanks, Dad," De'marco said humbly.

Martzu stood. He looked over to his son, *"See you in the morning. I'm sure my Queen awaits me."* He said, as he gave a wink to De'marco, and disappeared down the hall.

* * * * * * * * * * * * * * * * * *

De'marco was up early as usual this Saturday. He knocked out all the tasks around the house he was responsible for. He showered and got dressed. He sat on the edge of his bed, staring at the piece of paper with Jennifer's name and number on it.

As he slowly picked up the receiver, he thought to himself, *"What will I say? What if she's not home?"*

He quickly stopped his ramblings. Realizing how silly he was being. He took a deep breath and dialed the number. After what seemed to be an eternity the phone was picked up, and the sound of a soft, but sleepy voice came through the line, *"Hello."*

Nervous De'marco asked, *"Is Jennifer in?"*

"This is me." The voice said, sounding more alert.

"Hi! It's De'marco. Did I awake you?"

"No," she lied. *"Not at all. I've been up."*

"Oh, I see," De'marco said, *"Well, I was wondering what you were doing today?"* It had come out without warning.

Jennifer had been lying down, but now she sat straight up in the bed.

"I didn't have anything planned. Why do you ask?"

"Let's meet up and hang out!" He said.

Jennifer was surprised he asked her to hang out so soon, but this was her chance and she wasn't going to let it pass her by. She was excited, but she knew she couldn't let on, so she pulled herself together and calmly said... *"Okay, I guess we can do that. What do you have in mind?"*

"Lets grab something to eat, and go see a movie?!?" De'marco suggested.

"Sounds good," Jennifer replied. *"And the time?"* She added.

De'marco being new to the jargon of dating looked over at the clock on his nightstand and said…. *"Eleven forty-five a.m."*

"What!?" Jennifer asked surprised. She then looked over at the clock on her nightstand, and loudly said, *"Oh, my god!"* She busted out with laughter.

De'marco sat there holding the phone, puzzled as to why she was laughing. Jennifer calming herself down to a slight giggle, said, *"Not what time it is now, silly. What time will we be meeting?"*

"Ohhhhhh!!" De'marco said, as they both broke out laughing. *"How about six o'clock this evening?"*

"Ok," Jennifer said, still giggling. *"And where?"*

"At Easton. How's that?" De'marco asked.

"Mmmmmh, okay, Easton's nice." She said trying to sound calm.

"So, I'll see you then. As for now, I'll let you go back to getting your rest."

"That'll work," Jennifer said. *"And I'll see you later,"* she added.

"Okay," De'marco said, *"See you later."*

"Ok, bye." Jennifer said.

"Bye." He said.

The two of them, feeling goofy, hung up the phone at the same time.

Jennifer fell back on her bed screaming, *"Yes, yes, yes!"* While beating her fist on the bed and kicking her feet hysterically in the air. *"A date with De'marco and at Easton… everyone will see us. How wonderful!"* She thought. *"What will I wear? I'll figure that out after I make a few phone calls. It's on!"* She thought.

De'marco fell back on the bed looking up at the ceiling asking himself what have I done? Surprised by his actions he wondered was it too soon for all this? He pondered on whether or not he should call back and cancel.

Finding something to wear was an easy task for De'marco. He had impeccable taste for a guy. Not to mention, because he went to private school, he wore a uniform and that left the majority of his clothes untouched for the most part. Many of them still had the price tag on them. De'marco went toward the window and raised it. The sun was shinning, and it was rather warm for March, especially in Ohio. With that being the case, he decided to wear some casual slacks and a long sleeve pullover shirt, with a pair of Perry Ellis casual loafers. He pulled out a belt to match his shoes. He figured, just in case the weather decides to change and get a little nippy, he would carry a lightweight blazer. With his outfit picked out, all the way down to his socks and drawers, he decided to make a call or two, to find out the happenin' spots at Easton, at least the eateries.

He called a guy from school named Leroy, not that Leroy was a friend, it was just that Leroy was the "go to" guy at school. You wanted the latest in music CD's? He had it. New artists, bootleg CD's, tapes, DVD movies, he even sold clothes. De'marco wondered about Leroy, how he would pass a card around with his name and number on it during lunch, or passing in the hall. Once, he had come to the homecoming football game, popped open the trunk of his car, and was selling Tupperware to people's moms.

And sure nuff with no shame, he would hand them a card and say... *"If you need it, want it, got to have it, Leroy can get it!"* Leroy didn't have a driver's license or a job. But, no one ever asked Leroy where he got those things.

"Hello?" A voice answered.

"Yes, can I speak with Leroy?" De'marco asked.

"You got 'em, what ya need?" Leroy answered.

"Leroy, this is De'marco. I need to ask you a question."

"What!? You mean to tell me this call ain't about money?!?" Leroy said.

"No, not at all," De'marco said.

"Well, hurry it up partna," Leroy said. *"Time is money, and money is time,"* he added. *"Not to mention, this is Saturday, the first of the month, I gots to get it. Now what's your question?"* He went on.

"I wanted to ask you..." De'marco started to say.

Leroy interrupted, *"Who'd you say this is?"*

"De'marco. De'marco Poitier," he said.

"Oh, yeah!" Leroy said, with a hint of excitement in his voice. *"You're the Mandingo kid the chicks at school are whispering about. You're a hot commodity at school. Heeey! Maybe, I should be selling YOU!"*

Leroy laughed. *"Nah! I'd never get that off. What's the question, buddy?"*

De'marco was starting to get a little frustrated with Leroy. He realized he talked too much.

"Well, I'm taking a girl from school on a date and would like your input on some hip things to do."

De'marco smiled and bounced his head up and down, feeling cool, cause he used the word "hip."

"Who's the chicken head?" Leroy asked.

"The what?" De'marco asked puzzled by the slang term "chicken head."

"The female, man. Who's the female?" Leroy explained.

"Oh, Jennifer," De'marco answered.

"Jen-ni-fer, who?" Leroy asked as he pronounced every syllable of her name.

"Jennifer Dyson," De'marco said. There was a brief silence…

Then, Leroy broke out saying, *"YOU MEAN, SWEET, SEXY BROWN JENNIFER!? BIG PRETTY ALMOND EYES, JENNIFER?? YOU MEAN, JUICY LIPS JENNIFER!? YOU MEAN, NO WAIST HAVING, TWO CANTELOPES IN THE FRONT, BASKETBALL RUMP JENNIFER!?"*

De'marco was shocked hearing all this. He knew she was an attractive girl but Leroy turned her into an "Exotic Goddess."

Playing it cool, he said, *"Yep, that's her."*

"Man," Leroy said, *"Now how in the flick did you end up going on a date with St. Francis DeSales finest senior? I will never know, but here's the deal."*

After what seemed like forever on the phone, Leroy finally answered De'marco's question and gave up the information he asked. Leroy went into a long drawn out thing. He referred to as "Macking 101", a whole bunch of say this, do that, stand like this, walk like that, crap. Leroy was known in school as a cool guy, but De'marco decided to use only his advice of going to "Game Works." Play a few games, share some conversation, and laughs, and then go eat at "Max and Erma's."

Time had passed, and he realized he should be getting ready. Within moments, De'marco was out the shower and dressed. He stepped out of his bedroom and into the living room where his parents were sitting.

"Wow!" His mother said, *"Where are we going this evening?"*

"I have a date," De'marco said blushing.
Martzu just sat smiling.

"Hey, Dad, do you think you'd mind dropping me off?!?"

"No, son, I don't think I'd mind," Martzu said.
"I have a few things I need to pick up while I'm out. I have a got date tonight myself," he said as he threw a naughty glance at his wife, who was trying to hold back a smile from De'marco who hadn't really caught on to what his father was insinuating. *"What time do you need to be there, son?"* Martzu asked.

"Six o'clock. However, I would like to get there a little early," De'marco responded.

"Well, give me a minute to slip my shoes on, warm up the truck, and we'll be on our way," said Martzu.

As they arrived at Easton, De'marco began to get nervous. It must have shown on his face.

Martzu asked, *"Butterflies, son? Don't worry, you'll get those from time to time. You'll get over it. Well, here we are. Enjoy yourself and call me when you're ready."*

"Will do," De'marco said cheerfully. *"Thanks for the ride dad."*

"Don't mention it," Martzu said. *"Alright, close my door, so I can get out of this traffic."*
De'marco looked at his watch. *"Good,"* he thought, *"It's early enough for me to walk around and check things out before I have to meet Jennifer."*

There were people everywhere. Rightfully so, Easton was said to be the most popular shopping center in Columbus. Having everything from clothing stores, restaurants, a movie theater, bars, and a comedy spot. Yep, this place was made to draw a crowd. And it did! Kids, teenagers, parents, couples, you name it. They were there for one reason or another. Shopping, watch a movie, or to just be seen. De'marco even saw a few people from school. Ah! The spot he had been looking for, "Game Works". Just wanted to see what was what.

"Hey, De'marco!" A voice called out. He turned around to see a little short chubby girl. He recognized her immediately. It was Melissa, from history class.

"Hey Melissa," he said smiling, glad someone recognized him.

"Whatcha doing here?" She asked.

"Jus hangin' out, ya know?!?" He said.

"By yourself?" She asked, while scrunching up her face.

"No, I'm meeting someone," he said, while giving her the, 'So there, how do you like that?!?' look.

Acting surprised, she asked, *"Oh yeah, who!?"* As if she didn't believe him.

De'marco wasn't feeling this. He then noticed three guys from his homeroom stop and look as they pointed in his direction, and snickered.

"Hey it's De'marco!" One of them said loudly enough to be heard throughout the entire mall. They walked toward them, looking back and forth between De'marco and Melissa with silly grins on their faces.

"Funny to find you two here," he paused, *"together."* The others laughed.

Melissa grinned a goofy grin that said she was glad they had thought the two of them were together.

De'marco not wanting to hurt Melissa's feelings, decided to leave it alone, until one of them remarked, *"So how long you two been seeing each other?"* He nudged one of the other guys in the side with his elbow.

"We're not seeing one another and we're not here together," De'marco said firmly. *"We just happened to bump into you three non-entity individuals."*

De'marco laughed out loud. Melissa held out her fist to give De'marco dap.

One of the guys said, *"Non-entity, let me tell you..."* a voice interrupted before he could finish.

"De'marco!" Everyone turned to see Jennifer waving at De'marco. The three guys, who were clowning on De'marco, now stood with their mouths gaping open.

Jennifer was looking gorgeous and she knew it as she walked over, all eyes were on her.

De'marco was blown away by her hourglass figure. It was not to go unnoticed. De'marco had put his blazer on earlier to show off his whole ensemble. And he looked damn good, but Jennifer! *"Whoa!"* He thought, as he took note of her outfit.

She had on a peach colored top, and although it had long sleeves, it only came mid stomach, exposing her lower stomach and back. Her dark blue denim jeans were trimmed in what appeared to be a peach or pinkish stitch. They were low cut at the waist, and as she got closer, you could see her butterfly navel ring shinning.

Whether it was diamond, or straight glass, it didn't matter it just added to her magnificence. The pants fit oh so well, showing every curve, at the bottom of each leg, they had a split that went up just enough to show her soft leather, peach colored, DKNY boots.

As she got close enough she said, *"Hey, De'marco sweetie, do I look good enough for you?"* She turned around so he could get a view of her from behind.

One of the three guys blurted out, *"Well, damn!"*

Another said, *"Say it ain't so?!?"* While biting down on his clenched fist.

De'marco took a deep breath. He had never seen Jennifer out of school uniform, and this was a bit much for him. Her rump looked so plump, so well shaped, it looked like an upside-down Valentine heart. There was no doubt. She looked brilliant! And he didn't hesitate to tell her.

"You look brilliant my Queen!" He didn't even know where the words came from. But everyone gasped and Jennifer's face lit up with joy.

"Thank you," she said, as she held out her arms for a hug.

As De'marco leaned forward he realized how happy he was, and he held her tight.

Jennifer determined to have De'marco as hers; decided this was as good a time as any to mark her territory (as all pussycats do). So, she placed her hand on De'marco's cheek and lined his face up with hers, she then placed such a succulent kiss on him, that Melissa said, *"No the hell she didn't!"* The three guys simultaneously yelled out, *"Daaamn!!"* As if in some comedy movie. Jennifer even surprised herself, when she separated her lips from De'marco's. Both of their eyes were glassy from the sudden attack, to their surprise.

People began to clap and whistle, and just to make sure she planted the right seed, Jennifer looked up at De'marco who appeared to be in a daze.

With one finger in her mouth, in a seductive manner, she said like a little baby, *"I'zz sorry, you mad at me?"* While batting her eyes.

De'marco, overwhelmed by the whole thing, simply said, *"No, everything's fine."*

"Good," she said quickly with a devilish grin. She linked her arms through his.

"Let's go my King. What are we doing first?"

The two of them looked very good together as they walked off and left everyone standing there. As Jennifer looked over her shoulder, she saw Melissa grab her cell phone, dial a number and put it to her ear, as she stood, with one hand on her hip.

"That's right baby girl, call everyone and let it be known, this one is off limits. This one belongs to Jennifer. Ms. Dyson if you're nasty!"

Jennifer laughed to herself and hugged up close to De'marco as they walked through the crowded mall.

The evening went well for the both of them. De'marco had mapped out things, and it was going well. First, they hit "Game Works". They played air hockey, shot some basketball on the little hoop game, and played Mrs. Pac Man. From there they went to "Max and Erma's". They shared a large shrimp and pasta with garlic bread, and a salad. After dinner, they had a few minutes before their movie started. So Jennifer suggested they go into one of the photo booths and take a couple of pictures.

After the movie, De'marco realized it had gotten rather late. He looked at Jennifer, who was smiling while in thought.

"Hey," he said, interrupting Jennifer's pleasant thoughts of how well the evening was going. She felt as if she was floating on a cloud. The evening could go on forever as far as she was concerned.

"It's getting late," he continued, *"I should probably be calling my dad to pick me up before it gets any later."*

Jennifer thought for a second, *"I could take you home. I mean, if it's okay with you!?"*

"I'd have to call my dad," De'marco said. Just as quickly as he had said it, she handed him her cell phone.

After making the call home, he asked her, *"So, you have a car?"*

"Well, its my mother's car, but I have my license," she stated excitedly.

As they rode, there was a brief moment of silence.

Jennifer wasn't having her mood or her plans blown. So she popped in one of her mothers' CD's, and hit play, seconds later R. Kelly's voice came through the speaker.

"I hear you calling, here I come baby, to saaave you..."

She looked over at De'marco, and thought, *"Okay how do I do this? Oh well, here go's."*

"Hey, I have to make a stop by my house. Do you mind?"

"No, not at all," De'marco said, failing to see the devilish look in Jennifer's eyes.

She said, *"Cool,"* turned the radio up, and placed her hand on his leg. She drove hurriedly to her house.

As they pulled up the driveway De'marco asked, *"Will you be long?"*

"No, no as a matter of fact, come in," she lied.

Truly, she wanted an intimate moment with De'marco and was determined to get it. This would definitely make him hers, or so she thought. As they entered the house, she wasted no time. She grabbed De'marco's hand and led him straight to her bedroom. As they stepped through the bedroom door, De'marco didn't have a chance. Jennifer spun him around, and pushed him on the bed. Just as quickly, she reached over grabbed a remote, hit play, flopped on the bed, clapped two times, the light went out, and she straddled De'marco, and started kissing him, tongue all down his throat. Then, he heard R. Kelly again, *"There's something in your eyes baby, telling me you want me*

*baby, tonight is your night, see you don't have to ask for
nothing, I'll give you everything you need. So, gurrrl
don't be shy, Oohh just, baby come inside, turn out the
lights..."*

As De'marco pried Jennifer's lips from his, he asked,
"Hey uh, where's your parents?"

*"I live here with my mother, and she always spends
the weekend over her boyfriend's. So we're okay,"*
Jennifer said quickly, putting her tongue back down
De'marco's throat.

De'marco couldn't help but wonder how many other
guys may have starred in his present situation? What he
didn't know was, Jennifer was just as much a virgin as
he. She'd done no more than kissed a guy or two. What
sparked this little rendezvous is that Jennifer's mom was
relatively young and they were close, so Jennifer was
able to discuss certain matters with her mom and get raw
undiluted feedback.

She told her of the time De'marco came to school with
his father, whose size and looks not only intimidated
everyone, but also had all the female's mouths watering.
She also told her mother what she had overheard about
them being original descendants of the legendary
"Mandingo" tribe.

At that point her mother's mouth flew open, *"What!
Are you serious, a Mandingo man here in Columbus,
Ohio!?"* Her mother jumped up and called one of her
gossiping buddies from church.

She heard her mother on the phone saying everything
from how strong they are, how well they make love, and
on and on. She even caught wind of her speaking of the
rumors of how well hung they were. Jennifer was able
to testify to that, thanks to the little incident in gym
class. She never told her mother about that. Partly,
because she didn't want her mother to think she was
being frisky at school doing such things. As well as, she
wasn't sure she saw what she thought she saw. She'd
peeked at guys before. She had guys even pull their

privates out and flash them at her. But absolutely never had she seen such a sight in her life! Not even when she sneaked and watched the porn channels. However, she was already attracted to De'marco and every other chick at school wanted him, along with the rumors circulating around about his heritage made her want him all the more.

So, when she said to her mom, *"Well, what do you think?"* She remembered her moms eyes looked straight up and she placed a finger on her lip and quickly said, *"Uuuh, stay away from that boy!"* With a not so serious look on her face. All this is what led up to Jennifer looking forward to this night. Although, it came so suddenly, she felt like she was ready, or so she thought. The CD started skipping, *"that honey love, …that honey love, …that honey love."*

"Man!" Jennifer thought, as she felt around for the remote. Still kissing De'marco, who hadn't moved one inch since being pushed on the bed. She pointed the remote and clicked to the next song. She dismounted De'marco, and laid beside him. She continued to rub on him. He was solid, very firm and had a nice chest on him, she thought. As she slid her hand down, his stomach was as flat as hers. She dared herself to go down further into the 'forbidden territory.'

"Oh, well," she thought. She started rubbing the area where she figured his manhood should be.

"Excuse me," De'marco said, *"Uuhumm, what are you doing?"*

She was at a lost for words.

"Nothing, be quiet," she said as she took a deep breath and quickly unzipped his pants, and undid his belt buckle. She slid her hand in his boxers, looking for his…

"Oh, My God!" She thought as she discovered it. She was searching for the end of it, but her hand kept going further down. She got nervous and knew at that point, she couldn't have sex with him. She was afraid.

De'marco laid there tense, with his eyes closed tight. She pulled his manhood from down beside his leg, and positioned it to where it was pointing upward, so she could feel on it for a moment. She was amazed at it, as well as at herself, for what she was doing. This had really become too much for her. But, she didn't want De'marco to know she was afraid. So, she slowly slid her hand out of his pants, and zipped them back up. She didn't know what to do. She had come this far and she thought that she might disappoint De'marco if she didn't do it. She remembered a conversation she had with her friend Michelle who was hot in the ass.

"If you're not going to go all the way, you'd better do something."

She pulled her pants off and straddled De'marco.

Once more, he realized what she had done, and asked her, *"What are you doing?"*

"Shhhhhh!" Was all she gave him in response, as she positioned herself on top of him. His penis felt hard against her. It had never touched a vagina before. She started moving around back and forth. It actually was uncomfortable, and why she kept going, she had no idea. De'marco began to move with her. Although it hurt both of them, they continued moving around and grinding each other, possibly because there was a hint of pleasure, if they could just figure out how to bring this about. They had no idea of what they were doing. The sight was pitiful. After Jennifer became so sore, she couldn't take it anymore. She fell over on the side. De'marco had no complaints, although he was sore also.

"How was it?" She asked De'marco, as if they had really done something.

De'marco not sure what answer she was looking for said… *"I don't know."*

Jennifer lying there with her hand in her panties, feeling how wet and sore she was, became embarrassed.

"Maybe, I should take you home now?"

3

"GOODBYE VIRGINITY"

The time flew by with De'marco and Jennifer spending as much time together as they possibly could. With Jennifer's mother gone every weekend they would go to the mall, movie or whatever, just to be seen, as if they were celebrities. Then they wasted no time getting back to the house for one of their many grinding sessions. They hadn't advanced much further from their first encounter, other than now Jennifer would take her shirt off. Now there were a couple of occasions were they grinded so much Jennifer's leg would kinda start shaking. She would lose her breath and black out for a second or two. Although, these were the times they grinded the hardest and would end up extremely sore, she enjoyed them the most, for some reason. All this was fun and De'marco enjoyed it, however, it had gotten to the point where he wanted to know was there more to what they were doing…than what they were doing! De'marco was eager to move forward. Everything was okay, though.

Tomorrow was graduation and Jennifer had plans of her own for the two of them. Besides, she figured, it was the least she could do. From the very start she branded De'marco as her territory.

"He never had a chance," she thought smiling, *"I'm so bad."*

But that didn't stop the other females from throwing themselves at De'marco when she wasn't looking. So she knew she had to do something fast, before one of them stank booty chicken heads gave him a shot at the nappy, and he go for it.

Happy about tomorrow, she dialed De'marco's cell phone. The cell phone she'd got for him. She told him she got it because he would look cute with it.

Truthfully, it was so she could reach him whenever she wanted.

Because of her running her mouth, he had become Mr. Popularity. Some of everybody had become his friend.

"Hello," De'marco said.

"Hi, my King," Jennifer said cheerfully.

"Jennifer, how are you?" De'marco asked.

"I'm good. Are you ready for tomorrow?" Jennifer asked.

"I believe so," De'marco said.

"Let me get this straight… after graduation, we'll attend the bar-be-que, then we're on our way?"

"Yep, that's right," Jennifer said, *"And don't ask me where. I'll see you tomorrow. Okaaay? Bye."* She hung up the phone, and thought to herself, *"It's on, like never before."*

* * * * * * * * * * * * * * * * * *

The graduation was packed. People from everywhere, some folks who didn't even think they would graduate made it. As Martzu and De'shawntu stood with friends and a few family members, Connie appeared. She was running late because she had received a collect call from Sly in prison. The conversation they had put her behind schedule.

"Hey, everybody!" She said as she reached out her arms to give De'shawntu a hug.

"Hey lady," De'shawntu said, *"Everybody, this is Connie, De'marco's old babysitter."*

Everyone spoke, some shook her hand, those who couldn't reach her waved.

"Hey, big guy," Connie said loudly, reaching up to pat Martzu on the back. Martzu glanced behind him, and seeing Connie, began to smile.

"Hey there," he said, *"How's it been?"*

"Good, just working hard. I opened up two more shops," she said smiling.

"Did you?" Martzu said excitingly, *"Did you hear that De'shawntu?"*

"Yes, I did," she said, *"And congratulations on that,"* De'shawntu said.

"So, that makes how many now?" Martzu questioned.

"Five," Connie said. *"And I named them all "HOUSE OF BEAUTY".*

Shortly after this conversation they called De'marco's name, as he walked the stage.

Connie clapped and said, *"He's so tall now."*

"Like his dad," De'shawntu said as she elbowed Martzu in the side.

"Yes, yes he is. I wonder what else is like his father?" Connie thought, noticing how attractive he had become.

After graduation they all stood around outside talking and waiting for De'marco so they could take pictures, give cards of congratulations and gifts. De'marco finally made it over, with Jennifer on his side.

"Hello, everyone!" He said excitedly.

He introduced Jennifer to those not familiar with her.

Connie recognized her. She'd done her mother's hair before.

As she looked at Jennifer and De'marco, it dawned on her. She remembered hearing Jennifer's mother talk about an African Mandingo her daughter was dating from school. She never paid much attention because the woman never really went into detail. Now it all came together. De'marco caught her staring.

"So Connie, haven't seen you in forever," De'marco said.

"Yeah," Connie said.

"You're a young man now. Graduating from high school and all, got you a girlfriend. What's next?"

"Maybe I can get a business or two and become rich like you?" He said jokingly, with a big smile, showing his straight white teeth.

Connie tried to remain humble, though the comment swelled her head a bit. She cheesed a little.

"No, I'm not rich. Doing good, but not rich."

"Ok, remain modest if you must. What are you going to do with all that money?" De'marco asked.

"De'marco! How dare you!?" His mother exclaimed, *"What she does with her money is her business!"*

"I don't know," Connie said, starring De'marco in the eyes thinking to herself, *"I have a good idea though."*

De'marco had come out of his cap and gown, showing his frame and signs of how one day soon he'd be a large man like his father. She couldn't help but to think back to her days of babysitting De'marco. Catching Martzu's eyes peering at her on several occasions. She took it upon herself to see what was what?

Coming to baby sit one Saturday evening, she had come through the door wearing a mini skirt, a blouse that came down mid way, with some open toe heels. De'shawntu asked her why she was dressed in such a way, just to sit with De'marco? She lied, and said originally she was going to go on a date, but was stood up. As De'shawntu went out the door to the car, Martzu was explaining where they would be, and to call the cell phone in case of an emergency.

Once she noticed him looking attentively. She purposely turned around and bent over to pick De'marco up off the couch. She spread her legs in a wicked stance, and bent over so her mini skirt rose up on top of her ass. As she reached out to pick up De'marco, she held the position for a few seconds, allowing Martzu to notice the see-thru lace thong. She knew she had his attention, because he stopped talking. So, she let him get a good look. She knew he was staring at her fat pussy lips, they stuck out like a fist between her legs and just before she stood back up with De'marco, she wiggled from side to side, then stood and turned around, with De'marco in her arms.

She looked Martzu straight in the eyes, and said, *"I'm sorry. What were you saying?"*

Martzu was no fool when it came to the ladies. He showed no sign of being overwhelmed or turned on.

When he spoke, he simply said, *"I'll be talking to you later."*

No words were needed to be spoken. The look they shared said it all.

"Hello Connie, you there?" De'shawntu said, bringing Connie out of her little fantasy.

"Yeah, I'm here," Connie said regaining her composure. *"What's up?"*

"Well, we're having a bar-be-que at the house, you're more than welcome to come."

"I have to get back to the shop and stop and get a money order to send to Sly. If I have time later, I'll at least come by and get a plate. Is that OK?" She said every word while staring De'marco down as if he was bar-be-que.

"Do what you have to girl. We'll see you later, if you make it," De'shawntu said.

They hugged and said their goodbyes. Jennifer was standing there quietly, she noticed a great deal. She said to De'marco, *"That woman wants you."*

"What!?" De'marco said with his face scrunched up.

"I said, THAT WOMAN WANTS YOU! Did you hear that!?"

"No, she don't silly. That's Connie, my old babysitter," De'marco insisted.

Jennifer knew better. She may have been young, but her mother taught her about female intuition. She didn't want to spoil the evening she had planned, so she let that situation go for now. Yep, big things were going down tonight. No need to allow some insecure thoughts mess things up. The thought of tonight turned her on so she reached and palmed De'marco on the butt as they followed behind his parents to the parking lot.

The bar-be-que was going well. A lot of their friends showed up. Jennifer was amazed at how much

De'marco could eat, he and his father. They were putting away whole slabs of ribs.

De'shawntu asked Jennifer, *"You ready to feed that appetite?"*

It made Jennifer happy to say, *"Yes, ma'am,"* knowing she couldn't cook worth a lick. It had started getting dark, and her friends, as well as other females started to flirt with De'marco. Jennifer figured this was the opportune time to exit.

She leaned over and whispered in De'marco's ear, *"Remember, we have plans tonight,"* as she stuck her tongue in his ear. The act had sent chills through his body. Martzu noticed what was taking place. So he had a few words with his son before he left. He made sure he had his door key and told him, *"Don't worry about it if you're going to be out tonight. See ya in the morning,"* said Martzu.

As they rode away in the car, De'marco asked, *"So, where we headed?"*

"Let's just say, tonight I don't plan on being a virtuous woman," Jennifer purred, smiling.

De'marco raised one eyebrow, *"No?"*

She reached over and scratched at his leg like a cat, *"No, not at all."*

De'marco smiled, *"So, I don't have to be a young man of gentry, do I?"*

"You sure don't, not tonight. Tonight we both will be nefarious animals in heat, indulging in that which is illicit, so, hopefully you will find me to be enviable."

De'marco looked at her, *"Yeah, you must have been drinking, cause your conversation is sounding rather erratic and seeing that you just graduated, I know your vocabulary is somewhat erudite."*

They both laughed at their ability to express themselves above layman vernacular.

"Here we are!" Jennifer said happily as they pulled up in front of the Radisson Hotel on Cassady Avenue.

De'marco looked up at the hotel with anticipation in his eyes. He'd been waiting for this moment. Jennifer hit the button to pop the trunk.

She was out the car quickly, yelling, *"Make sure the doors are locked!"* As she slammed the drivers side door. De'marco got out noticing Jennifer grabbing over night bags and bottles of what looked to be alcohol. Man she planned to do it up. They went in, walked straight to the elevator.

"Don't we have to check in?" De'marco inquired.

"All that has been taken care of," she said smiling.

She couldn't stop looking at him. She had gotten all types of advice from her friends. The elevator door opened and she stepped out.

"This way," she said looking over her shoulder. De'marco wondered when she'd had time to do all this.

As they stepped into the room there were balloons everywhere, *"Congratulations!" "Yeaaa, Hurray!"* Were just a few of the words on the multi-colored balloons. No sooner than De'marco sat the bags down, Jennifer was digging in them, pulling out all sorts of things. She instructed him to go get ice, while she got ready to jump in the shower.

As he was about to walk out the door, she shouted, *"And grab a small bottle of cranberry juice!"*

When De'marco returned she was in the shower singing. He knew what time it was. He saw the bottle of liquor and thought he'd just fix himself a drink. He picked up the bottle and read the label, *"Absolute Vodka. Man, how did she buy this?"*

He made a drink. It was strong. He poured about half the cranberry juice in his drink to make it suitable for him to drink. By the time Jennifer came out the bathroom De'marco had three drinks. He didn't want to drink up all the cranberry juice, just in case Jennifer wanted some in her drink. So, two of his three was taken straight! Straight to the head! He was feeling pretty good. Drunk was more like it.

Jennifer came out the bathroom like, *"TAH DAH!"*
With her hands in the air like a model. The room
quickly filled with the aroma of vanilla. De'marco took
a big sniff, partially because he was drunk.

"Oh, I see you like my 'Vanilla Jasmine' body lotion."

That's not the only thing he liked. Jennifer stepped
out the bathroom in a red lace teddy. She spun around
showing the thong back. De'marco's eyes got wide as
pool table cue balls, as he followed the thin strap that
disappeared between her two fully round, firm ass
cheeks! He couldn't believe it. He stood and walked
straight to her with a look of hunger in his eyes.

Jennifer reacted quickly, *"Wait, wait, baby!"* She
pleaded, as his arms reached her, she went up on her
tippy toes, kissed him quickly, and spun out his arms.

"I have something for you too baby," she grabbed a
bag and pulled out a pair of red silk boxers.

"You like, baby?" She asked, pleased with her gift for
him.

"Yeah, they're nice." He started at her again with the
look of hunger. This time when he reached his arms out,
like a karate expert, she blocked, ducked, spun him
around, and led him into the bathroom, all in one
motion.

*"You take a shower first, then when you come out,
we'll talk, share a few drinks, make a toast, then we can
begin to osculate."*

She giggled, *"And take this,"* she said, placing the silk
boxers in his hand.

"And hurry up!" She said shutting the door.

"No you didn't!" De'marco yelled back feeling a bit
impatient.

"Oh, I know he don't have an attitude," she said.

De'marco being in the shower gave her time to light a
few candles and take a drink to the head herself. It was
too strong! She spit it right out! *"Paaah!"* The alcohol
shot out her mouth, straight into the flame of one of the

candles sitting on the stand. *SWOOSH!* The flame went up.

"Oh my God!" She grabbed a pillow and put out the small fire on the lampshade.

"Damn, damn, damn!" She said, *"Almost burnt the place down."* She laughed once she realized everything was okay. She tried fixing herself another drink, this time with the cranberry juice. Every time she went to turn it up, she would start laughing. *"Drink the damn drink,"* she told herself, *"Stop being silly."* She heard the water to the shower stop. She got nervous and gulped the drink down. *"There you go girl! Be a soldier,"* she said to herself, while tapping her fist on her chest with a scrunched up face, eyes watering.

De'marco stepped out the bathroom into the dimly lit room.

"TAH DAH!" He mimicked her, *"Oh yeah, don't let me forget,"* he put his hands over his head as Jennifer had done earlier and spun around.

Jennifer studied him. She hadn't seen him semi-naked before. She liked what she saw. The boxers fit well. Wait a minute! What the hell!? Because of the lack of light, she wasn't sure but it looked like the tip of his meat was hanging out one of the legs of the boxers.

"So, do you like, or what?" He asked.

"You look wonderful! Now come over here and have a drink with me," she said, before realizing what she'd said.

Neither of them needed to drink anymore. The drink was too strong for her and De'marco. He was even drunker now than before he got into the shower, thanks to the hot water.

De'marco headed toward Jennifer. He grabbed her and looked straight into her eyes, then said, *"What's that smell? Was something on fire?"*

Jennifer was caught off guard because she had momentarily forgot about her little arson attempt.

"I don't smell anything," she said quickly, making a cock-eyed look.

"Give me a kiss," she raised her head to meet De'marco's mouth.

He wrapped his arms around her small waist and began rubbing her. They kissed passionately, she held on to him, as his hands explored. He caressed her back allowing his hands to slide down to her exposed butt cheeks.

Immediately upon contact, he became erect. She felt his manhood rise, it felt strong, firm and ready as it pressed up against her lower stomach. As De'marco allowed his hands to find their way to her breast, she realized she wanted to control this moment. It was both of their first time, but she wanted it to go the way *she* wanted it to go. She was adamant about that. So, as De'marco went to pull down the tiny strap on her teddy, she pulled back.

"Wait," she said, *"I want to see you."*

De'marco didn't know what she meant, but he allowed her to continue on as she pulled him close to the edge of the bed, she continued to shower him with kisses on his neck and chest. As she went to sit down on the edge of the bed, she let her tongue slowly slide down the middle of his stomach, until she found his navel. She made circles around it with the tip of her tongue, and then she probed her tongue in and out his navel. It made De'marco get chills up his back. She stopped as her butt made full contact with the bed.

"What? What is it?" De'marco asked.

"I told you, I want to see you," she said, as she began pulling down his boxers. She slowly pulled them down; she looked at his manhood as it began to appear.

"Man!" She thought, as she caught sight of the first couple of inches. Her eyes widened, as she pulled his boxers down closer to his knees, but had not yet reached the end of his massive meat. Then, BAMM! It popped out. The head hitting her chin at the same time. She

gasped, as she leaned back with one hand on her chest, shocked by what she saw. Her mouth hung open, her eyes were bucked. She looked like a fish gasping for air.

De'marco noticed her reaction, and was slightly embarrassed. He went to pull up his boxers. Jennifer quickly stopped him.

"No! Let me see, please!" She said with a look of amazement on her face.

She pulled his boxers the rest of the way down, once they reached his feet he stepped out of them. When he did this, it caused his meat to bounce up and down. She couldn't believe it. The vision from gym class that day was real, it was long, it had to be at least 12 to 12 1/2 inches. And the girth, was like the bottom of a soda can. His nuts looked like two big baseballs. You could see the veins in it and it was all the same color of his body. Exxccept! Except the head was a deep dark red! The head of it shinned from the light of the candles. Jennifer reached for it.

"My God!" She thought, *"It is massive, and it has weight to it,"* as she lifted it.

"Are you going to observe me like I'm an alien or what!?" He asked.

"Hell yeah!" Jennifer thought to herself. *"Be quiet. I got you,"* she said.

Suddenly something clicked inside her. She took noticed of herself. Her breast were swollen, nipples hard, she could feel how wet she was between her legs. Her mouth was watering. She swallowed hard and said, *"Fuck it."*

She lifted his meat up and leaned forward to put it into her mouth. She opened her mouth wide to take him in. It felt as if the corners of her mouth were tearing.

De'marco took a deep breath, as he felt the wet warmth of her mouth on his manhood. He was surprised at her actions as well as the feeling he was receiving. Jennifer had no idea of what she was doing, but, lust, desire, and curiosity got the best of her. She realized her mouth was not doing much, partly because he was so large and her mouth couldn't take much of him in, as well as she was new to this act of sex. But she had already decided that tonight she would be uninhibited, so she did what she thought was right until her jaws and neck were tired. She pulled back and De'marco's eyes rolled back in his head and looked at her. Inexperienced or not, he enjoyed it.

"What's up?" He asked.

She said nothing as she scooted back on the bed. She simply gestured with her finger for him to follow. She slid out the teddy with ease.

De'marco positioned himself between her legs and after several attempts, and her sliding around trying to escape him, she finally lay still, ready for him to penetrate and explore the unchartered walls of her precious vagina. She didn't know what to expect, but she knew what she had seen. So she spread her legs wide, so he could enter. Only to quickly clamp them to his sides as she felt the head entering.

"Oooooh, oooh, ooohhh," she let out, as he went deeper and deeper. It felt like her whole body was tearing in half. She held him tightly, as he thrust back and forth in her. It felt like he was touching every part of her body with his enormous meat.

Many thoughts went through her head, *"Why am I doing this? Should I be doing this? Is he the right one to do this with? Does he love me? Does he want me? I'm the one who persuaded him to do this,"* she told herself.

He started really putting it to her. He wrapped his arms under her shoulders and began thrusting his hips as he did on the many occasions they had grinded. But this time, he was in her.

She felt her leg shake a couple of times. He had really been working her. She didn't know if this was how long it was suppose to last or if he was just drunk or if the rumor of Mandingos having great stamina was true. There were times, he would go slow and easy, but deep.

She could hear smacking sounds from the wetness between her legs. What really sent her for a ride is when she took the advice from one of her hot ass friends and let him hit it from the back. She got on her hands and knees, stuck her butt in the air, and put her face down. That's when the thunder struck! All she could do was put her face in the pillow and holler, as he held her waist and put it to her, it was as if he had entered her stomach. Her feet went up, toes curled.

"Why am I confused?" She thought.

She couldn't figure it out if it hurt or felt good. It's both, she told herself, but how could that be, a pleasurable pain? He was going to town on her. He had her ass cheeks jumping up and down. Her stomach hurt, but she felt good. Her breasts were bouncing back and forth. She tried holding them but one would always pop loose. She felt herself soaking from sweat, with her ass jumping, titties bouncing, and she moaning loudly into the pillow.

She lifted her head up from the pillow, and yelled out, *"I THINK I'M GOING CRAZY! Oh my God, you're fucking me till I'm CRAAAZZZY!"*

De'marco started moaning.

"What's that?" She thought. He started going faster, harder.

"Oh no, no. He can't cum in me. He doesn't have on a condom."

Reality kicked in, *"It feels good but don't get pregnant,"* her friend told her, *"Your life will be hell."* *"But, I don't want to disappoint him."* She thought.

With that on her mind she quickly came from under De'marco and turned over, before he could say anything. She took him in her mouth. Just in time too. As he moaned louder and grabbed her head he hit the back of her throat with his manhood. She tried to pull back, not knowing what to expect. It was too late, she felt him exploding and contracting. Shocked at his reaction, she froze, and then her mouth began to fill up. He jerked and ooze came out the corners of her mouth. She pulled back and ran to the bathroom. Leaving De'marco on the bed as she spit in the toilet.

She was like, *"What the hell!?"*

She looked at the contents in the toilet. She said, *"Eechh viscid!"* She lay back on the cold bathroom floor. It was a bathroom floor in a hotel, but it was cool and it felt good. She held her stomach. She reached down to touch between her legs it was swollen and sore. She was worn out physically and that she was aware of. But the fact that she was turned out mentally hadn't dawned on her yet.

"Hey you," De'marco said standing in the doorway, ass naked, *"Are you okay?"*

She looked over at him, his large meat hanging down.

"Damn that mother's big!" She thought, then she laughed a deep laugh, *"And it's all mine."* She saw the puzzled look on De'marco's face, *"Help me up boy, I'm okay."*

They returned to where the bed was, *"Daaammn!"*

Jennifer said, *"Did we do this?"*

"I think so," De'marco snickered.

There was a pillow across the room. Jennifer's teddy, somehow was hanging from the lampshade, the covers were on the floor and the sheets had popped from the corners of the mattress.

They made up the bed and lay down. De'marco wanted more, however, Jennifer asked him could he wait a few minutes so she could recuperate.

"Here, watch some T.V.," she told him as she pointed to the remote.

"Was everything okay for you?" She asked.

"Yes, it was wonderful," De'marco yawned and laid back. She laid her head on his chest. They both held each other tightly. De'marco fell off to sleep. Jennifer thought of what she and De'marco had just done. She

surprised herself. She liked it, and she was glad it was with him.

"Damn," she thought, *"I'm falling in love."* She fell asleep.

The next few weeks went smooth for De'marco and Jennifer. They were doing their thing on the regular. There was no sign of her getting used to the size of De'marco, however, they got it on all the same, several times a week. Once, she learned the technique of soaking in a hot bath to ease the soreness, she accepted the pleasurable pain of De'marco's unorthodox stroking.

They had been hooking up on the regular, and each time Jennifer told her friends and from what she shared, he had no idea how to honestly please a female. Once, Jennifer's friend told her she would teach De'marco if she wanted her to. Jennifer got pissed off. Her friend said to her, *"Okay, let all that meat go to waste."*

Jennifer had shared her first experience with her mother, who would have preferred that she waited before getting sexual. However, she gave her credit for graduating first, and advised her, not to bring any babies home. Jennifer's mother in return told her friend at church. And at the hair salon, Connie caught wind of the happenings.

"So, your daughter done bit off more than she can chew, hunh?" A woman said.

"Girl, I don't know what to say about that situation. She thinks she's grown. I try to give her the benefit of the doubt, she is 18 now, she finished high school and plans to go to college."

"What's the problem?" Connie asked, prying for more information.

"She claims it's hurting every time, and she told me he suppose to be this big and shit!" Jennifer's mom said, gesturing her hands far apart.

"Girl stop!" Connie said loudly, *"You know ain't no big ole dick good for nobody. The boy pounding her and don't know what he's doing. He'll been done*

messed her insides up, or have her ass sprung," Connie said with humor in her voice. *"Or have her ass walking like this,"* she walked around with her legs gaped open and bowed outward, rocking from side to side.

Everyone laughed.

"I'm serious," Jennifer's mother said with concern in her voice. *"She says she doesn't think he knows what he's doing at all!"*

Connie raised and eyebrow, *"He don't?"*

"Nah girl, she says he don't." Jennifer's mother attested.

"Just beating it up?" Connie inquired, trying to hold in a laugh.

The conversation caused Connie to think back on the days she babysat De'marco. One evening after she had given Martzu a peek at her goods, he was giving her a ride home and had stopped at the ATM to get the money to pay her.

"That was quite a little show you put on a week ago," Martzu said.

Connie had to think back, she had kinda forgotten, because he hadn't really responded to the enticing moves that she'd made that day. Once, she caught remembrance of what he was talking about, she thought quickly and chose her words wisely.

"I thought you said you would talk to me later?!? What's up?" She looked out the corner of her eye from the passenger seat, trying to catch a reaction. But Martzu was calm, he knew what he had heard.

"Listen," he said, as he spoke he explained how he had women, including De'shawntu back home in Africa. And he missed that and would like it that way again, but De'shawntu has gotten used to not having to deal with the other women. And he didn't care to put her through that again after all this time. He still wanted a lady friend on the side.

Connie was hip and needed money at the time, so when he handed her the money for babysitting that week, she held it up and waved it back and forth as she told him, *"Some more of these and we can do whatever you want, whenever you want."* That was the start of their arrangement. She remembered the early stages. She was hot in the ass and thought she was all that, until she saw Martzu naked for the first time.

She screamed, *"That ain't real!"*

Indeed it was. And when Martzu put it on her, he would deeply penetrate her, it was unbelievable. It never fit all the way in her, but that which did, he put it on her. He had her so open, the other guy friends she had couldn't compete, or live up to, or even fit after dealing with Martzu, so they fell off.

Even Sly was very sexual and freaky, but he was no Martzu. Messing with Martzu, Connie had developed a very noticeable gap and her lips stayed stretch. She would try to ride him never really attempting to take much of him in her. Mostly, she would play with the tip. It in itself was satisfying to her. She thought of the first time she lay there on her back, waiting as he allowed her a good long look at what she was receiving. She just stared at what looked to be another leg protruding from between his other two legs.

He grabbed it with his hand and asked her was she ready, while tapping it on her stomach. She murmured a *"yes"* and although he was large as all get back he was gentle, he was skilled. He filled her with such a feeling, her whole insides cried out with pain and pleasure. He laid into her for hours. He knew she felt pain, but he made sure she took it and enjoyed it.

Afterwards, she was so amazed as Martzu slept, she would rub on his manhood, lifting it up and talking to it like it was a lost friend come home. As time went on, she was addicted, straight sprung, dick on the brain. Martzu had to call things off. Connie started calling the house all hours of the night and De'shawntu, although she never said anything, was not dumb. It took Connie a while to get her head right and get back on track.

"So, Mr. De'marco Poitier needs a little schooling on how to work the middle? Okay." Connie thought to herself.

"Connie, Connie!" Jennifer's mother called out, *"This damn perm starting to burn! What you doing? Shit, burn my hair out if you want. I'll own this muther. What you doing anyway, with yo' hot tail. Thinking about that little Mandingo boy, and how you can get your hands on him?"*

All the ladies in the shop started giggling.

"More than you know," Connie thought to herself, *"Shut up messing with me for you be bald in here."*

"Play if you want to," Jennifer's mother said, *"I done told you, I date lawyers."*

Connie not feeling her smart mouth, fronted on her,

"Make up your mind, do you date lawyers with an "s" or you date Jesus with an "s" with your supposed to be church going self."

"Oooh, no you didn't?!?"

"Yes, I did, now lean your head back, so I can rinse this stuff out and if you say something I'm gonna squirt water in your mouth."

"Go ahead, you'll learn real quick if I'm dating Jesus or a lawyer."

"Why you playing?" Connie's attitude changed quickly, not wanting to lose a customer behind some B.S.

"I'm just playing gurrrl, let me make you beautiful."

* * * * * * * * * * * * * * * * * *

With Jennifer and her mother discussing all Jennifer's and De'marco's business around town, he was becoming very popular, and most women wanted to see what all the fuss was about. A few of Jennifer's friends had even called De'marco's house, he told her. Jennifer wasn't feeling this, and thought quickly on how to put a stop to it. She called De'marco on his cell phone.

"Hello, my Queen, how can I help you?"

"How'd you know it was me?" Jennifer said acting surprised.

"How about the caller ID you put on the phone?!?" De'marco said sarcastically.

"Oh yeaaah, that's right. So what you doing, my King?"

"Talking to you," he said, *"What is it? I can hear something in your voice."*

Jennifer took a deep breath, *"Well, I figured since we're both working, it might be a good idea if we get an apartment together. What you think?"* Before he could answer, she added, *"It'll let us both get out our parents house and we can save money together for other things, ok baby? Please,"* she said in a whiny voice. *"Pretty, pretty, please."*

"What about when I'm ready to go to college as well as yourself?" De'marco asked.

Damn! She forgot that.

"We'll work something out," she said not sure how they would do that.

"Let me think on that a day or two," responded De'marco.

Jennifer already knew that meant he was going to run it by his dad.

"Okay let me know."

"You know I will baby, Okay?!?"

"Alright, call you later." She hung up. *"Damn! Now what?"* She thought.

Back at the shop, people were clearing out. It had started to get late and Connie was still pondering on the conversation that had taken place earlier about De'marco and thinking of his father. She couldn't help wonder if Martzu had passed the bed skills of the Mandingo down to his son. As conversation had it, he hadn't. Damn, that would be a waste of some prime USDA meat.

"Hey, girl what you over there thinking about?"
Jerome asked in his girlish tone. Jerome was a flaming faggot that works at the shop.

"Nothing," Connie responded.

"You don't have to lie to me. You thinking about that young meat ain't you?!? Wondering if he got what his daddy got. Ummm, hmmm, I know you izzz."

Jerome was the only one who knew about Connie and Martzu.

"No, I ain't, and mind yo business."

"Oh, okay Miss Thang if you ain't gonna get 'em, I will. He can kill this thang here," Jerome said smacking himself on the ass, *"Please believe."*

Connie's mouth dropped open, *"Jerome please! Plus you know me, and you know I don't get down like that."*

"Shiiiit you don't. I get down like what evah!" He said loudly with two snaps in a circle. *"Shit after all I've heard about the boy. You better give'em some of that thure fish, before I break'em off some of this main diiish! Yep, yep, think I won't. Get'em up, drink'em up, flip him over like BAAM! Here I am."*

Connie gave Jerome a look of disgust.

"Shut up would you?!? And hurry up getting your station straight. I need to be getting out of here. I done made my money, you come in here all late thinking somebody gonna wait on you all day."

"I know girl, I'm sorry. I went out to Club Flex last night, had too many Apple Martinis. Next thing I knew, I leave the club and end up in a threesome with two fine straight men."

"First!" Connie said, *"You're sick, second, if they done you, they ain't straight."*

"Them two muscle bound men were straight gurrrl!" Jerome corrected.

"No!" Connie said. *"I hate to bust your bubble, but if they, the two muscle bound meeeen, as you call them, had sex with you, AAA punk, faggot, sissy, a.k.a twinkle toes, then they gaaaay!"*

"Oh, you trippin'! I done told you I was sorry triick! So, why you riding a bitch? Ain't my fault you ain't been able to find nobody to hit that fish like Mr. Martzu, ooow!" Exclaimed Jerome rolling his eyes. *"By the way, why don't you just wait for Sly? He's gonna be old...er, but so are you, but I'm sure y'all can work something out. Besides, I'm sure he's still kinda cute."*

"Pwsst, thinks not, and hurry up," Connie said rolling her eyes back while walking to the front door to hit the lights. *"Yeah, that's okay,"* she thought. *"I'm gonna get somebody to hit it, yes siiiir. Real soon like, please believe me."*

"Hurry up! With yo ole punk ass!" Connie yelled at Jerome.

"Oow! Miss Thang is hot. Let me get moving."

Martzu was proud of his son. He graduated from High School with a 4.0 GPA, and immediately afterwards, he landed him a job. He wasted no time setting a foundation for his life. He even liked the decision he made in Jennifer being his first, because they were headed in the same direction with college and all. Martzu felt it important for a couple to have like goals especially when starting out young. However, the thought of the two of them moving in together, at this point in their lives, didn't sit well with him. Plus the thought of what the Elders had told him of what was to come still, after all these years it was still on his mind, so he waited patiently.

"Son, to live with a woman is a very big step. You will have to provide for her, for she will depend on you in more ways than one. She will expect you to deliver with no excuses."

"Dad, you have taught me well. I can do it," De'marco said.

"There's no question in my mind of whether or not you can do it. It's a matter of if you can do for her and

*still accomplish the other things in life you've set out to
do. Do you overstand?"* Martzu explained.

*"Yes, very much so. So, I need to take things into
serious consideration, and either way have a well
thought out plan?!?"*

"That's my boy!" Martzu looked at his son well
pleased. However, Martzu was no spring chicken when
it came to this game called life, for he had played it well.
And not without error, he knew many a man had failed
for following his heart and his 'Love Rod', instead of
his mind. He was really against the move, but he would
let his son, who was becoming a young man, make this
decision on his own. It will affect no one's life but his
own. He had confidence in his son, yet, he knew we are
human and for that reason, and that reason alone, he
knew we were all allowed mistakes.

After speaking with his father, De'marco thought
about all they had discussed, and he went over a few
other things in his mind. After doing this, he figured
this was as good a time as any to call Jennifer and
discuss the matter. Besides, he was feeling a little
needy. So, he picked up the phone and called his little
lady.

"Hey! De'marco," Jennifer said happily, as she picked
up the phone.

"Hey beautiful, what you up to?"

"I was waiting for you to call, Mister."

"Oh, were you?"

"Yes, I wuus."

"So you want to get together?" De'marco asked with
a hint of mischief in his voice.

Returning the mischievous tone, Jennifer said, *"Why
yeeesss, what do you suggest?"*

*"Let's go over on Broad Street to Franklin Park and
talk, how's that?"*

"Fine with me, but izz talking aaallllzz we gonna do?"
She asked in a whiney voice.

"Yes, wezz gonna talk fo' sho, and if its okay with you, wezz gonna use some body language!"

"Fine with me," Jennifer said with a happy tone.

"Well, what ya still on the phone for gurrl!?"

Jennifer said bye and hung up quickly.

Jennifer picked De'marco up moments later. As they drove to the park, they flirted with each other and discussed the day's events. Jennifer was eager to hear De'marco's answer to her question of them living together. She thought on it herself, and just like all females do, she went over in her mind how the conversation should go, word for word, and even had a plan B, if needed. They parked and got out, meeting in front of the car to hold hands. They strolled through the park, looking up at the stars. The air was fresh and the temperature was just right.

"I bet you can't do a cartwheel…" Jennifer said, as she skipped forward and twisted sideways, as she sprang to her hands and turned upside-down. Her summer dress slid down, revealing she had no panties on.

"Oh, no you didn't!" De'marco said, as he started to give chase. Jennifer screamed, and tried to run. But he was on her too quickly.

"So you want to come out here with no panties, hunh?!? I got something for that. You bad girl." Sounding like a pirate, *"Come 'er lil one!"*

He grabbed her to him firmly and started kissing her. He didn't waste any time. He undid his pants, and lifted her dress up, feeling her wetness with his hand. He knew she was ready, so he lifted her up, catching her by surprise.

"Oh, my god, what are you doing?"

"Shhhh!" As he placed his tongue in her mouth. She wrapped her legs around him. He cupped both butt cheeks as he slid her down on his awaiting massive joystick.

"Ohhh, oh,oh,oh," Jennifer let out. They had had sex several times, but she was not yet used to his size. His

girth felt so good to her. It sent the sensation of thousands of massage nodules throughout her entire body. With her hands around his neck, he bounced her up and down, she opened her eyes, she couldn't believe they were making love outside at the park. She looked over his shoulder and saw a couple in the distance looking at them. She didn't even care. It felt too good to care, as she kissed him on his lips, neck, rubbing his face.

Not knowing what compelled her, she whispered in his ear, *"Hold me by my waist tightly."*

As soon as he did this she allowed herself to fall backwards. He held her waist, as she practically hung from him upside-down, this turned De'marco on even more. He began to bounce her back and forth as he thrusted in and out of her. There was no controlling the depth of penetration. It caught Jennifer off guard as he slid to the fullest depth of her.

She screamed aloud, *"Oh my God, De'marcoooo!!! Oh! Oh! Oh!"*

She was over come by the pleasure that delivered so much pain. She couldn't stop him, wouldn't stop him. She just went for the ride. It was like a slow motion movie. She moaned with each stroke, as her head bounced around like a rag doll. She caught glimpse of the stars, this added even more to the pleasure she was receiving. Yes, De'marco was applying his virile and she felt every inch of it. But there was no stopping it. No, not now, and as far as Jennifer was concerned, not ever. Besides this is the reason she made the hasty decision that they should move in together. She also was very much in love and wanted him all to herself. She would do what she had to do to make this a reality. Yep, she sure would.

The drive home started out pretty good. The radio was playing MusiqSoulChild. Singing came through the speakers, *"Looove so many people use your name in vain, Looove, those who have faith in you sometimes go astray, Looove, through all the ups and downs of joy and hurt..."* The cool breeze came through the open sunroof top. But, it all came to a stop, when De'marco said he wasn't sure about moving in with Jennifer.

"What do you mean you're not sure?" Jennifer asked with a worried look on her face.

"I mean, don't you love me?"

De'marco twisted around in the passenger seat. He started to feel very uncomfortable as he remembered the talk he and his dad had.

"You know I care for you deeply, but to live together is a big step and what about college?"

Jennifer had expected this (remember she had went over it in her head already on how *SHE* felt it should go), seeing that he would run it by his dad, who taught him to jump into nothing without thinking it out first. She respected this about him. It was one thing out of many that made her want him so bad. A man of gentry he was to be. But she was prepared for this, she had that plan B.

"Okay, you're right. Let's say we do this.... I'll get an apartment, give you a key, and we go from there?!? I'll be going to OSU anyway so it won't hurt me none."

De'marco felt what it was like to be trapped by a woman for the first time in his life. How could he say no? What would be his reason? He looked over at her, and thought, *"I do love her,"* although the thought of other females went through his mind. Not to mention, he had received numbers and talked on the phone to a couple females. Nothing serious, just talk, so no harm done, he thought. He didn't tell Jennifer. He figured the ones he did tell her about were enough. After letting out a deep breath, he said, *"Okay, we'll see how this arrangement works out."*

"Cool," Jennifer smiled and turned the radio back up. Next part of the plan is I'll feed'em and sex'em till all he does is sleep. She looked out the corner of her eye in a devious way and thought, *"Yep, I sure will."*

Once De'marco returned home his father was still awake.

"So, son, how'd it go? Did you talk with her?" De'marco flashed back to the walk in the park and the steamy sex he and Jennifer had shared.

"We talked," De'marco blurted out, realizing how little they had discussed things.

"Annnd?" Martzu questioned.

At that De'marco went into the brief conversation he and Jennifer had in the car on the way back from the park. Martzu stood there listening intently to his son. He realized from what De'marco told him, that neither he nor Jennifer had spoken clearly with each other about what they want in life or from each other. From the sound of things, it seemed that Jennifer might be caught up in her emotions.

"She's a good girl," Martzu thought. *"She couldn't possibly mean any harm."* Besides, he was determined to let his son, for the most part, learn life by experience.

"Okay," he said as he turned to walk away and headed to his bedroom.

"It seems as though you have it all together."

De'marco heard the words, but for some reason he begged to differ.

As he entered his room he noticed the note on his bed. He picked it up. It was in his mother's handwriting.

It read, *"I am not your secretary."* And a list of all whom had called him. As his eyes scanned the list of callers. He noticed Connie's name.

"Connie?" He wondered. *"I'll call everyone tomorrow,"* he said to himself, as he placed the list on the nightstand. He lay back on his bed, feeling good all over. He was still turned on from his sex escapade earlier. He placed his hand down his pants, to fondle himself, only to come across wet stickiness. He quickly pulled his hand out. He lifted his hand to his nose, and smelled it.

"Whoa! I'd better get in the shower."

4

"LADIES, NO SKILLS"

*D*e'marco's schedule was rather tight. Working, studying, and attending class Monday through Friday, was no easy task. And college was nowhere near like being in high school. He made sure he studied hard so he could get where he wanted to be in his career. However, college exposed him to more females, and the way Jennifer acted when she came up on campus made chicks wonder what all the fuss was about. De'marco received several offers for dates. Many he declined. Jennifer had begun to get extremely clingy since she moved in the apartment, he wondered about that. He also wondered how he ended up paying a part of the rent every month?

Her clinginess is what caused him to go on a few dates with a female he'd met in the library. She was all over him the first date. He refused to let things go too far. Until the third date, he could not resist her and how she seduced him. She had cooked, made him relaxed by way of a massage, poured him wine mixed with Gin, and even popped in a porno tape. He had never experienced that! While he watched the tape amazed, she took this as a time to change into an all red fishnet bodysuit. When she came out of her room, she said nothing, not one word. De'marco knew she meant business by the look in her eyes. She walked straight over to him and undid his pants.

He had begun to open his mouth to ask her what she was doing? But before he could get, *"What are you..."* out his mouth.

She took her hand and pushed his head back and said, *"Shut up boy. I got this!"* She pulled his pants down, aggressively, popping the button.

"Stand up!" She said. A tenth of a second later, she yelled, *"Now!"*

De'marco stood up quick, like a soldier at the command of a high-ranking officer. She yanked his pants and boxers down at the same time and in one motion, he and his penis stood at attention. At the very first sight of his manhood, she let out a wicked yell, filled with joy.

"Oh, hell nah! I know you ain't packing like this!"

She pushed him back down on the couch, and climbed on him like an animal, kissing him all on his lips, cheeks, sticking her tongue in his ear, calling him a 'fine muther sucker'. The whole time, she was trying to put him inside her, and couldn't. It was a sight! It was as if she were trying to poke herself to death. Finally, she flopped on her back pulling him on top of her by the ears.

When De'marco entered her, he didn't know what to think. She yelled and apparently became confused, because, for the first 10 minutes she kept saying... *"Oh, my god! Hold up! Stop! Go ahead! Stop! Go ahead one more time."* She told him, *"Hold it right there, don't move for about five minutes."*

De'marco's arms were getting tired. So, he moved.

"I told you don't move!!" She scolded. He couldn't take the abuse so he jumped up to put his clothes on. She was fighting him, trying to stop him. She asked him if he was a faggot or something? Needless to say, he didn't deal with her ever again. He'd even dodge her on campus.

At the time he felt guilty because he and Jennifer had gotten closer. They talked more and she definitely confided in him a lot. Once during their talks she asked him did he remember in school how they used to call him G.M.D.?

He was like, *"Yeah, what did that mean?"*

She revealed how all the girls at school back then referred to him as "Grown Man Dick."

He was shocked! He didn't believe her until she called one of her ghetto-acting friends and she verified it. She was laughing and talking about, *"Sho did,"* so excited she kept running her mouth, telling Jennifer, *"Hell, the way you tell it, it should have been M.D. Monster Dick!"*

At that point Jennifer hung up the phone saying, *"She silly. That's why she can't keep no man, she run her mouth too much,"* as if *she* wasn't in the girls club of 'tell all'.

However, his guilt didn't stop him from other experiences with the ladies at school. There was the professor in his lab that asked him, could she pay him to move some things at her house into the basement. Ready to make a quick buck, he told her, *"Sure"*. Only to find out the art of seduction ran deep in women. She snatched opened the front door before he could even ring the doorbell.

As soon as he stepped in, he knew she had something other than moving in mind. She had on a pair of shorts sooo tight and rode up so high, you could see her entire hips fully. Not to mention, you could see the print of both vagina lips and if you stared long enough you could see the hair print. And if that wasn't enough, the T-shirt she had on was cut to the point you saw the round bottom of her breast. He wanted to excuse her get-up as sleepwear, but it just didn't appear that way.

She shut the door and locked it, then quickly said, *"The stuff I want you to move is up here."*

She turned to go up the stairs, and what do you know?!? Her butt cheeks were hanging out the back. One cheek had a tattoo of a flower on it.

"Follow me," she said looking over her shoulder to notice the look on his face. She entered a room, with him following close behind. She turned and looked in his eyes.

"Look," she said, *"By now you should be aware that you're not here to move anything for me."*

De'marco nodded, *"Ye, Yeah, I kinda figured that. So, what's up?"* He said, shrugging his shoulders curiously.

"Well, do as I do," she said as she stepped out of her shorts and just as quickly, pulled off her T-shirt.

De'marco hesitated, so she walked behind him.

"Here, let me help you."

He still moved reluctantly. She raised up on her tippy toes and placed her mouth to his ear and whispered… *"Look baby, you fucking up my fantasy."* At the same time pinching him on the butt. De'marco began to untie the string in the front of his sweat pants and out of nowhere… *SLAP!* A sting across his butt!

"What the…?" He said, turning around to face this woman standing there with what looked like a bullwhip, or better yet, a three in one bullwhip. *SLAP!* She caught him across the front of his legs. De'marco ran to seek safety on the other side of the bed.

"What are you doing?" He asked shocked and afraid.

"Do like I tell you and you won't have to get this here whippin'" she growled.

De'marco was at a lost on what to do. But another lashing he did not want. So, he came out of his clothes. He wasn't erect, because the lashing had taken all the arousal out of him. However, she was still impressed.

"Well look at that there," she said, *"I done came up. Lay on the bed!"* She said, catching him looking towards his clothes. *"Here, put these on,"* she threw two sets of handcuffs on the bed. De'marco's eyes got wide.

"Put them on for what?" He asked as she raised the whip to strike him.

"Okay, okay," he said fumbling with the cuffs.

"Put those on your ankles and those on your wrists. Now, lay back! I said!"

De'marco laid back shaking. She placed a blindfold over his eyes. And as if that and the handcuffs weren't enough, he felt himself being tied to the bed. She fondled him from head to toe rubbing, kissing, biting and grabbing, his manhood. Asking him, *"What do you have here?!"* And answering for him, *"You don't even know, do you?!?"* He felt her licking his manhood as if it was an ice cream cone. De'marco had told her if she would untie him he would help her.

"I don't need your help! I got this!" She exclaimed. *"Yeah, I got this."*

After what seemed to be an hour of licking, kissing, rubbing and sucking on his body. De'marco had to admit; he was turned on in a weird way. It was as if the restraints and the blindfold enhanced the sensations.

All she kept saying was, *"I got this, trust and believe, I got this,"* as she worked her magic. She mounted him with more ease than the others, but at no point did she go all the way down.

"No, no, no," she said, *"Too much going on here. Don't need much for what I'm trying to do anyway."* She kept De'marco tied up for hours, doing some of everything. He even remembered feeling her tongue go down between his legs, sucking, and licking his scrotum.

She yelled, *"Yes! Yes! Yes!"* And clamped down on De'marco tightly and it was over. She untied him, handed him his clothes, threw fifty dollars on the bed and said, *"Let yourself out."* She walked into the bathroom and turned on the shower. The following Monday at school, she acted as if she didn't even know him.

"Mr. Poitier is there a problem? If you continue to stare off as if you are not following the lesson, I have no problem failing you."

He wasted no time he dropped the class.

Then there was Melissa and Malinda, they were twins, at least that's what they told people. Really, their birthdays just happen to be on the same day and they had been hanging around each other since they were kids. They acted alike, but in no way looked alike. They offered to take him out to eat for helping them with a class assignment. Somehow, after that, the three

of them ended up in the back of Malinda's Expedition
with the radio blasting Missy Elliott's *"Pussy don't fail
me now. I got to turn this nigga out, so he don't want
nobody else..."* The three of them, hot, naked, in the
truck. The two girls took turns doing the most
pleasurable things to him. Yes, they were skilled! They
even had times where they kissed and caressed each
other. They held back nothing. They may not have
looked alike, but they shared everything, so it seemed.
They would taste his manhood then each other's love
pocket. They made a sandwich out of him. They even
had a contest with him. The amazing part to De'marco,
was all this not only took place in the backseat of a
truck, but in the middle of the afternoon in the
McDonalds parking lot with people parking next to
them, going in and out.

This erotic ceremony caused him to drip green pus and
to piss fire when he urinated. Oh yeah, and a trip to the
hospital. He had to bring his father in on this one, cause
he had no medical insurance and his money was too
tight to afford a hospital bill.

After the hospital visit, his father handed him a black
box that read "Magnum" in gold letters. His father
explained the importance of the condoms. De'marco
wondered, why not before now! Also, his father
explained to him the importance for preserving himself.
He asked him about Jennifer. Telling him, had you
given her something like that, that would have been
terrible and a disaster to their relationship. De'marco
knew his father was right and decided it was time to get
control of himself and calm down on his sexual
escapades. However, this didn't stop until after several
rendezvous, the last being unwarranted, as if the others
weren't. This incident was very much unseen. A young
lady named Tangie. He would run into her at the library
occasionally and from time to time, she'd speak and
what have you. So, one day she asked De'marco could
she ask a favor of him.

He said, *"Sure"*.

She had explained how she was moving and needed a little help but only with the unloading. She told him it would be her and her mother there. De'marco remembered moving Jennifer and although she didn't have a lot, it was a pain and at the time he was glad to have a little help from Leroy. So, he told her he would help and got the address. He figured if anything didn't look right, he would just keep going. So, he borrowed Jennifer's car as he did times before. As he pulled up, there they sat in a U-Haul truck. They were happy to see him. They didn't think he was going to show. They had gotten the few things moved in, and they begged De'marco to allow them to fix him something to eat. He accepted the offer. They made sandwiches and talked about De'marco's background. Tangie pulled out a blender and just so happened to have a bottle of "Bacardi 151 Rum". Before long, they were sitting, drinking daiquiris, while Tangie's mom spoke on her childhood. They listened to music, even danced a little, before De'marco knew it he was drunker than Cootie Brown. When he woke up, he lay there on his back with a splitting headache, okay, a hangover no doubt.

So, he lay there with his eyes closed trying to put together what lead to this hangover, but before he could piece things together, the person on his right rolls over and says, *"Oh, I have to be going."* He opens his eyes to see a lady putting on her pants, saying, *"Tangie, I have to go, your father's going to kill me."*

"Okay mama, call me later," the voice coming from the person lying snug on his left side.

"Okay baby, I will, and whatever you do don't try to tackle that Mandingo by yourself. You could get yourself in a lotta trouble." She said giggling.

De'marco looked up with blurry eyes to catch the figure of the woman whom was seconds ago sliding her pants on, now waving goodbye and exiting the door. He figured he better get a move on, he had Jennifer's car.

And from the looks of things, it was daylight, the next morning. But before he could move he felt the person next to him fumbling around under the cover, his manhood being sought out. First, a hand, then the feel of a warm wet mouth, the wiggling of a soft, gentle tongue followed by the sound of sucking and slurping. He raised his head to see the cover bobbing up and down. He dropped his head back on the pillow and thought, damn what next?

De'marco started feeling drained from all his erotic adventures, he decided to slow it down. He took note of the many females and pleasures he was introduced to. He noticed after two or three get-togethers that would be it.

Some even would tell him, they liked him and enjoyed themselves, but they were straight. He didn't mind but, there were a few he would not have mind frolicking with one more time.

The thought of it all made him realize he loved Jennifer, so he decided to spend some quality time with her. Besides, he needed to get right.

He allowed himself to get behind in a class, and that was not allowed. Not just because he was studying law, but because he was "De'marco Martzu Poitier" and he didn't play that.

Ever since Jennifer had gotten the apartment, De'marco was more so in and out, not really staying but a night or two, here and there. So, when he called her and said he will be coming to stay and was bringing clothes Jennifer was excited. She hoped he would have been moved in with her, she didn't care for those lonely nights. Many a night she would call his cell phone to get no answer. Her friends would try to tell her he was with other females. That made her want to go find him in the middle of the night, but after speaking with her mother, she thought against it.

Her mother told her, *"If you go looking for something, you will find it. And that could be emotionally and mentally damaging and something you don't want or need at this point in your life. Your college education is more important. If he loves you he'll be there."*

She held strong to those words, and there was truth in them.

De'marco began to think living with Jennifer wasn't all too bad, she cooked, she cleaned and it seemed every free moment she got she tried to sex his brains out. The only time there even seemed to be a problem, was that dreadful week before her menstruation. He didn't know what to expect during that week, an argument, a fight, tears for what seemed to be for no reason. Hell, it was so crazy, yet so predictable, he had learned to time it, and spend that week staying away from the apartment the most he could.

Other than that, things were fine, from what he could recall. De'marco figured he would put a little more thought into it. And maybe, just maybe he would move all the way in.

* * * * * * * * * * * * * * * * * *

Two years had gone by since De'marco's graduation from high school, and the buzz was out on the young "Mandingo" stud that was packing a mean twelve inches and had all night stamina. However, Connie noticed at the end of every conversation concerning De'marco and one of his sexual stalkers, they would all say it was good and he was extremely large, but he was either unaware of his size, or he didn't know what he was doing. Either way, it was said he had the tools, but no skills. That was okay though, Connie had the fix for that. She knew how to help the young naïve man out and get her groove back too. She just needed to locate De'marco and get him to take the bait, which she figured wouldn't be too difficult, compared to some of the lame moves those who had him pulled, she knew she could come up.

She decided she wouldn't even go too far with it, *"Easy money,"* she thought, *"Like taking candy from a baby."*

5
"REMINISCENCE"

*C*onnie stepped from the tub and dried off. She reached in the closet and grabbed a plum colored cotton robe. She marveled over its softness and the elegant white stitched flowers that lined the sleeves of the robe. After looking at herself in the mirror for a few moments, she walked downstairs. As she entered her highly decorated sitting room she thought, *"What am I going to do today? Nothing!"* She giggled to herself. *"It's Sunday, no work, just got off my period yesterday. Just got out a nice hot bubble bath. Time for a drink and some T.V."* She fixed herself an apple martini, her favorite no doubt.

"Aaah, delicious," she said after taking a sip of the cold intoxicating drink. She placed it on the table, grabbed the remote and flopped on the couch aiming the remote and the power button all in one motion. As she drank her martini and flipped through the channels, she pondered on her game plan for De'marco. That's all she had been thinking about lately. Connie had become a woman who went after what she wanted regardless of how forbidden it was, and 9 times out of 10 she got it. She figured De'marco wouldn't be an exception. She smiled as she thought of the young tender specimen.

Her lustful thoughts were interrupted by the sound of the telephone ringing. She wondered who it was? She picked up the receiver, *"House of Beau... I mean, hello."*

A recording came on, *"This is a collect call from an inmate at Fort Worth, Texas federal penitentiary..."*

"Sly," she said to herself.

"If you wish to except this call press 3. For rates and..." Connie pressed 3.

"Hello Sly," she said, although she wasn't too happy he had called. She figured she wouldn't be rude and not except the call. It was the least she could do seeing she had picked up the receiver.

"Hello there beautiful," Sly said in a tone she was familiar with. *"How are you?"* He asked.

"I'm fine, Sly. And yourself?"

"As well as could be expected I guess. I won't complain though. Not that you'd care to listen if I did."

"No, I don't think I would," Connie told him. *"So this call, is it personal or business?"*

"Wow!" Sly said sounding truly surprised, *"Talk about cutting to the chase..."*

"What is it, Sly? You're a man now. I mean, after all these years I would hope that was the case. So cough it up, what is it? Why'd ya call?"

"To see if there's still any room in that warm loving heart of yours for me?" He said, continuing to sound charming.

"Why of course..." Connie told him, *"Just not much,"* she added.

"Ouch! Baby that hurt. So tell me what do I need to do to get the love back?"

"Nothing, Sly. Now seeing that this is a long distance call and collect mind you, I take it I'm getting charged twice for one phone call. So give it up baby. What's happening?"

"Look Connie baby, I'll be getting out soon, within the next year. You have to have your papers and things right when you're released, as far as where you're going, who you're gonna be living with, so on and so forth. And I was just thinking that maybe you would consider looking out for me. I mean, it would even give us a chance to get reacquainted. Sometimes I reminisce on the times we've shared. You have to admit Connie we had some good ones."

Connie sighed, *"I don't deny that Sly."*

She knew he'd be getting out in the following year or so, and was also aware of the assistance he would need. But the part about getting reacquainted, was something she definitely wasn't trying to do. She knew the chances of her being willing to do one, without him trying to do the other was slim. She was a woman now and knew better than to set herself up like that.

"Sly baby, I wish you well, but I'm not going to be able to do it."

"Man Connie, it's like that?!? I mean after all I've done. You still got the shops I helped you get. Not to mention, I haven't said anything about how after a while you just disappeared on me. What'd you do, fall off the earth?"

"First of all Sly, this is where this conversation comes to an end. But! Before I go, allow me to address your remarks…Yes, I do still have the shops, and I'll thank you again, just as I did back then when you helped me get them, yet I'm sure I've repaid you, because it was me who paid your lawyer fees. Also, not to bring up the not so good times, but I also covered your little debt you owed to the bookie. And if I remember correctly, they had intentions on paying you a visit if you didn't give them their money."

Sly knew he had screwed up. Her words were slow and calm. It had been years, but he knew what that meant, she was angry and had enough. She had even brought up an incident they agreed to let stay in the past, the debt. He owed $20,000 to a bookie behind a football game. He was going to pay them, as he always did, until he went to jail. He figured they would leave it alone. Until another inmate whom he didn't know at all, approached him with an 'amount due bill' from the bookie and let him know, *"Handle your business, so we don't have to handle you!"*

Connie somehow came through for him and made good on the debt.

Continuing on Connie said, *"The part where you claim I just disappeared, I held you down for 10 years straight. Money, visits, letters, only to find out you had 3 kids while we were together and check this out, BY 3 DIFFERENT WOMEN! OH, BUT NO! Let's not overlook the fact of you being engaged to one of them. Sly, I was that bitch and you know it. The one who had your back. Yeah, baby,"* Connie said to him, *"You've done a lot, but the problem was, the pain you caused began to outweigh the pleasure."*

"I know Connie baby." Sly said, *"Do me a favor? Just think about it."*

"Oh yeah," Connie said with a slight laugh, *"That's exactly what I'll do...just think about it. Now with that, you have a nice life. I'll be needing to go now. I'm sure my bill is more than I care to pay at this time. Goodbye Sly."*

"I still love you Connie. Never forget that."

"I won't Sly," she said and then hung up.

She couldn't believe Sly had called her with that foolishness. He would have been better off letting it be known that he just needed a place to stay, with no commitments and no strings attached.

"Reacquainted? Yeah, right!" Connie thought, as she walked over to her bar.

She poured a double shot of Grey Goose Vodka. She drank it straight down, and poured another one. She looked through her CD's until she found what she was looking for. Mary J. Blige's "What's the 411?" She popped it in, hit play, grabbed the bottle of Grey Goose, and headed for the couch. As she sat down, a tear ran down her face. She couldn't help but think of how Sly was her first in a lot of things. She leaned back to listen to the music. Mary's voice was a work of art! *"Yooou, you remind of a love that I once knew..."* It's often said that music soothes the savage beast and the sounds of Mary surely began to have a calming effect over Connie, with the help of the Vodka.

She couldn't help but to give into the reminiscent thought that began to pour into her mind. The thoughts brought on by a phone call from a love that she once knew. She wanted to help Sly, she truly did. But, not in the way he wanted help. Sly wasn't totally bad. She could recall times he showed acts of goodness. Like when they first met, she had fallen out with her mother, because her mothers' boyfriend made a pass at her, physically and verbally.

Her mother was so blinded by love and this man's dick, that she constantly gave acknowledgement to it, *"Oh that dick, it's so pretty, so nice, so perfect. It makes me feel so good. I've never had the taste of nothing so good in my life,"* are some the accolades her mother would give to this man's manhood. When Connie told her mother about her boyfriend's misconduct, her mom kicked her out of the house and stayed with him. Connie remembered the incident so clearly, as if it were yesterday. It was something that she would never forget, how could she? It was the beginning of the end for her and her mother's relationship.

She was standing in the shower soaping up and singing to herself. When she felt a cold breeze from the bathroom door being opened, *"Mom?"* She called out. She didn't get an answer so she peeked out the shower only to see Calvin, her mother's boyfriend standing there.

"Oh, hey," she said embarrassed.

"I'm sorry for taking so long, I'll be out in a sec," she said figuring he had to use the bathroom and couldn't wait.

What threw her off is when he pulled the shower curtain back, looked in and said, *"Take your time."*

She figured he'd leave out angry or something and she didn't intend to be rude to the man so she hurriedly rinsed off and turned off the water. She removed her shower cap and hung it on the hook. When she pulled the shower curtain back, she was taken by surprise to see him now standing there with nothing on except his underwear, and a towel in his hand. She placed her hands over her private area and her breasts in an attempt to cover up.

"If you would have just given me a moment longer I could have been out your way," she said to him, as nervous a teenage girl could possibly be. Why was this man standing here in his underwear she wondered, afraid to move.

"Here you go," he said holding out the towel, *"I brought this for you."*

As she reached to take the towel from his hand, he grabbed her arm. At first it seemed as though he was helping her step out the tub. But when she was out he pulled her close to him.

"Let me dry you off," he said, already doing so.

Connie was nervous, she was no fool, she realized this man's intentions were no good.

"Here, let me get out the bathroom," she said, *"So you can do what you need to do,"* attempting to walk away.

"No, no, no. Stay, its okay," he told her. *"I see you're built like your mother, nice and thick. You gonna be a bad mutha when you get older,"* he told her as he rubbed her breast and stomach. Connie looked down shaking and noticed he was fully erect. He caught her looking at his erect penis.

Then he told her, *"Yeah baby, let me take care of you like I do your mother."*

"Th...th...that's okay," Connie told him.

He was rubbing her thigh, *"You know your mother loves me and the way I make her feel. Let me do the same for you."*

Then Connie froze as he placed his finger on her clit and began rubbing in circles. Connie knew this wasn't supposed to be taking place and began crying.

"Where's my mom?" She asked Calvin.

"Shhh," he said, as he probed his finger inside her vaginal opening.

"Ouch!" Connie said, *"You're hurting me."*

She pulled away and pushed him, as she did, they both took notice of the blood on his finger. Connie had been so scared she had forgotten she was on her period.

"You nasty bitch!" Calvin scolded, as he went out the bathroom. Once Connie pulled herself together, she was surprised to find her mom right down the hall lying on her bed drunk. When she woke her up and told her what had happened, she couldn't believe how her mother acted. Calling her names, accusing her of wanting Calvin. At first thought, Connie figured it was the alcohol talking. But when her mom threw her out and never let her return home, she learned quickly what a man could do to a woman's mind. Oddly enough, Connie would see Calvin again later in life at court.

Now, Connie was 17 and homeless, and didn't know anything about the streets or life, for that matter. She was sitting at the bus stop waiting to catch the bus to a friend's house that she had called and said they were willing to sneak and let her stay at their house without telling their parents.

While waiting on the bus, here comes Sly, pulling up in a blue Cavalier. He didn't just roll down the window and holler out. He pulled the car over, parked and got out, walked over and sat down at the bus stop and started talking to her as if he'd known Connie forever.

The first thing that came out of his mouth was, *"Man, let me tell you, people crazy. How my boy gonna use my dog and get him killed, then say, "My bad?"*

Apparently, this was the beginning of his career as a hustler. At the time, pit bull fighting was the 'in' thing. He kept on about how he was mad, but not really mad.

"It's the principle of the matter," he said. *"It's principalities in this."*

Connie looked at him and asked, *"Do you even know what the word principalities mean?"*

He paused for a minute and the goofy look he gave along with his answer caused them both to start laughing. Connie was sad as could be at that moment, but he made her laugh and for that brief moment, the pain was gone. By the time the bus pulled up, they talked so much, Connie felt comfortable with him. So when he told her she could ride with him to get something to eat, she didn't see a problem with it, plus, she was starving! While they ate, she could tell he hadn't finished school by the use of his improper grammar. Yet, she could tell he was mature. She picked up on that when he asked, *"Sooo, what's your story?"*

"What?" Connie asked.

"What's going on in your life? You have a look in your eyes as if all has failed you."

Once she told him, he leaned back in his seat like an older man would and said, *"Well, what are you going to do? Go back to mama's or try to make it on your own?"*

Because Connie hadn't given much thought into it, she began to cry.

"Oh, I'm sorry," he told her, *"I didn't know you hadn't put any thought into your life."*

At that moment, he suggested she go home with him and from that point on, they were inseparable.

As Connie brought that thought to an end, she poured more Vodka in her glass. After she took a sip she yelled, *"That's right, Mary! Sing it!"* She then pointed her glass towards the stereo and nodded her head as if she and Mary were toasting together.

"Old Sly," she began to think again of the times shared by them. She remembered how Sly would always talk tough, then say my mama told me this, my mama told me that.

Connie would asked him, *"Boy, where yo' mama at? Why I ain't never met her?"*

He asked her, *"You wanna meet my mama? We can go visit her this Sunday."*

Connie got dressed as clean as she could with what little she had. They drove way out to a town called Sandusky, Ohio. They pulled up to a building that at first glance looked like old military housing. They walked in and went straight past the front desk to room 27. There laid Sly's mother, speechless with IV's in her arm.

"Hi mama!" He said to her, *"I have someone I want you to meet. I guess you could call her my girlfriend seeing that she eats off my plate, drinks from the same glass after me, and the other day she even had the nerve to fart in front of me. I didn't care for that mama, but she did it. Mama this is Connie. Connie this is my mama, Mrs. Fountain."* He said finishing introducing them. Although the woman was apparently in poor medical conditions, Connie didn't want to come across rude, this was his mother.

So she raised her hand as to wave and said, *"Hi, Mrs. Fountain."*

"She can't hear you," Sly said, *"She has cancer so bad, it has caused her to slip into some kinda coma."* Connie stood there looking back and forth between the terminally ill woman and her son. He looked just like his mother. Then as luck would have it, as Connie stood there for the first time meeting his mother, ill fate had to show its face. The heart monitor began to beat strangely, then show a straight, flat line across the screen.

Connie panicked, *"You want me to get a nurse!?"*

"No," Sly said as he ran and shut the room door and propped a chair up against it to keep the nurses and doctors out.

As they beat on the door, Sly walked over and unplugged all the devices his mother was hooked up to. He then leaned over and kissed her.

"Bye, mama," he said, *"You don't have to hurt no mo'."*

Walking towards the door, he grabbed Connie's arm as he moved the chair from the door. The doctors and nurses rushed in with all types of medical equipment. Sly just kept walking, pulling Connie with him.

Connie asked, *"Aren't you going to tell them what happened?"*

"There's no need," Sly said, *"The ultimate reality is, she's dead. I'll miss her, but I promised I wouldn't cry."*

As they jumped in the car, Connie was so upset. She had never seen death take place ever.

"What about a funeral?" Connie asked.

"I don't have the money," Sly told her, *"I spent all my money trying to pay the $1,200 dollars a month it cost for her to stay there."*

It dawned on Connie that this was the reason he'd been in his apartment a year, hustling everyday, and only had a mattress on the floor of his bedroom, with a 19" black and white T.V.

"What about your family?"

"Don't have none that I know," he told her.

"There's got to be somebody...," Connie said, determined not to allow him to carry the burden of his mother's death alone.

"Where's your father?"

"Oh yeah!" He said, as if excited, *"I've never even thought of my dad. We can go by his place now."*

"Good!" Connie said, *"Let's go."*

Connie, glad that there would be an adult involved, felt somewhat better. As they pulled up besides a large building and drove around the back, up an alley, Connie figured his dad must live in one of those big lofts like in the movies.

When Sly stopped the car and jumped out telling her to follow him, it really made her feel as though all wasn't lost. His father could handle everything and give the lady a descent burial. She thought maybe Sly had to take a leak or something, he started moving a pile of old boxes. But to her surprise, there laid a drunken man with a white woman beside him. The woman looked up and started shaking the drunken man until he awoke.

"What woman!?" He snapped.

"Get up, your son is here."

The thought of that caused Connie to snap out of her moment of reminiscing. That was a sad moment in life. It was also the first time Sly had her suck his dick. She did it out of compassion for what he'd been through. From that day forth it seemed as though he kept his dick in her mouth. That's also when he stepped his hustle game up from pit bull fighting and stealing, to selling drugs. From then on, life wasn't the same.

Connie stood up, *"Am I tipsy?"* She asked herself, as she walked over to the stereo. She was wobbling and tripping over nothing.

She answered herself, *"Naw bitch, you drunk."*

Sitting on the floor, she pulled out a Stevie Wonder CD.

"Heeey, Stevie baby!" She said holding the CD case close to her face as if she was going to kiss it. She popped in the CD and pushed play.

"Sing to me Stevie!" She screamed, and he did, or so she thought.

She glanced over at the couch, as she did she measured the distance and told herself she wasn't getting up to walk over there. Then her eyes caught sight of the half-empty bottle of Vodka, *"Here I am, come here baby,"* she said, *"Mama ain't gonna leave youzz byzzz yo' self now."*

Once she made it back to the couch, she grabbed the bottle and flopped on the couch. She pointed the remote and turned the volume up.

"Over time, I've been building my castle of love. Just for two, though you never knew you were my reason...," are the words she heard Stevie Wonder sing as she went back to reminiscing on the times she and Sly shared.

"Sylvester Fountain," she thought.

He had become something else over the years, but the boy had a good heart at one time and he showed it more so within the first few months they had been dating.

Summer was over and school was starting. Sly asked Connie what was she going to do about her education? She asked him how could she go to school with no new clothes and without the supplies she needed to attend class. Plus, everyone probably knew her mother threw her out for some man. She told him she wasn't feeling school no more.

Sly snapped, *"You going to school. Ain't no need for two uneducated people sitting around bringing each other down. You going to school, you hear me!?"* He grabbed her up in the neck.. *"I'll buy what you need. But you going to school!"*

And she did. He bought what she needed, as well as, drove her there everyday, rain, snow, or shine. They were happy when she graduated. He was the only one who came to see her graduate. Connie and her mother didn't speak much, if at all, during that time. When graduation was over, Sly handed her a small box with a gold herringbone bracelet inside. It was the nicest thing anyone had ever done for her and she was glad all her friends saw him give it to her.

Some time later, he'd gotten mad and snatched it off her arm while they were riding in the car and threw it out the window. It was a long time after that, before he bought her anything again. It hurt her, because it was the first thing anybody ever bought for her. She excused the incident by telling herself, at least she had graduated and it was because of him and all his support.

So much took place during the summer that followed her graduation. It's hard to believe so much could have happened in such a little time. Sly started making more money and the shopping sprees started taking place frequently, along with a lot of partying. Connie's body was starting to take form and shape like never before. Her hips swelled up, her ass went out and so did her breast. That gave rise to Sly's insecurities, which he dealt with by cursing her out, wanting to fight, or having the most outrageous sex with her. Every time he did something new to her he would tell her *she* was a freak.

As time went on, she began to believe it and started desiring more and more sex. At the time, it was cool because Sly was freaky too. He was so freaky he had her put on a dress with no panties or bra. They went to Columbus, Ohio International Airport, bought 2 round trip tickets to Atlanta. They went to downtown Atlanta, to the Sheraton Hotel, which has a glass elevator on the outside of it. They got on it, about half way up, hit the emergency stop button, he turned her around, bent her over, threw her dress up on her back and knocked sparks out of her kitty cat while she stared out the elevator window at the traffic and people walking by. That was just one of her most memorable moments and also one of the times she came the hardest. Yeah, she was weak in the knees from that experience.

"Oh, yes," Connie thought to herself, *"Let me not forget that July, for my 18th birthday, our trip to Cancun."*

She and Sly flew out to Cancun, Mexico for a week. They got a hotel suite on the beach where they could look out at the ocean. The sight was beautiful! To add to the romance of it, they made love on the beach 2 nights in a row. Under the light of the moon, which appeared to be sitting right on top of the water, casting a sparkling path from it to the sands of the beach where they laid hunching away. And just as she thought it could get no better, they spent the last 2 days on a cruise ship right off the shore. They partied and drank some of the most expensive champagne money could buy. The last night on the cruise they walked to the front of the ship where Sly rolled up some weed, then told her, *"Tonight, you get to smoke with me."*

They stood at the back of the ship smoking away and looking at the immense waters in front of them. After flicking the cigarette of weed over the side, Sly grabbed Connie and started kissing her. She was so high that she could barely function. She began to comprehend things once Sly began guiding her down to her knees and undoing his pants and dropped his boxers to his ankles.

Connie thought to protest, *"Sly...,"* she started to say, but didn't get to finish. He had pulled her head back by her hair and gave her a mouth full of his manhood.

"Oh well," she thought, *"We're on a cruise and we're high. What happens here, stays here. No one will know but us."*

So she worked overtime like never before and as he started to swell for release, she tried to pull away, but he held her head in place with one hand and threw the other hand up with a balled up fist and yelled, *"I'M THE KING OF THE WORLD!"*

Once he was done, she stood up spitting and to what she thought was the clapping of water against the ship, was none other than a small audience of people watching the miniature porno Connie and Sly put on. Sly had a little bit more to offer... As they walked away, a guy they were passing happened to say, *"Hey sexy,"* to Connie, no doubt turned on by what he'd just seen. Connie looked over at the guy for a brief second. When she turned her head back, she was met with a slap!

"You know him?" Asked Sly.

"No," Connie pleaded.

The rest of the night, Sly made Connie stay in the cabin while he ran about the ship partying. She excused that by saying, it was cool, with it being their first time on a cruise ship. Thinking about it later, it was also the first time Sly came in her mouth and the first time he slapped her... both in front of people, that is.

That same summer, they visited New York and stayed at the Waldorf Astoria, Sly spent hella money for that place. New York was New York. Connie didn't care for it, too many people, too much, *"Yo, yo, peep this son. Yo, kid...*" so on and so forth. The buildings were worth seeing, but all in all, it wasn't her cup of tea.

Connie, momentarily coming out of her daydream, sat there on the couch with a blank stare, not knowing if she should laugh or cry. A vacuous feeling overtook her for a moment. She took another drink, this time straight from the bottle, no need for a glass when you start out as a borderline drunk and are already inebriated. Strange thing about the moment to her, was that she enjoyed remembering about the past. She even challenged herself to see if she could remember the craziest thing that they'd done? She thought for a minute, and then it hit her, she let out a deep laugh and said out loud, *"That's what he gets!"*

She recalled the event that took place when Sly had some partners who had talked him into coming to what they referred to as a "freak party." They told him to bring her. When they arrived, everything seemed cool. There were people in the front living room of this large mansion, just drinking, talking. A few people were kinda dancing where they stood. As the night went on, folks started migrating to the back of the crib. One of Sly's friends told him to bring her and come to the back. They entered a large room. So large she wouldn't have believed it, had she not seen it for herself. Yet, that wasn't the most surprising part... What took Connie aback was the large beds and couches throughout the room and people fucking everywhere you looked! Even on the floor!

Connie and Sly were the only ones in the room with their clothes on, and those that noticed began clapping and chanting, *"Take it off! Take it off!"*

Sly wasted no time. Connie was rather hesitant, but eventually did it. Needless to say, she had the tightest body throughout the place, causing males and females alike, to gawk. Guys winked, chicks stuck out and flicked their tongues. So, how did Connie and Sly get separated? She felt it was intentional on Sly's part, leaving her to fight off the vultures by herself. The people were like animals! The chicks would surround her, as if to talk and before long they would start rubbing on her curves. What would start out as a gesture of admiration, turned into an invitation to sex. Sly returned finally, with some guy and a chick with him. They stood there smiling.

"Hey baby," Sly said, *"Check this out..., me and my dude here have been chit chatting. As you can see, this is a real adult party, people having fun and all. We were discussing swapping ladies."*

"What!?" Connie asked.

"You know babe..., you and him, me and her," he said as he pointed from her to the guy and then himself to the girl. Connie was truly reluctant, until Sly pulled her to the side and had a very strong grip on her arm.

"Look!" He told her, *"You are truly beginning to embarrass me. His girl down, and my girl need to be getting down. Do you follow me?"* He demanded, adding a firm jerk to her arm.

"Ok Sly, let's do it," Connie said, mad as all get out.

So they all walked over to a semi-vacant bed. The guy she was to have sex with had a towel wrapped around him the entire time. Once he pulled the towel off, Sly who was already indulging with the other female, noticed that the enormous totem pole of a dick the guy was packing, had him beat by far, width and length. He had a look in his eyes as if he'd seen a ghost. When he looked at Connie, she pretended not to see him and pulled the guy down on top of her.

The guy did everything to Connie that night! He kissed her from head to toe, to eating her out from the front and the back, to having her stand up, bend over and hold her ankles. One time, he had her put her hands on the floor as if to do a handstand, then he wrapped her legs around his waist and went to town. He put on such a show, that other people having sex stopped what they were doing to watch. He worked Connie so good, he had her screaming, moaning, and asking him, *"Why you doing this to me, hunh?! Why you fucking me so good!?"*

He even got her to do the 69 in front of Sly. There was nothing he could do or say, because he started it. When the party was over, Connie was worn out. The guy, although he didn't know Connie from Jack, had treated her like a queen all night. When Sly got her home, for some reason his jealousy took him there and he beat her ass. That was the night she came to her senses. She began paying attention to things. Why she hadn't left Sly, is what she wondered to herself. Then, she realized she couldn't. She didn't have money or a car. Sly kept her totally dependent on him, for everything. He kept her in the house. She didn't move unless he moved her. Had he not gotten busted, there's no telling how long that foolishness would have lasted?!?

"Well," she thought, *"Those were the adventures we shared brought on by the hardships life dealt us."* A lot of times they found it unfair, but it was theirs all the same. At that, Connie went to sleep drunk.

6

"LESSONS IN LOVE MAKING"

*A*fter putting her ear to the street, it only took Connie a few days to find out what she pretty much already knew. De'marco had been staying at the apartment with Jennifer. She was going to call there and ask for him since she used to babysit him and knew the family well. But after she remembered back to the graduation how Jennifer cut her eyes at her a few times, she decided against it. She had come up with the cell phone number and that was good enough. As she thought out her plan, not only did it make her anxious, it also aroused her. If De'marco was like all she had been hearing, and anything like his father, it would be all to the good. She heard De'marco must have been chilling out, staying out the way, because no one had seen or heard from him other than up on campus during class. Connie had a good feeling about that too because that meant it was possible he was horny and down for something different, you know what they say?!?

"Ain't no pussy better than old pussy, but new pussy!" She couldn't help but laugh at herself.

"Let me call this tender young thang and get the ball rolling," she thought.

She dialed De'marco's cell. As it rang she couldn't help but smile. She knew she was up to no good and that alone turned her on. De'marco being subjected to the streets over the last couple of years, answered his phone with a, *"Yep, yep?"*

"De'marco?" Connie asked lightweight surprised.

"This me, who dis?"

"This is Connie, baby. How you doing?" Looking at Connie as a friend of his parents and one who knew him as a child, made him lose the so-called hip demeanor.

"Oh, I'm fine. How are you?"

92

"Fine baby, you busy?"

"No, why. What's up?"

"Look baby, I need to know if you can get away this Friday evening?" Before he could even answer, she blurted out, *"And where you been? I done called your father's house looking for you."*

That was kind of a lie, because although she had called his fathers' house for him, it was some time ago. De'marco remembered the note his mother had left on his bed with Connie's number on it. But that was so long ago, he thought.

"I'm sorry, I've been busy. You know college, working this part-time job."

"That's right, you going to ah, uh, Franklin University. Taking up law, right?!?"

"Yeah, that's right."

"How's it going for you?" Connie was determined not to give him a chance to think.

"It's going good," De'marco managed to squeeze in, *"Now about this Friday, what's the deal?"*

"Look, do you know where my shop is on 161 and Cleveland Ave?"

"Yeah, I'm familiar with where it's at."

"Well, meet me at the shop say about nine in the evening, ok?"

Before De'marco could answer, she asked, *"How long you have left in school?"*

De'marco was tired of being interrupted, *"Probably another four and a half years. I only have in two."*

"Well, hurry up and finish so you can be my Johnny Cochran," she laughed. *"So Friday, right?"*

De'marco realized her persistence.

"Yeah, okay. I'll stop by there."

"Oh, and De'marco baby, don't tell nobody. Tah, tah, smooches." She hung up the phone abruptly.

He didn't have a chance to question her. She knew he was still wet behind the ears, and used that to control the conversation. She called Jerome and briefed him on what she was up to. He called her a stanky cunt trick, and told her she was just trying to get the meat before he did. She told him he was tired and confused and should think about getting a life.

He screamed like a female, and said, *"Oh, no you didn't bitch! You a fish named Stella,"* then hung up on her.

Meanwhile, De'marco was pondering the conversation he just had, *"Why would Connie call me? What did she want?"*

He remembered graduation, when Jennifer had told him Connie wanted him.

"Could that be the case?" He thought. *"Naaaahh, not Connie, not me. She's too fine, too rich, and much older. Ain't nothing I could do for her. Maybe she has some work for me. But, nine in the evening, on a Friday, man I'm tripping,"* he thought.

Maybe he should call her back and tell her he couldn't make it. Then he figured Connie was a friend of his mother and father, so he would go see what was up. If she really didn't want anything he'd just take off and go on about his way. De'marco couldn't help to think about his life and how it was becoming filled with short accounts of interesting and humorous incidents.

"What'd you call that?" He asked himself.

"An anecdote! Yeah, that's it. Whatever the case, I'll do just fine, for I am a man of self- confidence, and poise. 'Aplomb' is the word, I think describes me."

He laughed, if Jennifer could hear his use of vernacular, she would be very pleased.

For some reason, Friday came faster than normally. He wondered what Connie needed him for. He still pondered on whether or not to call her and say he couldn't make it. But, he had given his word. Or, she had volunteered him, if he remembered the phone conversation correctly. He was running late as he zipped through the evening trafficors probably headed out to a club or something for the night. He figured a courtesy call couldn't hurt.

Connie picked up her cell phone and looked at the number.

"Helllooo?"

"Hi, Connie, this is De'marco. I'm running a little late, so I figured I'd call and tell you."

"No problem sweetie. Take your time. I'll be waiting here for ya."

"Okay, well, I'll be pulling up in about twenty minutes."

"Okay, see you then," Connie said, as she hung up.

De'marco wondered why she sounded short. Connie spun the chair around so her client could see her hair.

"Here you go. You like it?"

"Yes, as always, here's your money. I need to be getting home. So, I'll chat with you another time. You take care, thank you."

"You do the same, De'shawntu," Connie said waving goodbye, raising her hand and wiggling her fingers. Jerome just sat there looking at Connie with his lips twisted up.

"What Jerome!? Don't say nothing."

"I ain't got to say nothing, bitch. You know you ain't shit! First her husband, now her son. Damn! You could at least do her hair for free. You trying to break up her happy home."

Connie placed her hands on her hips, *"Look Miss Thang! And a thang you are. I ain't breaking up shit!"*

Jerome's mouth hung open.

"I know you didn't just refer to me as a thang?!? It's that thaang between your legs that got you out to have a sex-capade. You need to close it, before it swallows somebody up and they be on the news as a missing person. Then yo ass be walking through the mall somewhere and they fall out. Then yo ass going down for kidnapping."

Connie waived her hand.

"Ha, ha, shit that's the problem, it done been closed too long,"

Jerome smiled.

"So, that's why the quality of air is getting better in the city?!?

Connie was about to throw a brush, when the door chimed.

In walked De'marco, *"Hey Connie, I'm late, but I made it."*

Connie smiled and her eyes got wide.

"Hiiii, De'marcooo, its okay. Like you said you made it. Give me a sec, I was just finishing up."

Jerome loudly pretended to be clearing his throat.

"Oh, so rude of me," Connie said.

"De'marco, Jerome, Jerome, De'marco."

As De'marco turned to speak, he was shocked to see Jerome sitting there, big-eyed, and chopping his teeth at him, like some hungry animal.

"Jerome stop it!" Connie yelled.

Jerome looked De'marco head to toe.

"Hey Mr. Man, how you dooooing?"

"Pretty good," De'marco said wondering, *"What in the hell would make a grown man talk like a woman and act like a belligerent fool."*

Connie walked up to De'marco, stood in front of him and put on her best innocent look.

"I need you to take a ride with me somewhere, please baby."

Jerome was behind her with his hands on his hips, walking back and forth at a fast pace, jerking his head from right to left like a chicken. De'marco looked over at him and thought anything to get out of here.

"Okay, lets go," he said quickly. Connie looked over her shoulder at Jerome, as he stood there with his legs gapped open and quickly dropped his butt down and up as if in a rump shaker video.

"I'm out, lock up fool," Connie said.

"Yeah, okay. You go ahead and beguile the poor boy, you serpent. Run! De'marco, run! The evil witch is going to get you!"

Connie noticed De'marco looking wonderingly back at Jerome as he once again put on a show that made him look like a chicken, chomping his mouth open and closed.

"Don't pay him no mind, he gets beside himself sometimes."

De'marco looked over at her, *"Ya don't say?!?"*

Connie grabbed his hand, *"Here, lets take my car."*

As they approached Connie's ride, De'marco realized just how well things were going for her. She hit the button on the remote, and not only did the doors on the silver Range Rover unlock, the engine started up. As they climbed in, the radio came on playing Sade, "Smooth Operator."

"Smoooooth Operator, Coast to coast L.A. to Chicago....." At the same time, four T.V. screens lit up. Connie quickly pushed a button and the screen that appeared to have a porno on it, went black. As they pulled away De'marco was concerned about leaving Jennifer's car in the parking lot.

"So, where we headed?" He looked at Connie.

"Curious, don't worry baby, we won't be long."

Connie lived on the outskirts of town. It took a minute to get there. But she kept De'marco's brain occupied by asking him a thousand and one questions. As they pulled up De'marco was taken by surprise to be pulling up at a house.

"Where we at?"

"This is my crib." Connie said proudly.

"You live here by yourself?"

"Yep, sure do."

She hit the remote on the visor and the three-car garage door went up, and a light came on. As they entered the house, Connie told De'marco to take his shoes off. They walked through the kitchen that was done in black marble with bronze toned wood grain trim.

"Here or there. Have a seat in the living room. I'll be out in a minute to tell you why you're here".

De'marco stepped in the living room and couldn't believe his eyes, the scenery was like something in the movies. The living room was round, with thick plush carpet on the floor with a leopard skinned rug, complete with the head and paws on it. He wondered if it were real. It sat in front of a fireplace that was marble with gold trim around it. On top of the fireplace was a four and a half foot portrait of Connie in an all white leather outfit. The stereo was in the wall, the T.V. as well, and a seventy-five gallon fish tank that was rounded like the part of the wall it was in.

"So, are you going to have a seat or are you just gonna stand there?" Connie asked.

It sounded like her voice had come through the walls.

De'marco looked around.

"Psssst! Up here," she said.

He looked up amazed. The ceiling was high and about mid way up, there was an opening, and there she stood looking down at him.

"Have a seat," she said once again.

De'marco made his way over to the rounded couch that had large pillows everywhere. As he sat down, he touched the pillows. They had embossed paisley patterns on what felt like silk. Connie stepped in the living room with two drinks in her hand. She handed one to De'marco.

"Let's get down to why you're here," she said with a smile, flopping down on the couch.

She held back no punches. She let De'marco know he was well known and discussed, regularly, amongst the ladies in town. She didn't even hold back when telling him how many of them said he had no real bedroom skills. Big? Yes. Stamina? Yes. But, no skills. At that point his eyes showed signs of embarrassment. He also turned his drink up and downed it at that moment. To let things soak in she stopped and went to make him another drink.

Before De'marco started in on his second drink he couldn't help but ask, *"So, you have me here to tell me this?"*

"YES!" Connie said in a perky tone, as she sat up straight, *"Also to help you, help me, to help us."*

De'marco raised an eyebrow, *"What!?"*

"I'm going to make a deal with you and in return you'll give me what I want."

"Which is?"

Her eyes shot directly between De'marco's legs. He couldn't believe what was taking place.

"So you're going to teach me how to have good sex?"

De'marco found this to be ludicrous, because he was a "Mandingo." And they were known for their sexual prowess.

"No, I'm going to teach you how to be a good lover. Something few men are capable of, because of the same thing you have ozzing out your ear right now."

De'marco touched his ear looking to find something, *"What?"* He asked.

Connie smiled as she brought her drink down from her mouth, *"EGO De'marco. Your egos won't allow many of you to listen or to take time and learn a few good pointers."*

De'marco turned and faced Connie, *"And just what are these pointers?"* He asked sarcastically, but honestly wanted to know. She knew he was serious despite him trying to act as though he wasn't. What man wouldn't want love making tips from a woman? Especially a man as young and inexperienced as De'marco.

"Well, De'marco, first men need to realize that women are mental and can be stimulated and or turned on by something as simple as a conversation. Let me clear that up for you. Not just any 'ole bla-zay, bla-zay type

talking, more like conversation that stimulates the mind. You could be having a conversation with a woman and the things you say can stimulate her mind to the point you arouse her and not even be aware of it. That's another thing I'll teach you. To know when to, and when not to, timing!" She said sharply.

De'marco thought for a second, then he tried her.

"So, how do I know your not trying to bring about some form of machination?"

Connie laughed, almost choking on her drink.

"Good one," she told De'marco.

"I can assure you this is not an hostile or evil scheme, okay?!? So, let's stay away from the malarkey." She continued to giggle, *"Look, you have more to gain than I. I'll teach you some things and while doing so I'll get a little something from it too. Once the schooling is over, my gain is over."* She raised an eyebrow, *"Unless you plan on blessing a sister from time to time?!? All in all, you keep something with you, well into your old age. Something you can perfect over the years."*

De'marco couldn't believe his ears. Connie the babysitter sitting right next to him with her pretty eyes, sexy lips, perfect body. Wanting to teach him lovemaking tips.

"What else will this class consist of?"

"How to talk, touch, when to touch, where, how to dress, what cologne to wear, CONFIDENCE! Don't worry, you're a neophyte but, once I'm done with you, you'll be 'Confection Penis,'" she started cracking up.

De'marco missing the joke asked, *"I'll be con what?"*

Her eyes were watering from laughing.

"So much Sweet Food baby, Sweet Food." He still looked lost.

"Don't worry about it," she said, and held out her hand, *"So, do we have a deal?"*

Connie hoped her plan worked. At first, she was going to bring De'marco over and just jump his bones, and be done with it. But, after thinking it out, she realized this way she could get repeat performances until she had her fill and then she would dismiss the young lad.

De'marco took her hand in his, *"Deal,"* he said.

"So, when do we start?" He asked with an anxious look in his eye.

"Right now," she said, *"Make a mental note of this, never come across desperate, no matter how bad you want the person. Stay calm, in control. Be pleased to have the opportunity to indulge, however, be a man who can take it or leave it, got it?"*

"Yeah," De'marco replied, realizing she was talking about him at that moment.

"Good then, let's go. I'll take you back to your car, and seeing that you know how to get here now, be here tomorrow at ten o'clock sharp," she added.

De'marco stood up to follow her into the kitchen, when Connie spun around and threw her arms over his shoulders and began kissing him very seductively. When he started to kiss her back she reached down and rubbed his manhood through his pants, until it became swollen. She squeezed it checking for girth and slid her hand up and down it checking for length. Once she did that she quickly pulled away leaving De'marco with his lips puckered up.

"Okay baby, let's go," she told him as she moved briskly towards the way they came upon arrival.

De'marco was unsure about the arrangement he and Connie had, but in the same token he looked forward to this evening. He made sure he had spent all day with Jennifer and broke her off real good throughout the day. So once he left out she wouldn't be tripping. He had learned to do that much before stepping out. Even as he kissed her before leaving out the door, she told him her female intuition was telling her he was doing more than just going bowling. He just looked at her and told her he would see her when he returned. He left out a couple hours early. He needed to make a few stops and pick up a couple Magnums from the house, just in case.

Meanwhile, at the shop, Connie was stressing, it was a little after eight and she had a head left to do.

Jerome noticed her stressing and decided to pry a little, *"So what's up with Baby Boy?"*

Connie caught up in what she was doing and not really paying him any attention.

"Who Jerome?" She asked with an attitude.

"Don't play me Cow! You know who. Junior Stud, that's who."

Connie came off nonchalantly, *"Ohhh! You talking about De'marco?!?"*

Jerome's mouth hung open, *"Oh, you got amnesia, huh?!? That's cool, why don't you forget I owe you booth rental this month? Yeah, De'marco, what he do girl? Done rung your bell already?"*

"Nah, I decided against it. I ain't even gonna waste my time."

She lied to Jerome figuring the less he knew the better. Especially after how he acted yesterday when De'marco came to the shop.

"Look Miss Thang, you could have just said none of your business. You ain't halfa lie. Hell, it's written all over your face. And then you have the nerve to be trying to get out of here early on a Saturday."

Connie looked over at him, wishing he would shut up!

"Well, none of your business then!" She stated coldly.

"Seeee," Jerome said, *"That's why I'm glad I don't have one of those thangs between my legs. Y'all don't know if y'all coming or going."*

Connie didn't have time to lollygag with Jerome. She needed to get these heads done and beat De'marco to the house. She was hoping he hadn't changed his mind and reneged on her. Whatever the case, she would soon find out, and if he did show, it would be on!

* * * * * * * * * * * * * * * * * *

102

De'marco finished his little running around and figured it was time to head to Connie's. It was nine fifteen, and he was clear across town. So he headed toward the expressway, feeling a little gangster, thuggish. De'marco popped in the "West Side Connection" CD. He thought for a second about what he was doing.

Then said, *"Oh, well, its on!"*

Turned up the radio and Mack Ten's voice came through the speakers, *"Bitch you say you love me, that shits absurd, wanna show your love for me, hop on a plane with a bird....!"*

Meanwhile, Connie finally broke from the shop as soon as she finished her last head. She grabbed her purse and headed to the door, telling Jerome to lock up. He started in with his candid remarks. Connie paid him no attention. She had no time for his gay shit tonight. She was on a mission.

She didn't play, she hit the expressway in the Range and stood up on the gas pedal. She weaved in and out of traffic. She was home in no time. She looked at her watch and realized she had thirty minutes before De'marco was to arrive. Not much time, she thought. But it would do. She made herself a bikini martini and headed for the shower. She washed herself gently, slowly. The hot water and suds had already put her in the mood, as she scrubbed her body. She purposely rubbed places in a teasing way, allowing the slippery touch to arouse her. She took note of herself. She still had the legs, hips, and ass and the small waist, thanks to working out at the gym a couple times a week. Her body was still nice and firm. Even her breast remained perky, nipples firm. The abortion she had, to keep from having Martzu's baby hadn't affected her body at all. The thought of that time caused her to snap back, rinse off and get out the shower. She dried off and made herself another bikini martini, and sipped on it while she lotioned up. She wasn't going to go all out tonight. So, she just sprayed a little Tommy Girl here and there. She saw the headlights hit the window. De'marco was pulling into the driveway.

As he entered the screen on the front porch, Connie's voice came over the speaker, *"Come in baby, its open."* That reminded him of the incident with his teacher from his lab class.

"Oh, no!" He thought, he couldn't go for that again. He still hadn't been able to explain to Jennifer the mark the whip left on his butt cheek. He laughed while taking his shoes off.

Connie's voice came over the speaker again, *"Share with me what's so funny?!?"*

De'marco didn't see where the speaker was, he just spoke in no particular direction.

"Maybe next time, where are you?" De'marco walked in the round living room, noticing a china cabinet that had oriental crystal figurines on each shelf. Each piece shinned and reflected off the glass shelves. He walked over to get a closer look.

"How in the world did I miss this yesterday?" He questioned himself.

Connie peered over at him, *"What you know about crystal?"* She asked.

De'marco looked up at her, seeing only her face, *"Nothing, other than its expensive."*

"Yeah, that's true, I'll be down in a minute." She paused, *"On second thought, come up here. Go through the other door that branches off from the kitchen, pass the foyer up the first set of stairs."*

"Oooookay," De'marco thought. *"Why not just get an elevator?"* De'marco joked.

"If I could I would," Connie said with a giggle. *"Why don't you buy me a house with one?"*

De'marco didn't answer quickly enough, so Connie turned around to see what the problem was. De'marco stood in the doorway admiring her. His astonishment showed on his face. Connie had on a two-piece set. It was light purple, and fit nicely on her. You could see her toned frame. She turned around to give him a good look. The lace allowed you to get a peak of her butt crack. Hell, that was nothing because you could definitely see the V-shaped mound of hair in the front. Not to mention, her nipples were both doing a peek-a-boo, through the sheer design on the top piece. Connie was about five foot four inches, 36-24-34. Her finger and toenails were done, matching what little she had on. The purple went so well with her caramel skin. Connie made a smacking noise with her mouth and pointed a finger at De'marco, as to say, what'd I tell you?

De'marco caught himself and remembered, *"Oh yeah, pleased to be here, but not desperate."*

Connie turned around to light a couple candles, and he noticed her big round firm butt that made her already small waist look as though it was not there.

"My," he thought as he noticed the two dimples at the bottom of her back.

"Have a seat, on the bed," she added quickly.

De'marco had been staring at Connie so hard he failed to notice the bed. As he got closer he thought, *"What is the deal here?"* A heart-shaped, pillow top, California Cow king size bed with silk sheets, a matching heart-shaped comforter, nine heart-shaped pillows, and what he thought was a wall unit behind the bed was the headboard with a large mirror in the middle of it, with a built in stereo.

De'marco sat on the bed, *"You have a very nice place here, Connie,"* he said as he went to lie back on the bed and enjoy its soft but firm mattress.

"Thank you. Here..." Connie said, handing him a drink.

De'marco noticed the mirrors on the ceiling, and as he looked around, there were mirrors everywhere.

"What's up with all the mirrors?" De'marco asked.

"Look De'marco, let me tell you what you don't know, but need to." She turned her drink up until the contents of it were gone. She placed her glass down and motioned for De'marco to drink up. Holding back no punches as before, she looked him straight in the eye, and told him, *"I'm a freak, and a big one at that."*

He swallowed and held out his glass.

He remembered what she told him before, and tried playing it cool.

"Okay, that's cool."

"Alright, tonight will be a test to see what you working with and how you work it. Don't worry I'll be talking you through it."

The truth of the matter is, Connie felt as if tonight were her night, and she was going to toy with De'marco.

"Stand up!" She snapped at him.

She had a devious grin on her face. She sat on the bottom at the tip of the heart-shaped bed. She slid her hands up his shirt, rubbing on his stomach.

She looked up at him, *"Put this in your notes, touch is good. The right place, the right time, the right caresses. Take your shirt off."*

As he let his shirt drop to the floor she slid her hands up and rubbed his chest. She pinched his nipples. De'marco's eyes grew big. She leaned over and placed her tongue on his stomach, and started making circles around his navel. She undid his pants, they fell to the floor, she probed her tongue deep into his bellybutton. She leaned back to get a look at him. His long lean body looked good to her, fresh, firm, she thought. She looked down at his manhood. It hung there like a mean beastie piece of meat.

"De'marco!" She said, as if surprised, *"All this for me?"*

She moved in closer and raised his stiff penis up to her mouth. She took the tip between her teeth and gently bit down. De'marco responded by flinching. He wanted to say something, but it was too late, Connie had begun performing on him orally. She wasted no time, as she took him into her mouth. Smoothly she stroked the length of him with one hand while she caressed his balls with the other. She looked up at De'marco, he had been taken by surprise and was being overwhelmed by it. He had experienced it before, but not like this. Yep, Connie had plans of getting her groove on and turning De'marco out in more ways than one. He was going to be her pet.

"I ain't no good," she thought, as she began to speed up and put concentrated effort into her oral performance. De'marco's eyes rolled to the back of his head and he began to moan. At that point, with a loud smack that came from the suction of her mouth, she stopped and looked up at him.

"You okay, baby?" De'marco nodded a yes. Connie released him and rolled over backwards like a kid on a mat. She came out the roll and sprang up to her feet. She stood there on the mattress looking at De'marco.

She said, *"Note, anything goes, and is accepted as long as you build up to it properly."*

She slid her bottoms down over her hips and let them fall the rest of the way to her feet. She slid her top off, as De'marco stood there looking at her. She held her top out to the side, she let it drop from between her thumb and index finger.

De'marco followed it with his eyes. She cupped both breast in her hands and began rubbing them and pulling at the nipples.

"You ready Marco baby?" She asked him with her eyes looking devilish and her lips puckered.

Just as he went to answer, with one smooth move of her foot she flicked the bottom of her sexy two-piece set right in his face. He felt something wet on his lips and smelled the sexual aroma that permeates from between a woman's legs when she's aroused. He removed the clothing from his face to see Connie walking across the mattress to him. She stopped in front of him.

"How do you want it Marco? Always know how you want it. How you're going to give it to her. Be confident or else your moves become sporadic and clumsy."

She leaned his head back and kissed him. Putting much tongue into his mouth, and he returned the kiss. She took his tongue between her lips and sucked on it in the same manner she had done his manhood moments earlier. She moved smoothly, controlled. She released his tongue and turned his head to the side.

She whispered in his ear, *"You can touch me baby."*

De'marco began rubbing her, as she placed her tongue in his ear, it was wet and warm. It felt strange, but good. She slid down, kissing his neck, nibbling him with her teeth, she kissed his shoulders, top of his chest, then she began sucking his nipples, this sent him. She sucked, nibbled, and licked with her tongue. She even lightly bit him. He flinched and she stood again.

"So, you didn't tell me how'd you want it?"

She stood in front of him, legs gapped open, caressing herself. She slid her finger between her vagina lips, it was wet when she brought it up. She stuck out her tongue, placed her finger in her mouth and sucked it. She repeated the same act, only this time she rubbed her finger across his mouth leaving the moistness of her pussy on his lips.

"This what you want Marco?" She turned around and slightly spread her legs and bent all the way over placing her hands on the bed.

De'marco's mouth came open. Once he saw the size of her pussy. It looked like a large muffin, perfectly baked. The clit poked out, as if it were peeking at him. The hair was long but neatly shaven around the edges. You could see her pink lips and the moisture that oozed from between them. Connie was teasing him to the fullest. She was doing a good job at it too. He could feel spasms in his meat. He wanted her and he wanted her now! Judging by the juice coming from those lips, she had to want it just as bad. Connie scooted back so as to have her sexpot right in his face.

"Stick your tongue out!" She said sharply.

De'marco did as he was told and she reached back and pulled his mouth to her vagina, she grinded her lips to his lips. De'marco got tired of being a puppet and grabbed her hips firmly and started licking her all up and down, wildly probing his tongue in and out of her slit.

"There you go!" She yelled, *"Go boy!"*

After soaking his face with her love juices, she slid down from his grasp. On all fours with her rump tooted up, she reached back and began rubbing the head of his meat up and down her wet lips. De'marco grabbed her hips once again ready to drop anchor.

"Hold on baby," she turned over on her back and slid up on the bed. She realized that she wasn't ready to get hit off like that. Not just yet. Plus, he was ready to break something off in her. Not right now, not with that.

She opened her legs, *"Come here baby."*

As De'marco came across the large bed, she reached for the button on the radio and pushed play. When De'marco got right up between her legs, she pushed his head down, and pointed at her clit.

"Here is where all the action is. Take your tongue and spell your name on it, ten times. After each time, dip your tongue twice in the hole to get some more ink, then start back writing."

De'marco started doing as he was told.

Then she said, *"Middle name too."*

Sometimes fast, then slow. She giggled and reached to turn up the volume. Adina Howards' voice came through the speakers, *"I'ma be a freak all through the night, until the dawnnn!"* Connie looked at De'marco, who was catching on pretty good, and thought, *"I'm gonna teach the boy, but tonight is my night!"* She grabbed his head by the ears and started raising up her hips, *"He gonna learn."* She grinded and grinded until she began to feel what she was looking for, that spot, and she worked it. De'marco was some dumb, but not plum dumb. He had a move up his sleeve too. He watched Connie and paid close attention to her actions. As she locked his head in place and started making quick jerking movements, then the words slipped from her mouth, as she moaned.

"Ohhh, here it comes, here it comes!" Right then De'marco slid his thumb in her ass.

At the same time, she screamed, *"Ohhh no you didn't?!?"*

She jerked and grinded and slid down so his thumb could go further in her.

"Yes, yes, yes!" She yelled. She pulled De'marco up to her, wiped his mouth and started kissing him. He didn't answer, he just slid himself up in her, she moaned, and let out a, *"Damn!"* He filled her up from top to bottom, just like his father used to. It brought back memories.

"Martzu was much more skilled. But, we'll get you there," she thought, and in one smooth move, rolled him over and was on top. She placed her hands on his chest and just worked the head. She knew better than to go sliding down all out of control. She had done that to Martzu, and when that thang hit the bottom, she thought she was paralyzed. She had to stop and ask Martzu to help her up off of him. She was done that night. But tonight, she would do her thang and hook herself up. Sure nuff! She leaned forward and spread her legs further apart, and bounced and rolled her hips, making the tip of him touch all sides of her vagina walls, while it slid deeper inch by inch slowly. She reached over and grabbed his hand and placed it in the crease of her ass cheeks. And had him slide his finger deep inside her anus.

She whispered, *"I'll explain that to you later,"* and started sucking his nipples.

With his other hand, he began caressing her back, rubbing her sides and pulling and pinching her breast.

She moaned and found her spot and bounced and stroked his manhood. The more she worked it, the deeper it went. The further De'marco's finger slid into her ass the harder she sucked his chest. They found a rhythm together and worked it. De'marco paid attention to what was taking place. Every now and then he would push deeper and watch her reaction. Connie was in the zone, total ecstasy. She just worked it, as she allowed herself to be worked. She was gone. Caught up in the moment. She was no longer sucking De'marco's chest, her mouth was open on it, as she breathed hard and moaned, slobber dripping down his chest. She just rode the wave, and waited for her river to flow. She was totally unaware of her surrounding. All she felt was the pleasure. She was gone.

As the months went by, De'marco and Connie continued their classes. They went from the bedroom, to the park, from the movie theater, to the back seat of Connie's Range Rover, from the back seat of the rental car parked on the side of the highway, her office at the shop on Mondays. She even flew De'marco to Atlanta, just to get busy in the restroom on the plane.

Connie kept her word and taught De'marco all he needed to know to be a good lover. From techniques on touching, caressing, biting, pinching, stroking, when, when not, how, how not, how to dress, cologne, conversation, how to teach a female how to take it anally, how to get head from any female. All the while she was getting what she wanted. Things got good to Connie.

She bought De'marco plenty of clothes and shoes. And if that weren't enough, she put the icing on the cake, when she bought him a car. He was her project and her pet. She was his teacher of things never to be forgotten, at least that's the game they played to keep the feelings from growing. As things came to a sort of halt, they made an agreement, although they would go their way in life, if either called the other, they would be there to wear the springs out of a mattress or whatever else they may need each other for.

She told De'marco, *"Always take care of home first. Never jeopardize that! Make sure you stay on top your game and keep your shit tight. Females watch for that. And make sure they earn any dime you give them. It makes them respect you more."*

Connie showed him how to save his money by putting up ten percent of every dime he earned.

She told him, *"It don't sound like much, but over time it'll grow. Trust me,"* she said. *"You'll never have to ask anyone for anything and that's the way it's supposed to be."*

De'marco went from being impecunious, to being a well-desired man that have got.

7

"CONFECTION PENIS"

After months spent with Connie, De'marco was ready, new clothes, new thoughts, new ideas and a new BMW 740. Yeah, it had a couple of years on it, but to him, it was new all the same. He looked good in it. He turned heads before, but now mouths dropped open with the same quickness. Last night Connie and De'marco decided they would put some space between them for a while. It was cool they ate dinner and talked.

"A woman's mind is where you want it to be, De'marco baby," Connie told him. *"Her heart will follow. She's a beautiful creature, but equally dangerous if her mind isn't right. She talks a good bluff game, but in all honesty, nine times out of ten, has no idea of what she wants. That's where you come in baby. Do you think you can handle it?"*

With the same confidence she used to help him sharpen himself, he looked over the table at her and calmly said... *"There's not a problem I can't solve, and no question I can't answer. Handling a woman is the least of my worries."* Taking charge of the conversation he told Connie, *"Stop running your mouth baby and finish your dinner."*

She let out a giggle and got her grub on. She was pleased at what she had created, although she couldn't really answer why. She felt good about it. Not to mention, she got her fill sexually. Yep, she got her groove back, several times.

* * * * * * * * * * * * * * * * * *

Class was as usual today, females winking, pssst here and there, the fella's mean mugging. De'marco didn't care. He refused to sweat the small stuff.

113

Connie told him, *"You're a Black Man who has his stuff together. That alone gives you the right to be choosey when you select the women you deal with, whether you bed them or not."*

As he pulled up at the apartment, he noticed Jennifer peeking out the window. Once he stepped from the car the front door came open.

"Hey baby!" Jennifer said, happy to see him.

He reached in the back seat and grabbed the dozen roses. As he walked towards her he smiled a big smile.

"Hey, baby, you messin' up my surprise."

"I didn't see anything," she said looking up in the air, as to pretend she really didn't see the roses.

De'marco reached, and he pulled her to him, *"Come here beautiful,"* he said in a seductive voice. He kissed her in such a passionate way, Jennifer became light-headed, *"These are for you baby,"* as he handed her the flowers.

"Oh, thank you De'marco! They're pretty." She told him as she put her nose to them and smelled them, *"They're so fresh."*

"Like our love," De'marco added.

"Yes baby, like our love."

As she turned and walked in the door, De'marco gave her a firm pat on her rump. She giggled as she hopped forward like a little kid. De'marco had taken things to another level. Jennifer set out to have his heart and mind. But thanks to Connie, De'marco had changed the game and it was cool, because he meant Jennifer no harm. It was just that being the man, he had to be in charge. He controlled the flow of things even down to the lovemaking. Jennifer had no problem with all this. At all times he treated her like a queen. She didn't know what had taken over him. His talk, his touch, everything was as if he were romancing her. She even had times of being aroused just by thinking of him and the things he did to her. The lovemaking seemed to have enhanced a thousand times over. It wasn't rough and uncontrolled, although it still had its painful moments. It was as if he had so much confidence and control, he applied a burst of pain with the pleasure when he wanted to and it was always at the right moment. He would flip her, turn her, squeeze her, stroke her, it was so good every time. She always ended up sweating and shaking uncontrollably. Some days, he would put it to her three, four times a day. Those were the days she would damn near forget her name.

She noticed the change in De'marco's conversation, clothes, everything, however, it seemed like the more he changed, the better. Things between them were better. Lovemaking would last practically all night and be filled with stimulating conversation. He bought flowers, candy, sexy panties and cards, just because. Yes, De'marco had changed to Jennifer, but in such a way he made her feel like some sort of goddess.

As far as she was concerned, it was all good.

De'marco knew he had taken Jennifer's heart and mind to another level. And it was cool because he planned on staying with her. Yeah, he was going to do his thang, but he was going to keep his first. It was a life long investment.

De'marco had become a well-known person in the small city of Columbus, Ohio and his mouth along with every thing else had him staying in demand. Females he didn't even know and had never met would end up calling him with all types of invites. Married and single women, young and old, sisters, cousins, it was something else, but he took it in stride. He couldn't lie though, the ones who would call and try to manipulate him into letting them just see it. *"Just for a second,"* he would say. Then, tell them to promise that was all they wanted to do. They would, but once he pulled it out, it would go from, *"Ooow, can I touch it?!?"* To them leaning over and quickly placing their mouth on it and putting down the oral game. He would just turn up the radio and let his seat back. Many of them would get in over their heads and would have to come up for air. Their neck and jaw would be tired. Others were beastie with it, doing all types of stuff from gagging themselves to humming while doing it, to putting their hands down their pants and working themselves at the same time. All would finish and ask, *"When can we do the real thing?"*

De'marco made no promises, he would simply smile and tell them, *"I'ma get at you."*

When they put themselves out like that, he made no attempt to get back with them, for what? Oftentimes, he missed Connie, she had taught him well. Oddly enough, no females compared or even came close to what they shared in the bedroom, with the exception of Jennifer, and that was because she was his first and he is madly in love with her.

Connie told him, *"Now that you have a basic knowledge and overstanding of good love making, you'll get to see just how many women don't know what they want in the bed or life for that matter."*

De'marco found it to be all too true. He would sit with some females and just talk to see where their heads were and how they were living. Many of them talked in circles, and some just came straight out and said it, *"I don't know what I want."*

Some of them he would add to their confusion by sexing them for hours, afterwards they would say things like, *"I might not know what I want in life just yet, but I do know, I want you."*

De'marco realized that the mind of a woman was not only fragile, but because she would over think everything, she would confuse herself and mix up her own emotions and cause herself a lot of strife. De'marco had a few rolls in the hay with a couple of women much older than he and they weren't much different. Sure they had no problem paying the bill on a few outings, and they may have had their own place, but once they hit the bed, a couple of times he noticed the emotions kicked in and they would come out the mouth with some type of immature game. Trying to come across as if they wanted a relationship. He would have to remind them of the age difference and how in time, that would cause them to grow apart. It was cool and exciting at times. He also found it to be outrageous!

Another Saturday evening had come and De'marco was looking to take it easy. With Jennifer studying medicine at OSU, she interned at a local twenty-four hour CVS pharmacy and was working this evening six to six. So he figured he would go by his parents to see what they were up to and head back to the apartment, order pizza and call it a day. He hadn't spoken with Connie and wondered what she was up to. His cell sat in the cup holder of the Beamer vibrating, causing the change to vibrate also. He picked it up and looked at the number on the screen, it was Connie.

He placed the phone to his ear, *"Speak of the Devil!"*

Connie laughed, *"Not quite, but we done had a run in or two. He's mad 'cuz I'm taking over."*

"Oh, yeah?!?" De'marco exclaimed. *"If he knew what I know, he'd better do a JayZ and bow out gracefully."*

They both bust out laughing.

"So what my baby up to?" Connie questioned in a sexy voice De'marco caught the change in demeanor.

"What's up, Connie?"

Realizing there was no need to prolong her reason for calling, *"I need you to come by this evening for a sec."*

"What's a sec?" De'marco questioned hesitantly.

"Baby, just a couple hours."

"What?!" De'marco said, *"I thought we was going to chill out for a minute?!?"*

"Baby, it's not even what you think. Just come by tonight about ten thirty, OK?"

De'marco wanted to play hard, *"I'll have to see."*

Connie peeped game quick, *"If you have something else to do baby, then it don't have to be tonight. Maybe another time."*

She listened close as De'marco sighed, *"I'll be there."* *"Okay baby, see you then, smooches!"* She hung up. De'marco figured, *"Oh well, there goes my Saturday."*

He went on and stopped by his parents. They were fine. However, they complained he needed to cut the grass. So he promised to cut it first thing in the morning. He figured he could do that, seeing Jennifer would probably sleep most the morning away. While talking with his mother in the kitchen before he left, she noticed his watch.

"Nice Watch!" She told him, as she checked it out by raising his wrist so she could get a closer look. De'marco glad to be showing something off to his mom replied, *"It's just a little somethin' somethin'"* trying to sound cool.

"Yeah, I see it is." De'shawntu noticed the same exact model on her husband's wrist years ago. The only difference is De'marco's look to be a more up-to-date watch and it had a diamond where the twelve, three, six and nine should be. Whereas Martzu's just had a large diamond in place of the twelve on his watch. But you could tell these watches were both custom made by the same jeweler. De'marco left his parent's house kind of puzzled, because he had never told his mother where he got his car or anything else for that matter. So when she made her little remark at the door as he was leaving, it threw him off.

She said, *"Did you get the watch from the same place you got the car?"* And when he turned to look at her, she quickly said, *"Oh, that's right car lots don't sell watches, my bad."*

He questioned, *"Could she know about Connie? Nah, how?"* Although she got her hair done at Connie's shop, by Connie, there's no way such a conversation would take place. He dropped the thought and drove to the apartment. He figured he'd get cleaned up, and put on some smell goods. Connie called wanting to play, so he decided he was going to play alright, play hard to get.

After he showered, he slipped on a shirt that only buttoned up half way. Exposing his chest and a pair of partially faded jeans with no underwear. He matched his belt with his shoes and was ready to go. He figured he looked dapper enough in the outfit he got from Men's Express at the City Center Mall downtown. A couple squirts of "Armani Mania" cologne and he was out. He was going to call Connie when he got on the expressway to let her know he'd be there soon, and decided against it.

He was going to see Miss Connie and that called for a theme song. He decided to go old school and mellow out. So he popped in Mint Condition, leaned his seat back and turned up the volume. As he accelerated the big body Beamer, the engine made a suction noise and jetted. He bobbed his head and sang along to the words, *"Pret-ty brown eyes, you know I see them..."* He figured since Connie wasn't holding strong on their deal of putting some space between them, after tonight, he would play a game of hide and seek and dodge her for about a month or two. No phone calls or nothing.

"Yep, that's how I'll play it," he thought.

Only reason he was coming through tonight is because Jennifer had to work. If not for that, his cell would have been off and he would have been chilling with the woman he loved.

As he pulled up in Connie's driveway, he noticed another SUV with "NIC" on the plates. He'd seen it before, but couldn't put his finger on where. Once he stepped on Connie's porch, he was wondering what was up, seeing that it appeared she had company. She met him at the door as she had done on many occasions before.

119

"Hi baby," she said with excitement in her voice, *"Come on in!"* She rose up on her tippy toes, *"Give me a kiss."*

As he leaned over to kiss her, he noticed another lady sitting over on the couch.

"Nicole, this is De'marco, my sweetie. De'marco, this is Nicole. You may have noticed her at the shop."

"Right," then it dawned on him. He had noticed her at the shop before. But she always had on a smock with her hair pulled back. Now it was done up hanging down, causing her to look ever so foxy. De'marco felt bad that he thought Connie wanted to play frisky tonight, but he quickly realized that could not be the case. They both sat there in the living room with lightweight knee length blazers on and their purses on the table as if ready to leave. Connie brought him out of his thought with an elbow to the side, *"You gonna speak Mister?"* She asked.

"Why of course," he said. *"Hi Nicole. How are you?"*

"I'm fine De'marco. What's been going on?" She questioned as she lit a cigarette.

"Not a lot, trying to stay focused on school. How about yourself?"

"Money baby." She then blew the smoke out.

At that point, De'marco realized she was smoking a joint.

"Damn, I know they're going out now." He thought to himself.

Connie said her and her girls always blazed one before they hit the club. De'marco turned to Connie, somewhat frustrated.

"Say woman," he stated sharply. *"What's the deal? Why you have me come through?"*

Connie raised an eyebrow at Nicole and they shared a slight giggle. Nicole handed Connie the joint.

"Girl, tell this man why he here before he curse us out," Nicole said.

120

Connie stared at De'marco, while she hit the joint a couple times, taking long slow drags.
She was thinking, *"No he ain't a little teed after I taught him about patience. I always told him, good things come to those who wait."*

De'marco and Connie traded glances, he knew what she was thinking, but he figured she could have been courteous enough to have filled him in on whatever was up on the phone, instead of him driving to her house and they're about to go out.

Nicole looked at Connie and then said, *"Damn with all these gadgets you got in here you would think you would have a ceiling fan."* She unbuttoned the two buttons on her blazer.

"I do." Connie said, and hit a remote. Cool air began to come from the vents that were positioned slanted on the surrounding walls. She stood up and walked over to De'marco.

"Hey, Mr. Poitier, I don't appreciate you coming to my house with an attitude. "Stand up!" She said in what seemed to be an angry tone. *"I told Nicole you were pretty good with working on things around the house and she wanted to talk with you about it in person."*

De'marco stood there for a second, then asked, *"You mean to tell me, you couldn't call, with her on the phone? What is it she wants done?"*

Nicole stood up and said, *"Look, all I need to know is, can you help me out? Damn!"*

De'marco noticed the tone in her voice and looked over at her at that point. She unbuttoned the rest of the buttons on her blazer and let it slide from her shoulders to the floor. De'marco was surprised to see Nicole standing there butt ass naked. He looked down at Connie who was standing right in front of him, and gave her that "no you didn't" look.

Connie looked him in the eye, and started undoing his belt, *"I told you she wanted to talk to you in person."*

She smiled and stepped back as she let his pants fall to the floor. Nicole came towards him and grabbed his manhood.

"That's what I'm talking about." She looked over at Connie, *"Bitch I can't even believe you was holding out on some shit like this! This sucker is heavy,"* she said as she lifted his meat and fondled it. Connie came out her blazer. De'marco noticed their bodies were shaped similar, except Nicole's nipples were longer, much longer.

"So what," De'marco said, *"Am I a piece of meat you pass around?"*

Connie stepped behind him. *"De'marco baby, stop!"* She said in a whiney voice, as she began kissing and rubbing his back. Nicole undid his buttons on his shirt and slid it off. She rose up on her tippy toes to kiss De'marco's chest at the same time. She placed his hand between her legs. De'marco wanted to protest until he felt the piercing in Nicole's clit, then he thought, *"What the hell, this could be interesting."* He began rubbing her breast and grinding her. Connie kissed his back as she slid her index finger up and down the crack of his behind, *"That a boy, De'marco baby. Get with this."* Connie came in front of De'marco, along with Nicole. They pushed him down on the couch. They took turns orally satisfying him. De'marco looked at them both, unable to believe what he was experiencing. Two women, both in their forties. He watched Nicole as she took him deep into her mouth.

She made the sound, *"Ummm, um, umm,"* and looked at Connie.

"I told you, didn't I?" Connie said as she took a hand full of Nicole's hair and pulled her head up off De'marco.

Then, the two of them kissed in such an intimate and passionate way, it turned De'marco on even more.

"Go ahead girl. Get you some," Connie said to Nicole motioning to De'marco's love bone. As Nicole

stood up to straddle De'marco, Connie gave her a smack on her ass.

"Okay," Nicole said, *"You know I like that shit."*

That made Connie and De'marco both smack a cheek.

Nicole screamed, *"Oh, this is going to be a fun night here!"*

As she slid down on De'marco she moaned a deep erotic moan. Connie leaned in and sucked Nicole and De'marco's breast and chest, back and forth. As Nicole took the ride of her life, she grabbed De'marco and kissed him so passionately, De'marco felt as if she was trying to make him cum from her kiss alone. He placed a hand on her waist and thrust upward. She gasped for air, then asked him to do it again.

"Oh please do it again, and again."

"That's right baby, get that!" Connie said, once again smacking Nicole's butt cheek, then she slid her finger in Nicole's rectum, sending sensations up her spine. Suddenly, Nicole stopped.

"What?" Connie asked, *"What's up?"*

De'marco just looked at her. Then she stood up on the couch and turned around with her back facing De'marco. Right then, De'marco looked at her big round rump and told himself, *"Yep, tonight I'm gonna open that up."*

Connie looked at Nicole, *"What you gonna do now? I know you trying to do your thang, but you standing on my couch with your heels on!"*

Nicole rolled her eyes as to say, don't disturb my groove. She then squatted down on top of De'marco's love pole. She took one hand and guided it in, *"Oh, this thang here!"* She screamed as her entire body shook. She slowly bounced up and down. She then spread her legs and bent all the way over holding De'marco's ankles, she bounced. De'marco watched. He caught a shot at her anus that made him swear to himself he would slide up in it tonight. Since Connie set this little shindig up he was going to make her jealous by sexing

Nicole overtime. He figured it was the least he could
do, seeing that she was passing him around like he was a
piece of meat. Connie began sucking on his chest. He
placed both hands on Nicole's hips and began thrusting
up in her deep. She moaned loudly.

Connie whispered, *"Get her, De'marco. Get her
baby."*

Nicole lifted up and reached around and grabbed
Connie as she leaned back on De'marco.

"Come here baby girl," she said to Nicole as they
began kissing. Nicole caressed Connie and rubbed
between her legs as they kissed. Connie slid down and
kissed Nicole's neck and sucked her breast. Then she
began moving her hips in a circular motion as she placed
her hand on top of Connie's head and began pushing it
down between her legs.

"Take care of that baby girl," she said to Connie.
Connie got between both their legs and began to lick and
suck Nicole as she rode De'marco. Nicole just sat back
and enjoyed the ride, while De'marco worked his love
joystick up in her and sucked the back of her neck, while
turning her nipples as if they were knobs on a radio.
She moaned. He moaned. The lovemaking was good
and very pleasing for them all. They got to release
themselves several times.

As the night went on, so did they, changing positions,
moaning, rubbing, kissing, they exchanged everything
from looks, hugs, kisses, bites, squeezes, laughs, it was a
wonderful night! It went on until five o'clock in the
morning and the only reason it stopped was because
Nicole wanted to try and beat her husband home and
De'marco figured he should do the same with Jennifer.
Yep, that night ended, but it wasn't the last threesome
performance De'marco and Connie performed.
De'marco had pulled several stunts, wearing the woman
out, making Connie jealous or so he thought. It didn't
matter to Connie. She made him what he was and was
continuing to turn De'marco out in the world of sex,

passion, and eroticism. No, it didn't bother her what De'marco did, the more the better. She just wanted to make sure that the women who came through got their monies worth, so they would keep coming. All appeared to be going well, because she had a couple of repeat customers. At times, Connie wondered if she should let De'marco in on what was going down. That would make things much smoother when she called him to come through.

Then again, she thought against it, *"I mean hell, I was shocked when Nicole said she would pay money to frolic around with the young tender Mandingo stud. No telling how De'marco would take it. Better leave well enough alone,"* she thought.

* * * * * * * * * * * * * * * * * *

Back at the Poitier's resident, De'shawntu sat quietly in thought. She rarely said much concerning De'marco's dealings. She figured boys will be boys and men will be men. Plus, De'marco had graduated from high school and went straight to college. So she thought he must be keeping his focus. However, she couldn't help but wonder where he was getting the clothes, the car, and the watch! She knew good and well he wasn't able to buy those things working as a part-time paralegal during the week. Besides, that was part of his internship. So, a big check, he was not getting. That she was sure of. But where was he getting this extra stuff? De'shawntu wondered if Martzu noticed the change in De'marco?

"My King," she asked, *"Have you noticed a change in De'marco?"*

"What change might that be my Queen?" Martzu knew exactly what his wife was talking about.

*"The clothes, the car, not to mention, the watch that's very similar to the one you came home with **that time**!"* She placed emphasis on *"that time"*, causing Martzu to

look her way with a raised eyebrow. The fact that she hadn't let that go was one thing and he could accept it, but De'marco having a similar watch, would be a close to impossible coincidence. He knew the watch he had was one of a kind, and had to be custom hand crafted. He didn't want the watch, but Connie insisted. She said it was the least she could do for all he'd done for her. At the time, he figured she was just caught up. So to keep matters from getting worse, he accepted the watch from her with the promise that she wouldn't purchase him any other gifts. She agreed and that was that.

"*What watch?*" Martzu asked slowly.

De'shawntu spoke quickly, "*He had a watch that was gold, real gold mind you, with four half carat diamonds, one at each of the numbers, twelve, three, six, and nine. It didn't look to be a watch you could pick up at just any jewelry store. It had to be customed made, LIKKKE YOURS!*" She said with a hint of aggression.

"*Okay now,*" Martzu said catching her mood shift to an unpleasant one, "*Watch your tone, it's just a watch. I'll get in touch with De'marco and see what's what? I'm sure it's nothing.*"

De'shawntu got up, "*I'll watch my tone, sure nuff,*" she said as she walked away, down the hall to her bedroom. She knew where the watch Martzu worn had come from. She just never spoke on it. And she knew there was a time Connie wanted Martzu. A woman's intuition will not fail her. But, the thought of Connie possibly wanting, or dealing with De'marco disgusted her. She used to change the boy's diaper FOR CHRIST SAKE! Martzu appeared in the doorway of the bedroom looking at De'shawntu who was very upset.

"*Look,*" he said, "*You know how females can be when it comes to a guy they like. The things they'll do are unpredictable. This is no exception just because it's our son.*"

126

De'shawntu looked at Martzu with such vexation in her eyes you would have thought fire was going to jump from them and consume him.

*"Yes Martzu, but **what** female is the question?"* Martzu stared at her. He was shocked by the question. He had a blank look on his face.

"What female buys such expensive gifts for a guy? Not to mention a watch, similar to the one his father received years earlier?!? Can you tell me that one Martzu Poitier?!?"

Martzu was very much aware of where his wife was headed with all this. *"Like I told you,"* he said calmly, *"I'll speak with De'marco and see what's going on. I'm sure it's nothing. There's no need for you to be upset. Now is there?!?"*

"You tell me," she responded coldly.

Martzu turned and walked away from the door. He respected his wife and her concerns, but he was not going to stand there and allow her emotions to cause her to disrespect him. No, not in a million years, regardless of what was taking place. He wouldn't have that.

De'marco sat back on the couch waiting for Jennifer to finish preparing what she referred to as a surprise dinner. She told him it wasn't his favorite, Cajun shrimp with noodles and sherry wine sauce. But she assured him he would love it. So he waited patiently as he sipped on a double shot of "Grey Goose" and cranberry juice. He couldn't help but to reflect, on the last couple weeks Connie had him strung out. Two or three threesomes throughout the week, and the weekend guaranteed a sexual fiesta. How he was maintaining his grades in school was beyond him. The thought of that in itself was enough to make him want to call Connie and tell her not to call him for anymore of these orgies. That's what one voice was telling him to do. But, on the other hand, he couldn't lie, it was like he enjoyed the act of fulfilling these women's sexual fantasies. Not to mention, many of them had a few stunts up their sleeves.

Like the woman who had him turn her upside down and he ate her out while she sucked away at his love pole. They were actually doing the sixty-nine, but standing up. Then there was the time when two ladies were there and Connie just watched. They had him lay on his back with his legs up, while one orally sucked and massaged his love muscle. The other did what she happily referred to as "Dookie Love," where she savagely licked and probed her tongue in and out his anus. This felt so good to him. The next day he questioned his own sexuality. It was moments like this that made him not mind the many pleasurable episodes. All in all, he knew it was time to put a stop to it. Besides, there was one incident that took place that still stuck in his mind. One of the ladies he found to be very attractive. So, he decided to really work her over, just to mess with her mental. Afterwards, she told him, she gathered she would more than likely get her monies worth. But, she didn't think it would be so overwhelming, and if he wanted to, he could charge her more. What kept him from addressing it right at that moment; Connie grabbed her and started kissing her. She was really laying it into her. Later on, Connie dismissed the comment for being tipsy. Truly they all were pretty drunk that night. Although that may have been the case, the lady seemed serious about what she said. It was time to call Connie and use a little reverse psychology.

He reached for his cell phone and yelled to Jennifer in the kitchen, *"Hey lady, how long before I can eat!? Izza hungry in here."*

With a joyful giggle, Jennifer told him, *"Hold your horses, just another fifteen, twenty minutes. You'll be good to go."*

That's all he needed to hear. He hit speed dial and Connie's name slid across the screen. She picked up on the first ring.

"De'marco? How can I help you Mister?"

"You can help me by telling me how much money you been getting from our little parties."

Connie paused. She had been caught off guard. After all this time De'marco said nothing. She figured she had it made.

"What you talking about?"

Connie took too long to answer and that gave her away. Just as she had taught him, when dealing with a woman and a touchy situation, remain calm, but think quickly.

"Look Connie, we have been dealing with each other for a minute and through it all, I figured we are friends at the least." He let that sink in a little and continued, *"You have taught me a lot and have given me just as much. Honestly, there is no way I could repay you for the things you've done for me."* Realizing from her silence, he had her hanging on every word. *"I could even say you have made me a man before my time. So I ask you again, the sex, the money, how much?"*

Connie had to say something, even if De'marco was just trying her, she had to say something. *"To hell with it,"* she thought, *"I've put the game down this far with raw reality. Why turn back?"*

"De'marco listen baby, you are right about all you just said. We are friends and I must admit there were times my feelings for you grew even stronger than that."

De'marco cut in, *"Connie! You charged the people money to lay with me. Correct or not?!?"*

"Yes, I did"

"Why, why would you do something like that? Why would you involve me and not tell me?! What type of silly shit your old ass up to?" De'marco belted the words out before he knew what he was saying.

Silly? Old? The words hit Connie like bricks.

*"Look little boy, I got your old and silly alright. Don't blame me because you lack volition. Hell, I didn't **make** you do nothing. Don't fault me for setting out to become opulent."* She knew she was wrong. She

took advantage of De'marco. However, at this point, it didn't matter to her. His words and tone of voice hurt her. She warned him about a hurt or angry woman. And right now she was both.

So now, he gets to feel the venom, *"After all I taught you!"* She yelled through the phone, *"You would think you would have demanded emolument, just on G P!"*

There was silence on the phone for a few seconds then De'marco spoke calmly, *"So there we have it. I want to thank you for being so veracious and if it's okay with you, I'll leave everything at that. EVERYTHING! And return to my life amongst the proletariat."* De'marco hung up. Angry from what just transpired.

"Baby?" Jennifer called out to him. She noticed the look on his face. *"Is everything okay? Who was that?"*

De'marco knew a slew of questions were on the way, so he gained his composure quickly.

"Nothings wrong, baby. I called the B.M.W. Dealership about a custom stereo and they gave me a ridiculous price. I couldn't believe it," he said at the same time forcing a smile on his face. The smile caused Jennifer to feel as everything was okay.

"I told you when you pulled up in that car, yeah it's nice, but maintenance on a foreign car is crazy, especially at the dealer. You believe me now, don't you?" She stuck out her tongue, as to say I told you so. De'marco jumped from the couch quickly and grabbed her with both his hands, then wrapped his arms around her. It startled Jennifer. She let out a yelp that was smothered by De'marco's kiss. This excited Jennifer. She became aroused quickly and started kissing and rubbing his back. De'marco pulled back and looked deep into her eyes, *"Woman, you love me?"*

Jennifer was ready for some hot steamy sex right then and there. On the couch, on the floor, on the coffee table, it didn't matter.

She looked back into his eyes, and in the sexiest, oh so desperate voice and said, *"Yes baby, I lovvve you. Oh, I love me some you."*

De'marco spun her around and smacked her on the butt and said... *"Then where's my food? I'm hungry."*

Jennifer gasped, *"No you didn't. You punk! I got something you can eat alright."*

"And what's that?" De'marco mimicked, *"How about some vagina turnover? Or some cunt a'la carte? Or, how bout some rump roast! Or better yet, coochie a la cumm?"*

"OK, ok, ok, De'marco!" She cut in. *"After we eat, it's on. How bout that?"* Jennifer looked to see if he was serious.

"I promise," De'marco said knowing there was no turning back at this point.

"You better," Jennifer said in a whiney voice. *"Now sit down and let me fix my baby a big plate of food. He gon' need his energy,"* she mimicked, while sticking her lip out like a baby.

* * * * * * * * * * * * * * * * * *

Connie was wrong, dead wrong. She had been from the start and she knew it. The last thing she wanted was to fall out with De'marco. He may have been naïve, but that didn't make him a bad person. As a matter of fact, De'marco treated her with more respect than a lot of the guys her age did.

"But he can't call me old? And silly at that?"

Her pride had been hurt. But that was no excuse. She had to make good with De'marco if for nothing else than to have him as a companion. That she had to have. He made her feel vibrant. He made her feel good about herself.

She thought, *"A party! He would like that. I'll have a surprise party for him. Music, food, gifts, everything. I'll give it in a day or two. Let him calm down. Then*

I'll call and apologize and ask him to allow me to make things up to him."

Connie lay back on the bed, deep in thought about her times spent with De'marco and the direction she had taken things. Her phone rang. She smiled, knowing it was De'marco. She was willing to apologize right away.

She quickly grabbed the phone and put it to her ear, and in a sexy voice said, *"Yeesss De'marco?"*

"Connie?" The voice said on the other end.

Realizing it wasn't De'marco, she cleared her throat, *"This is Connie. Who's this?"*

"This is Martzu."

8

"STRAIGHT DRAMA"

*T*he next few days were crazy. Jerome was coming into the shop late, having one or two clients sitting, waiting on him. Nicole kept asking, *"What's up with the hook up? My money right and I'm about due,"* talking about De'marco. She couldn't even bring herself to tell her she had messed things up. She had led everyone to believe De'marco was not only a willing subject, but that he was also getting a piece of the money they were shelling out to party. If they only knew, she had used poor De'marco.

De'shawntu called and cancelled her hair appointment and when asked when would she like to reschedule, she said she didn't know, she'd call and let her know. That was a surprise, seeing that she'd been doing De'shawntu's hair twice a month for as long as she could remember. She hoped it wasn't behind Martzu's calling. He caught her off guard. He hadn't called her in who knows how long. She had just got off the phone with De'marco and didn't know what to expect. So, she told him she had company and she would call him back. Although, she never did. She called De'marco's cell phone a couple times, only to keep getting his voicemail. She let her feelings get the best of her and drove by the campus and the apartment. The car wasn't at either place. That kinda sent her.

As far as De'marco was concerned, this week was a pleasant one. Jennifer had no class and didn't have to work. Although he had class, when he returned home, they would just sit around the apartment laughing, playing, and enjoying each other's conversation and company. The closeness allowed them to learn even more about one another, which was cool with the two of them. Jennifer really enjoyed it. De'marco used her car all week, because he had the Beamer at the dealer getting a new sound system put in. They called and said it was ready so he figured he would have Jennifer drive him to pick it up this evening, as well as, he hadn't totally gotten over what Connie had done. So, he thought he would pay her a visit.

Martzu was still awaiting Connie's phone call. Although at this point, he really felt like she was dodging him. A few times he had contemplated leaving it alone. He tried picturing De'marco and Connie being involved. It was difficult for him, because he knew how outlandish Connie's lifestyle was at times and how laid back his son could be. Yet and still, knowing Connie, he wouldn't put anything past her. He figured he would still get in touch with her, but he couldn't help hope that it was just a matter of his wife jumping to conclusions.

* * * * * * * * * * * * * * * * * *

Connie made it her business to leave the shop early today. It just seemed to have been too much going on, more than she was trying to deal with. She left out with a few things on her mind; a bottle of Jack Daniels, 7up, and a hot bubble bath. When she arrived home, she had only been in the door a few seconds and her clothes were off. She left them where they landed, fixed her a drink and headed towards the bathroom to run her water.

"Nice and hot," she thought. As she prepared her water and she spared no bubble bath. As the water bubbled up and began to fill the tub, she went to fix another drink. She questioned whether or not she was tripping?!?

"Go ahead girl drink up," she told herself, *"You deserve it. You've come a long way from Greenbrier Apartments. To hell with it,"* she thought and grabbed the whole bottle, headed back upstairs to the bathroom. Bubbles were everywhere, *"Ooops!"* She giggled and turned the water off. She lit two candles, poured

another drink and killed the lights. She stepped into the tub, sat down, and leaned back and thought mission accomplished, as she made a toast to herself and turned her drink up. As she sat back, she could hear her cell phone vibrating on the counter downstairs in the kitchen, *"Oh, well,"* she thought. She wasn't about to let nothing disturb this moment.

Martzu decided because Connie wouldn't call him back he'd call his son and see what was what.

De'marco answered his cell phone happy to see it was his dad.

"Hey dad! How are you?" Hearing the excitement in his son's voice made Martzu happy also and assured him he had nothing to worry about.

"I'd be doing a lot better if my wonderful son would remember where his parents lived and come to cut the grass."

De'marco laughed, *"Dad I just cut your grass last weekend. It can't possibly need cut again."*

"Oh, that's right." Martzu said tensing. *"Just don't forget."*

"I won't dad," De'marco said. *"So what makes you call me?"*

"Well I wanted to talk to you about a few things. Where are you?"

"I'm about to pick the car up from the shop."

"The BMW?" Martzu inquired.

"Yep, sure nuff."

"That's part of what I wanted to speak with you about. The car and a few other things taking place with you. Your mother brought a few things to my attention. I figured she was just being Mom and worrying about nothing. All the same, I figured I'd give you a holler. You know how we do!?"

De'marco was caught off guard by his father's conversation. The first thing that came to mind was the watch and the conversation he'd had with his mother in the kitchen. That made him somewhat reluctant to talk, seeing that he had no idea where the conversation might go and Jennifer was sitting right beside him.

She blurted out, *"Tell your daddy I said hi! Tell your daddy I said hi, now De'marco!"*

"Look dad, Jennifer said hello and we're pulling up to the dealership. Once I handle the business with the car, can I call you right back?"

"Sure, son, handle your business and call me right back. And tell Precious I said hello," changing the tone of his voice. *"You have a good girl there son, don't mess that up."*

"Okay, I won't dad. Talk to you in a few minutes."

"Alright son, in a few minutes."

"Man," De'marco thought. *"What could it be?"* Well, he had a few minutes to think on how he would respond, depending on how the conversation went. De'marco sat in the lot of the BMW dealership for over an hour talking to his dad about the things he had received from Connie, even the car, although he wasn't totally honest about it. He made it seem as thought he'd saved up some money and Connie just pointed him in the right direction on a good deal with the car. Truthfully, Connie bought the car straight out for him. The conversation was rather uncomfortable for Martzu and De'marco, because they were both stretching the truth and withholding information from one another. They both knew it. The saddest part about it was, it was because of a woman.

Martzu knew his son and he knew Connie. With that and the bit of information he received from his son, he had a pretty good idea of what transpired. Rather disappointed, yet still willing to allow his son to live his life, he left it at that. However, not before warning him of the troubles and drama that came with certain women. De'marco apologized for any disappointment he may have caused his father and thanked him for the advice. As they hung up, De'marco was pissed and headed straight for Connie's with one thing on his mind.

* * * * * * * * * * * * * * * * * * *

Once Connie finished her bath, she stepped out and finished the glass of Jack and Seven in her hand. She was drunk like never before. She spoke to herself as she dried off.

"That was a good bath." She then looked at the half empty bottle of liquor, *"And this is some good Jack. Hey! Jack,"* she said looking at the bottle, *"Wanna be my man tonight? It's alright with me, if it's alright with you. Here baby, let me turn us on some good music."*

As she walked from the bathroom, she heard her cell phone still vibrating. It didn't sound as loud as before. It must have vibrated itself right off the counter onto the floor.

"Oh, well," she thought. *"They'll be okay. I'm about to listen to me some Luther. Is that alright with you baby!?"* She yelled towards the bathroom where the bottle was.

Then the phone on the nightstand by the bed rang.

"Who the hell is this?" She thought. She started not to answer, but she looked at the caller ID and saw it was the shop. *"Jerome,"* she thought. She picked up, *"Jerome, what in the devil, which is you, do you want?"*

"Ooowee, Miss Thang, you already T'd off, so you really about to kill my black behind."

"No Jerome, your gay. So, your black behind is already dead."

Jerome made a noise like a hissing cat. Then he meowed. Connie was not in the mood for Jerome and he was messing up her date with Jack.

"Look booyeee!"

"Okay, okay," Jerome interrupted, *"You need to come lock up the shop. I left my key at the house."*

"Oh, no the hell you didn't call me on some irresponsible bullshit?!?"

Jerome realizing he had really screwed up, got serious.

"I know I messed up Connie. I'm sorry, but you got to lock up. Like I said, I'm sorry. I, I, I'll be here girl. Take your time. I'll wait, okay?"
Connie was silent.

"Connie? Okay?" He said in a real mellow voice.

Connie said, *"Yeah, okay Jerome, I'll be there."* She hung up furious. *"Ain't this some shit?"* She thought. She went to her closet to put on something. *"To hell with it, I'll be right back."* She slipped her feet into some house shoes and grabbed her robe. She went into the bathroom and grabbed the bottle of Jack Daniels. As she reached the bottom of the stairs, she decided against taking the bottle with her. So, she placed it on the counter, grabbed her keys and headed out the door. She drove fast up the highway partially because she was mad and partially because she was drunk. As she turned to get off the exit, she saw the BMW with De'marco in it getting onto the expressway. She wanted to turn around and catch him, but thought about Jerome and the shop. She reached for the cup holder where her cell phone usually would be, only to remember she had left it on the floor at the house.

"Damn it! Damn it! Damn it!" She cursed, as she banged her fist on the steering wheel. Moments later, she pulled up at the shop and jumped out.

Jerome came to the door. He saw the anger in her eyes. As he opened the door, he tried being cordial, *"Hey!"* He said in an innocent tone.

Connie wasn't feeling him at all, *"Come on, come on, come on!"* She snapped, practically snatching him out the door. She stepped in, punched the alarm code, stepped back out, locked the door and headed towards her truck.

Jerome felt bad. It was the third time this month he had left his keys, but it didn't stop him from continuing to be his "Royal Gayness", *"Thank you girl."*

Connie threw up her middle finger, *"Do it one more time and you can find somewhere else to work."*

Jerome's eyes got big, *"Damn! It's like that!?"*

Connie kept walking, as she opened the door to the truck Jerome yelled, *"Anyway, I thought you might want to know that that booyfriend of yours came driving by."* He was determined to piss her off even more for threatening to fire him.

He yelled, *"He was probably looking for me."* He then two-snapped his fingers in a circle and walked off to his car mumbling to himself. Although Connie jumped in the truck, slammed door and drove off as if she hadn't heard a word Jerome said, it was quite the opposite, she heard every word. What was De'marco up to and where was he headed? She jumped on the expressway. As she floated to the house, she thought, *"Let me get home to call him and find out what's really popping."*

Connie was surprised when she pulled up in her driveway to find De'marco sitting there. She hit the garage opener and pulled in. She saw De'marco through her rear view mirror. As he walked towards the garage, she waited for him to step past the censor. Then she hit the button to let the door down. She looked over herself, *"Damn, I look crazy."*

De'marco thought about a million and one things on the way to Connie's. What ate at him the most was the conversation he and his father had. Although, his father didn't say it, you would have thought he and Connie might have had something at one time. But, why wouldn't his dad tell him? Stupid question De'marco, you didn't admit to your frolicking with Connie, now did you?!? Connie opened the door to the truck and jumped out.

"Hey baby!" She said, trying to be happy. When the alcohol on her breath hit his face and he saw what she had on, it made him even madder. He grabbed her by the arm and pulled her towards the door.

"Hey, now!" Connie said, *"Watch what you doing."* She didn't play the grabbing game and De'marco knew it. That had long been discussed, the do's and don'ts of

their relationship. Because he knew she wasn't with it, he held her arm tightly as he maneuvered her into the house.

"De'marco!" Connie yelled, as she looked up in his face. She saw the anger and the hurt she'd caused. *"If you give me a minute, I'll explain everything."*

"I bet you will!" De'marco said as he spun her around to face him.

"Look, let me make things up to you baby, Okay?"

As she said this De'marco was taking inventory of her clothes spread out on the floor and the half empty bottle of Jack Daniels on the counter. He then looked back at her in the house robe. He reached and pulled at the belt around her waist. As it unloosened, the robe came open exposing her completely nude body. He just shook his head. Realizing what he was possibly thinking, Connie put her hands up.

"Wait now De'marco. You're taking everything in too fast. Let's go sit down." She pulled him to the living room. *"I'll explain E-VERY-THING,"* she said pronouncing each syllable. *"And then I'll tell you what I have in mind for you to make things better between us."*

De'marco just stood there. Then he said, *"I know what you could do to make things better between us,"* as he unbuckled his pants and let them fall to the floor. Connie had never seen him like this. His eyes were red from anger. He seemed so cold. Her mouth flew open from the shock of what De'marco had done.

"That's right," he said, placing his hand on top of her head and pulling her down towards his limp meat. *"You got the idea."* Connie was floored. De'marco was playing her cheap, real cheap.

As De'marco pushed her head down and guided her towards his meat, Connie spoke, *"A party De'marco. A party for you."*

He wasn't hearing her. Her words were muffled as he placed his helmet in her mouth and began guiding her head back and forth.

"Go ahead Connie, suck it. Get it up baby. Do what you do."

The way things were going down hurt Connie. But, she told herself she would go along. Why? She didn't know, but she would. So, she started working De'marco's love pole the way she knew he liked it.

"There you go," De'marco said, *"Do your thing baby. I mean hell, this is what you about, right?"*

Connie fought back the hurt and continued doing what De'marco wanted.

"Things will be better after this." She told herself. She felt De'marco getting stiffer in her mouth and realized he was about to release. He had never done that to her before, even when she wanted him to.

He would pull away and tell her, *"You don't have to do that. Plus I don't know how I would look at you if that were to happen."* With that thought, Connie went to pull back.

"Aaat, aaat," De'marco said and held her head still. Before she knew it, he gasped and her mouth began to fill up with his baby making fluid. It was so much, she gagged and while some seeped out the corners of her mouth, some also ran from her nose. At the same time, a tear ran down her face. Connie was crushed. De'marco released his grip, as Connie pulled back, she tried to regroup. Before she could stand up, and say anything, De'marco pushed her back and spread her legs. She swallowed to keep from choking on the contents in her mouth.

"De'marco baby, listen. Where's your head at? Look, we can go upstairs and do this right, okay baby?"

De'marco was hearing nothing. He was rubbing the head of his johnson between her legs and as soon as he became erect, he began to slide it in and out. Connie looked in his eyes, he wasn't paying her no mind.

She still tried to reach him, *"Let me tell you about the party Marco baby."*

At the same time, he entered her while raising her legs up over her head until her feet were touching the floor. He began stroking, and then Connie's nightmare…De'marco raised up to penetrate all the way into her. She never had him completely in her, not every inch. She never even tried. She knew better. As he began to lower himself into her, she knew she caused his pain. He trusted her and she took advantage of that trust. She told herself she would play along since she created this anger, this monster. She watched the inches go inside her like a slow motion movie. She knew she could only take up to eight inches. They had played around and measured it before. So as it passed the depth, she was so familiar with, she braced herself and rightfully so. He began thrusting hard to make sure she felt it.

"Hey, Connie baby. This is what you want, ain't it baby? Dick, dick, dick. Right? Sex, sex, sex. Oh! That's right, you want some money for it. "Don't blame me for getting paid," ain't that what you said?!?"

The position she was in and the pressure made her pass gas, and not just once, three times. The third one was a long one and because of the alcohol and food she had eaten earlier, it stunk something fierce.

"Damn!" De'marco said. *"What've you done, shit or what?"*

Connie was in pain both from the words he spoke to her and the way he was stroking her. Not to mention, she was so embarrassed another tear escaped her eyes. As her phone began to ring, it set De'marco off even more.

"I wonder what poor foolish ass victim of yours is that?"

Little did he know, it was his father, Martzu, calling Connie, likewise, as the phone continued to ring, Martzu did not know that his son was over there punishing Connie's vagina, as he once did.

The whole evening had literally blown Connie's mind. She couldn't believe it. She thought about how things had gone down. She comes home to a nice hot bath, a good stiff drink to recharge herself after the week that was draining, silly Jerome calls with some more of his simple irresponsible B.S., she handles that, only to come home to an angry De'marco, who had every right to be. She would have liked the chance to clear things up before he showed just how angry he was, because this whole scene took the cake. He had punished her, releasing in her mouth, throwing her legs over her head, something she had never done in her life. The passing gas, his comment about it and he didn't stop there. With her legs still bent back, he pulled his johnson out her vagina and spit between her butt cheeks. He then began sliding his johnson into her anus. That was a way they'd never done it. After trying it once, it was very clear, he had too much going on for that type of activity. Today, however, De'marco refused to deny Connie the pain he felt. And felt it she did. She lay there on the living room floor sore inside and out. The skin between her legs felt as though it was torn up, not split, torn up! The muscles in the back of her legs and butt cheeks felt sore from being stretched back for so long. Her back was killing her. She had dried semen and tearstains on her face. And to top it off, when he finished, he stood, pulled up his pants, turned to walk through the kitchen, and yelled back at her, *"Oh yeah, let me know when the party is,"* as he grabbed the bottle of Jack Daniels and left.

Yeah, Connie felt the pain, mentally, physically, and emotionally. She lay there naked on her living room floor, unwilling and unable to move. As she laid there in her thoughts, she was unable to prevent the fart that escaped from her rear end.

"Damn! What next?" She said to herself out loud as if it had heard her and overstood. Her butt released an enormous fart that caused her cheeks to part. When the smell reached her nose, it just made her yell out, *"Why!?"*

Worn out, tired and stankin' she thought, *"I'm too old for this shit I'm going through."* She then drifted off to sleep. Upon awakening, the next morning Connie's condition was no better. She was even more sore than the evening before. On top of that, she was dehydrated from the consumption of too much alcohol. Which was more than likely the reason for the headache. She had to pull it together though and this she knew. She took a deep breath and counted to three. She rolled over and stood up, legs weak, head spinning. She climbed the stairs to the bathroom. She started running water in the tub, added bubble bath. She laughed to herself, *"Damn, what's this dejavu?"* She turned and looked in the mirror, *"What a sight!"* She thought. Eyes puffy with tearstains and along with what appeared to be a milky white mustache coming from her nose. *"What the…?"* She thought. She then realized, she didn't want to remember. She turned off the water in the tub and went in her bedroom. She called all the clients she could reach and cancelled. She called Jerome who came in on time today and told him to let her other clients know she had an emergency and would give them twenty dollars off their next appointment.

Jerome was like, *"Girl, you ain't coming in? Shit I guess there's a first time for everything. I'ma leave it alone doe."*

"Okay, now that's straight." She got her thoughts together and dialed De'marco's number. *"Why?"* She asked herself. She doubted if he would pick up. To her surprise, he picked up on the first ring.

"Hello, De'marco." He didn't answer. *"Look, okay, I'm sorry. I apologize for everything. Let me make it right by you, okay?"*

"I thought you was calling me about some party you was having."

Connie didn't appreciate this playing dumb and figured he was still mad and this was part of his punishment thingy.

"De'marco come by, let's talk."

De'marco smacked his lips, *"I don't think so."*

"Why not?" Connie asked.

"Is today the party?" De'marco asked sarcastically.

"Nooo, but I would like to talk to you."

"That's okay," De'marco said, *"Look, I'm about to go, how can I help you?"*

Connie was in no mood to play. She took a deep breath, *"So, you'll come to the party?"*

"Sure, let me know when my party is." De'marco said, *"Tah, tah."* Then hung up.

9

"STEALING A TASTE"

*T*he weeks went by and Connie prepared for
De'marco's party. He hadn't come by, and refused her
offer for lunch and dinner a couple times. Yet, he had
no problem talking to her on the phone. He'd even
called once or twice. But, he continued to carry on as if
nothing ever happened. Connie realized this must be his
way of dealing with what had taken place. So she let
him have that. Once again she played along. Her whole
thing was that she realized she was wrong from the very
beginning. She wanted from De'marco what she had
gotten from his father. But reality was, she was a young
naïve female when she dealt with Martzu. And although
he sexed her to the point of ecstasy, he also took time to
educate her on making her own life successful and
having something when she became too old to be out
there trying to get it. Her feelings got too caught up and
she wouldn't listen, so Martzu put an end to their
dealings. She applied a lot of what he told her, which is
why she had what she did to that day. He also, whether
he knew it or not, turned her out and let her go. That in
itself was a lesson to Connie. Because of this and her
sexual appetite, she caused unnecessary confusion. She
knew it was important to make things right again, and
she would. She had plans on keeping De'marco as a pet
for her own gratification, oh yeah, fo' sho, but she
wouldn't hurt him again. As of now, she needed to
make peace with him and get things together for his
party. De'marco's cell phone began to vibrate for what
seemed like the fiftieth time today and to look at it and
see Connie's number on the caller ID for what seemed
like the forty-ninth time today didn't make him any
happier.

   "Yes Connie, how can I help you this time?"

"Look De'marco, I can respect and overstand why you're taking the steps you are, however, I want to see you and I need to talk with you in person."

"Connie I don't think that will be happening, sorry."

"De'marco, I don't think I'm asking. Meet me at Franklin Park today at five-thirty." She hung up.

De'marco wasn't feeling this. He hadn't seen Connie since he put mad meat to her. He felt bad about it, but she had it coming and she knew it. As far as he was concerned, she was lucky he hadn't done more than that. Especially, after putting things together and realizing all she had done.

He looked at his watch. It was four-fifteen. He figured he should just not go and not even call to tell her. But, he also felt enough games had been played, so he decided to show and allow her to say whatever it was she needed to say face to face. He couldn't help laughing to himself about how a woman her age was running around doing the things she was.

Connie and De'marco met up a Franklin Park at five-thirty. It was a nice little park over on Broad Street. It had a little pond and a jogging trail that went around it, as well as a huge, elaborate flower and plant conservatory that also housed many interesting and educational exhibits.

She was very surprised, De'marco showed, she didn't think he would. Although he showed, she was aware of his reluctance from the jump. She held out her arms for a hug. He hugged her back, but it was brief with no feeling behind it. Yet and still, as they talked things began to look brighter. De'marco accepted her apology, but not without hella questions that put her on the spot and made her question her own level of maturity. De'marco even brought up the discussion he and his father had. Connie stayed as far away from that as she possibly could. At the end of the conversation, they were okay. There was an agreement that they would keep the sex activities on the low and only between them, unless they both agreed otherwise. Connie was cool with De'marco and the fact that he said he would never leave Jennifer. She knew this because of the age difference and her associations with his family they could never be together. She also knew she would never find another young stud like De'marco around town, maybe in the depths of Africa, amongst the "Mandingo" tribe, but not in little ole Columbus, Ohio.

As they walked to their cars, Connie asked, *"So, how's the Beamer holding up?"*

"Good" De'marco answered, *"Real good."*
That's not what she really wanted him to say, so she got her nerve up and tried it again.

"Hey, do you think you could come by later and hook a sister up?"

De'marco laughed, *"No Connie, not tonight."* He said it in kind of a snappy way.

She didn't want to end up back on his shit list.

"Okay, Okay, see you this Saturday at the party, right?!?"

"Yeah sure, and I'm bringing Jennifer."

She didn't like the thought of that, but played along, *"Okay, that's cool. I look forward to meeting her again."*

* * * * * * * * * * * * * * * * * *

Jennifer was excited about going to the party, even though she was unable to stay longer than a couple hours, because it was her Saturday to work at the pharmacy. She tried getting out of it by stating it probably wouldn't be busy. However, her supervisor assured her that people will be wanting to pick-up prescriptions late on Saturday evening. So, she carried her lab coat and nametag with her. She followed behind De'marco in her car. She was clean, and showing it all off. It raised an eyebrow when De'marco told her it was at Connie's. She still felt Connie wanted him, although he would quickly deny the accusation with disgust but she knew better. A woman's intuition is not to be messed with!

As they pulled up, there were cars everywhere, they barely had a place to park. De'marco jumped out his car and was pulling her door open before she could even get it in park good.

"Hold your horses De'marco. I'm coming."

"Yeah, but when?" He said being sarcastic. *"We're already late"*

"If you tell me that one mo' gin, I'm turning around and going home!" Jennifer snapped.

As they walked towards the house, Jennifer surveyed the type of cars and houses in the neighborhood. She questioned if she was ready to meet and mingle with what appeared to be such well-to-do folk. As they approached the house, the garage door was up. You could hear the music playing loud and clear, Too Shorts voice, "Bounce that Monkey."

They stepped into the kitchen through the garage. There were people everywhere, standing around all with drinks in hand. They passed couples and a female let out a, *"Hey there Mister!"* As if she knew him. He looked closer and it was one of the ladies that he and Connie had romped with. As they passed, he felt her pinch his butt. When they stepped in the living room, the furniture was moved out of the way and people were dancing. A female in a fishnet body suit was in the middle of two guys. The way she was dancing said she had to be a stripper or a super duper freak. Her butt cheeks were working so tough, you could here them clapping. Jennifer's eyes were bucked open along with her mouth. De'marco had to give her a slight nudge. De'marco noticed several of the woman whom he had bedded, most of them with husbands or boyfriends.

"Hey guy! Glad you could make it!" Connie said popping out of nowhere.

"Hey Connie."

Connie looked over at Jennifer and winked her eye, *"Hey girl, look at you. You looking good."*

Jennifer gave a big Kool-Aid smile, *"Thank you!"* She said bashfully, as people trying to dance were bumping them around.

"Hey, come in here."

They walked through a door into a large room with a pool table. As many times as De'marco had been here, he didn't even know this room was here. And why should he? The only time he ever came over was for one of Connie's sex set-ups. And those always went down on the living room floor or couch. Except for the time they were in the kitchen with the chick that had a food fetish. That was a mess. Across the room, was a long bar that ran along the wall. There was a sliding patio door with people standing out on a deck.

"Hey everybody, De'marco's here!" Connie shouted. *"Finally,"* she added with sarcasm, looking at him out the corner of her eye.

Several people walking over greeted him. He once again noticed some of the women he and Connie laid with. As he shook hands and mingled, Connie caught Jennifer's eye and they walked off somewhere together. De'marco wasn't too happy about that. But he played along, just to see what would take place. He spoke with different people about where they worked, and about him going to law school. Connie popped up, handed him a drink and was gone again.

Some chick stumbled over to him as if she had lost her balance. It was almost believable, but as she reached out towards him, she brushed her hand across the front of his pants and as smoothly as she wanted to be, she squeezed down on his manhood, giggled, then a *"Oops!"* Came out her mouth followed by, *"Call me,"* as she shoved a piece of paper in his pocket. As she walked off, she looked back and said, *"I mean it,"* with a look on her face that was suppose to be serious. He watched her as she walked with a guy who she must have come with, because as she took her seat, she kissed him on the cheek.

He looked out on the patio and saw Connie and Jennifer engaging in conversation. Something was apparently funny from the way they were laughing. Jennifer had a drink in her hand. That was a shock, seeing she had to be leaving to go to work in the next hour. De'marco continued to mingle with a group of guys. Then suddenly, he noticed that out of the four guys standing there, three of them had on the exact same watch as he did.

"Hell no!" He thought to himself. He walked off and made him a drink. He took three straight shots of a bottle, he didn't even read the label until after the fact, "1800 Cuervo Gold Tequila".

"Man, this shit is strong and nasty," he thought as he turned up his fourth drink. He then reached and grabbed a Miller Light. Let me find my lady and get a dance. He found Jennifer and Connie still on the patio.

"Hey lady! Can I get a dance?" He asked Jennifer as he pulled her to him and kissed her as if he hadn't seen her in weeks.

She was surprised, *"We can dance, come on baby."*

"Yeah, you two go dance." Connie said.

As they walked off, she smacked Jennifer on the butt. *"What you gonna do with it?"*

Jennifer looked over her shoulder at Connie with a half curious and half surprised smile on her face.

As they danced it was clear, De'marco looked at her as he never had before. They looked as if they were dancing to the words instead of the beat. The fact that he was buzzing from the Tequila and kept turning the beer up wasn't helping. They danced two or three songs and Jennifer threw her arms around him, *"Baby, I'm tired."*

De'marco was drunk by now.

"I bet you is. I'm out here turning out!"

Jennifer twisted her lips up in the "O dear!" position.

"Yeah, you doing your thang. I got to get to work. Walk me to the car."

"Okay, let's go. I probably need to be leaving myself."

"Let me find Connie and say goodbye."

De'marco was nice and drunk, yet he still wondered about the Connie and Jennifer conversation. He watched as they talked and said their goodbyes. They hugged. Connie was really drunk. She grabbed Jennifer on both sides of her face and kissed her smack on the lips and then her nose. Jennifer pulled away with an 'Oookay,' expression on her face.

De'marco was like, *"Hey what's up with that?"*

Connie waved him off and stumbled over and sat on some guys lap. As they were walking to the car, they saw Jerome walking up.

"Hey De'marco buddy!"

"Hey," Jerome said as he rolled his eyes at Jennifer.

Jennifer laughed, *"Damn baby, he want you."*

"Don't play!" De'marco snapped. *"That gay guy is crazy."*

De'marco was walking a little wobbly. Jennifer noticed.

"Baby before you pull off, maybe you should sit in the car and sober up a little."

"Yeah, you probably right," he said.

De'marco opened the car door and started rubbing her butt.

Jennifer looked at him, *"Oh, now you wanna play?!? Give me a kiss, I gotta go."*

They kissed and she pulled off, but not before rolling down the window and yelling out, *"Don't forget to sober up before you drive home!"*

"Yeah, yeah." De'marco waved and wobbled to his car.

Before he could put his key in, Connie spoke from the edge of the driveway, standing with her hands on her hips, *"Oh, so you gonna leave. No goodbye? Nothing?"*

De'marco went over and gave her a hug.

"Oh yeah, I see you was all chummy with Jennifer. What's that about?"

Connie laughed, *"Look, that's your lady, right?!?*

"And?!?"

"And you said you are gonna keep her and straighten me out sometime, right?!?"

De'marco looked in her face, although it was dark, he could see that look in her eyes, that game look.

"Okay then, I got this," she finished saying, *"I know what I'm doing. You ain't gonna keep both of us and we don't know nothing about each other or one don't know the other. That will cause you to have to lie and sneak. That's what a cheater with no game does because he really can't handle what's going down. To hell with that, I'm gonna make you a player, a true one at that. And a player comes real off the jump. No silly shit. Can you dig it?"*

De'marco wasn't sure if he wanted Connie dealing with Jennifer.

"Yeah, I hear you," he told Connie, *"But I'm watching you too."*

Connie responded quickly, *"Good. That way you'll learn something. Look,"* she said, *"Enough of that small talk. You need to sit down and pull yourself together a bit. You up here swaying from side to side like you gonna fall over. Plus, I got a gift for you. Come grab it before you leave. Come on."* She grabbed his wrist and started toward the house. When they stepped in, the party was still jumping. There was a Chug-a-lug contest going on. People were chanting, *"Drink, drink, drink!"*

Nicole came out of nowhere, drunk like nobody's business.

"What's up you two? Is it on or what?"

Connie realized she was tore back, *"Girl, calm down. Ain't nothing shaking and ain't that Melvin, your husband, over there?!?"*

153

"Oh yeah," Nicole laughed, *"That's right, forgot he was here wit me. Since that's the case, guess I can't lay and play. But look, De'marco baby, why don't we slide into the bathroom and you hit me off right quick?"*

"What the fuck?" Connie said as she took Nicole, spun her around and pushed her in the direction of her husband. De'marco just shook his head.

"Sorry," Connie said, *"Look, go upstairs..."*

Before she could finish De'marco blurted out, *"I ain't doing nothing with you!"*

"What?!" Connie just looked at him, *"Look, don't flatter yourself. You think I'm trying to be getting a nut with all these people in my house? I thinks not! Go upstairs, lie down and sober up a bit. Plus your gift is on the bed."*

De'marco scrunched up his face, *"What's the gift for? And who is it from?"*

Connie had enough of him. She just pointed, *"Go!"*

De'marco started walking off, then looked over at her and said, *"I ain't scared of you."*

Connie just walked off, *"A drunk ain't shit!"* She said to herself.

De'marco went upstairs and flopped on the bed. He grabbed a box that was nicely wrapped. Before he could start to open it, he began to think about his first night there. He was drunk, but the thought aroused him. He smiled and fell to sleep.

Meanwhile, the party downstairs continued to grow. It was only twelve-fifteen and people were still coming. Drinks were being poured, music was being played, off to the side, you saw people smoking and carrying on. Connie figured she would put some food out. So she headed to the kitchen, only to find Jerome there rummaging through her refrigerator.

"Excuse me," she said, *"Damn! I guess you hungry."*

Jerome shut the refrigerator door, put the pickle he grabbed in his mouth, while standing with one leg up like in a karate stance. He started moving his arms and hands like he was clawing at her. She grabbed his raised leg, snatched the pickle out his mouth.

"Gurrrl, you can make me fall if you want to. Your ass will be grass. I'm high and drunk too."

"Shut up punk!" Connie said, *"And help me fix some finger sandwiches."*

"Oh, now you want me to help you fix some shit to eat, but I can't eat a stanking pickle!"

Connie put up her middle finger, *"Punnkk! Is you gonna help or not?"*

"Or not," Jerome snapped back, *"I got one of those too,"* he said, putting up his middle finger.

Connie started pulling out dishes. Then she grabbed a knife and turned around holding it up. She looked at Jerome, *"You gonna help or what?"*

Jerome gasped, *"Let me go wash my hands. You psycho bi…"*

"Psycho what??!" Connie yelled as she poked the knife at him. He screamed like a girl and walked off.

"Hurry up!" Connie yelled, *"Before I cut you for real."*

Jerome went around the corner to the bathroom. The door was locked and he heard moaning. He put his mouth to the crack of the door and yelled, *"Get that pussy!"* And took off.

He went upstairs to use the bathroom. When he reached the top of the stairway, he looked in Connie's bedroom and saw De'marco lying on the bed sleeping and snoring away. He walked on into the bathroom. When he turned the water on, he looked in the mirror at himself. His eyes became little slits, as he told himself, *"You ain't shit."* He then turned the water off and tiptoed into the bedroom.

"Hey, Mr. De'marco. Hello there... Are you sleeping?"

De'marco snored away, unaware of the man he considered at as a crazed fool. Jerome set on the bed beside him. He placed his hand on De'marco's stomach.

"Hey Mr. De'marco," he whispered. Then in an instant he began telling himself, *"Go ahead. See what all the fuss is about."* So, he started undoing De'marco's pants. He slid his hand in his pants and grabbed his manhood. He pulled it out.

"Damn this bad boy feels thick and heavy."

He pulled his pants down further to get a better look.

His eyes got big, *"Well, I'll be damn! Look at this big tasty bar of chocolate we got here."*

Jerome turned evil in his thoughts and started rubbing and talking to De'marco's meat, *"Hey, I bet you give'em hell. But I'll break you off."* He then chomped his teeth at it as if to bite it.

De'marco moved his hand and coughed.

Jerome jumped down on the floor beside the bed.

"Oh my God! Oh my God! Please don't wake up, please don't. This man gonna kill me if he catch me in here."

He then noticed De'marco hadn't wakened up because he continued to snore. Jerome popped up from beside the bed like a Jack-in-the-box. He turned back evil. He reached and lifted up De'marco's meat.

"Damn!" he thought, *"It's all the way up by his navel and he ain't even hard. To hell with it,"* Jerome thought to himself, *"I'm stealing a taste of this!"*

He lowered his head and opened his mouth.

Connie had finished the finger sandwiches and filled a couple bowls with chips, when she realized Jerome hadn't come back. She carried the platter of food into the crowded room of people,

"Food, food, coming through." She put the platter down. As she did, it got swarmed. She walked over to the bathroom and tried the doorknob. It was locked.

She knocked, *"Jerome what you doing? Did you fall asleep in there?"*

She went back in the kitchen to get the rest of the food. Minutes later, as she finished up, she looked and saw Jerome downing a drink. She went over and slapped him hard on the back of his head.

"Punk, thanks for coming back to help me."

Jerome turned around looking like he'd seen a ghost.

"Girl, I am just too through. I need to be on my way. Ain't no men in here anyway."

Connie looked around at all the people and took note of the men throughout the party.

"No, Jerome. Ain't no fags in here. And if ya leaving," she said placing her hand in his face, *"Poof, be gone!"*

"Holler at ya!" Jerome put his arm around her to hug her goodbye then squeezed her butt.

She pushed him back, *"Punk don't play!"*

Jerome looked at her, *"Yeah right, you know you want me to hit that thang."* He then walked off.

Connie shook her head, *"That mother is sick in the head."*

She pulled out a joint and fired it up, as she inhaled the smoke a guy walked over and put his arm around her.

"What's up baby?"

She looked up, *"Oh, what's up Mic?!?"* Reading his thoughts she said, *"Yeah, you can hit it."*

* * * * * * * * * * * * * * * * * * *

De'marco woke up. He quickly realized three things. He was hungry, his mouth was dry, and his pants were undone. As he slid his hand in his pants, he fondled himself and pulled his hand out to see the slobber on it.

"Hell no!" He thought, *"Connie."*

He pulled himself together. Once he collected his bearings he got up and walked downstairs.

As he reached the bottom of the staircase, Connie came up to him, *"There he goes..."* she said. She placed her arms around him, *"You better now, or do you still want to bite my head off?"*

He just looked at her, *"My mouth is dry,"* he told her.

"Well hi, to you too," she said, *"Come in here."*

She opened up a bottle of PowerAde. *"Here drink this, you'll be okay in a minute."*

"How you gonna play me?" He asked.

"What now, De'marco?" She asked figuring he didn't like the gift.

"If you don't want it, I'll take it back."

"Don't play dumb. How you gonna do me while I'm sleeping, after I told you I wasn't trying to get at you like that tonight."

She saw he was serious, *"De'marco baby, I haven't done nothing to you."*

They stood in the kitchen and talked. De'marco told her how he had awakened. The thought of someone going into her room doing such a thing had her furious. She started clearing people out.

"It's three-thirty in the morning. You ain't got to go home, but you got to get the hell up outta here!"

De'marco was trailing behind her as she told people, *"Party over, bye. Get out!"*

There was a couple on the patio getting it on. The guy had the chick up against the banister spread open, going to town.

"Hey!" Connie said, *"Enough, go home!"* She yelled.

"Damn," De'marco said, *"What's their problem?"*

"X that's their problem."

"X what?"

"Ecstasy. If you don't know, you don't want to. And if someone says they have some, run!"

"Damn," De'marco said, *"It's like that?"*

Connie looked at him, *"You think someone took advantage of you tonight while you were in your little drunken sleep, take some X."*

The statement made De'marco mad, *"I'm out. Talk to you another time."*

Connie didn't have time for it. She was tired. It was late and somebody had pulled off some B.S. in her bedroom.

"Go ahead and go De'marco," she told him, *"Call me in the morning."*

He left thinking on whether or not Connie may have been lying.

"Whatever," he thought, *"You can have that one on G.P."*

De'marco left and Connie began to straighten things up. She was drunk and hot. So, she peeled her clothes off down to her panties and bra. She couldn't believe the evening, she set out to throw a nice little "make-up" party for De'marco, he falls out drunk and gets taken advantage of supposedly, and blames her, *"Check that shit out!"* However, the party wasn't a complete fiasco. She began picking up empty cups and napkins. Standing there with half filled cups, she said, *"People wasting my drinks and stuff!!"* As she picked up a napkin she couldn't believe what she saw on the coffee table.

"Now how somebody gonna leave an empty condom wrapper on my damn table!?" She went to flop down on the couch and when she did, the contents of one of the cups she held in her hand spilled right in between her legs. The ice and all the coldness made her scream and giggle at the same time. Then, her thoughts became devious.

"Hey," she told herself, *"That didn't feel too bad."* She looked at the ice holder over on the bar. *"I must be crazy,"* she told herself, heading towards the bucket full of ice. She stood there staring at the ice, then asked herself, *"Why? Why not?"* She said, *"It's my house. I'm home alone."* The statement made her think of the movie. She laughed and slid her panties down.

As she stepped out of them, she climbed up on one of the barstools. She grabbed the largest piece of ice and began rubbing it on her breast, *"Sssssssss...,"* was the sound she made as she rubbed the cold ice cube on her body. Her nipples became instantly hard, while she began sliding the ice down the middle of her body. She gripped one of her breast and raised it up as she bent her head down as far as she could. Her tongue was darting in and out of her mouth licking her nipple, the other hand rubbing the ice cube in circles around her navel. She spun the barstool so she was able to raise her legs and place her feet on the bar. Sliding the hand with the ice cube down in it, she let off another *"Ssssssss...."* It was cold, she was drunk and not to mention horny, and it felt good. She started making circles around the hood of her clit with the ice cube. She then rubbed on the sides of her vagina lips, then up the middle of her lips. Her body heat made the ice melt fast, causing the split of her vagina and butt cheeks to be soaked. She liked it... it added to the moment. Once again she rubbed the ice cube around her clit while she circled her breast with her middle finger, pinching them between her thumb and index finger, pulling them, turning them like little knobs. *"Oh, Ssssss...,"* she moaned. She liked what she was doing to herself, so much so, between the ice and the wetness of her kitty cat, the barstool had water mixed with juices from her honey pot dripping down the side of it. The ice cube melted to the point it was too small to be fooling with. So, she pushed it inside her vagina. *"Whoa!"* She exclaimed. She then leaned back in the barstool the best she could and spread her legs wide. With one hand, she parted her lips while pulling the hood back until the little man in the boat was fully exposed. She then began to put in work. She rubbed it in circles, up and down, side to side. She even flicked it with her finger real fast causing a vibrating sensation. She moaned, and in her drunken state thought about De'marco putting it to her. For some reason she couldn't help but to think of Jennifer too. She began probing her two fingers in and out of her vagina, first slow and easy, then she probed them deeper, faster, harder. As she stroked her fingers in and out, she quickly caused her hand to clap on her clit bringing a double sensation. The more it built up, the more she worked it. She then began to feel it... *"Come on baby! Come on baby! There we go! There we go!"* She was working the middle so tough, she began rolling her hips in a circle. *"Ohhh, ohhhh...!"* It was a sight to see, because she was so drunk. She began pumping in rhythm with her hand that she worked in and out, thrusting her hips to meet her hand like she would with a real dick. This caused the chair to rock so hard that she fell out of it right onto the floor.

"Damn! Damn! Damn!" She said. *"To hell with this."*

She got up and started limping to her bedroom. She hit the lights and flopped on the bed to go to sleep, but not before she licked the succulent flavor from her fingers, *"Slurp."*

10

"HUMILIATION"

*D*e'marco and Connie seemingly patched things up between the two of them, with the exception of what happened the night of the party. De'marco really believed Connie had done it. He figured no one but her would be that shallow to do such a thing.

Connie knew she hadn't done a thing to De'marco, she tried at best to stay away from the subject. De'marco was wondering about Connie. He was trying to give her the benefit of the doubt, overlooking all that had taken place between them. But, Connie never ceased to amaze him with her, "let me give you some game" tactics. One day, she called and asked him to let her take Jennifer shopping.

"I thinks not," De'marco told her.

Then she told him, *"You could at least let me take you two to dinner."*

"Why?" De'marco asked.

She responded by telling him, if Jennifer and she were going to be wife-in-laws, they needed to be getting to know each other better.

De'marco felt that Connie was acting up because he hadn't broke her off in a while.

Connie sat in the shop finishing up a head, when Jerome asked her, *"What we gonna eat today girl?"*

Connie frowned, *"I don't know what you gonna eat today... but, I'm bout to call my baby and have him pick me up some curry chicken and plantains from Red Snapper."*

Jerome clapped and jumped up and down like a little baby, *"Call'em girl and have him bring us some eat'em ups."*

Connie dialed up De'marco, *"Hey baby, you busy?"* she asked in a whiny voice.

"What's up Connie? I just left class and I'm tired."

"Wellll!" Connie wondered if she should continue, seeing that he was tired. *"I was going to ask you to bring me something to eat and I'd return your money when you get here."*

"From where Connie?"

"The Red Snapper. If you coming out of Franklin University, it's straight down Main Street."

"I know where it's at. What you want?" De'marco said irritably.

Connie told him what she wanted and had him grab a little something extra for Jerome.

An hour passed and Jerome hadn't heard whether or not Connie ordered him some food, so with an attitude he asked her, *"Excuse me, Cuntie. I mean Connie, did you happen to order me anything through your little Hercules?"*

Connie looked bug-eyed, *"What you call me?"*

"Look girl, I'm just asking before I call Pedros and order me a sub."

Connie caught his little attitude, *"Oh yeah, I ordered you something."*

His mood changed quickly, *"Oh, okay, what you get me, girl? Lord knows I'm hungry."*

Very calmly, Connie said to him, *"I got you some Curry penis, with red balls and rice, smothered in cum sauce with a large diet sissy drink."*
Everyone in the shop laughed.

Nicole told the two of them, *"Y'all need to stop. Everyday y'all at it. What is it? Gee whiz!"*

With an attempt to change the subject before things got out of hand between them, Nicole asked Connie, *"How De'marco doing? What he's been up to?"*

"He's cool," Connie said, *"Trying to get through law school."*

"What was the deal at the party?" Nicole asked. *"I heard you just started kicking people out."*

"Yeah, girl," Connie said, *"It was late, plus somebody pulled some silly shit up in my crib."*

Nicole looked over with curiosity on her face, cause she was drunk that night and hoped it wasn't her. She remembered when she approached De'marco that night, but she was too lit up to remember what happened.

"Girl, let me tell you, De'marco went upstairs to sleep off some of his drunkenness, so he would be able to drive home. Don't you know while he was sleeping, somebody gone up there and fondled him and got their rocks off!?"

The whole shop was like, *"What! You lying!"*

"No I ain't," Connie said, *"He come downstairs on some, 'I done it' shit!"*

"Hell no," Jerome said, *"That's some fucked up shit there."*

"Yeah," Connie said looking over at him, *"You didn't do it, did you?"* She asked just to be messing with him.

At that moment, De'marco came walking in with the food. Connie noticed the look on Jerome's face when she asked the question. Although she was BS-ing Jerome with the question, everybody else was looking for an answer from him.

Jerome felt the pressure of the eyes peering at him, *"Oh, goody, here's the food,"* his voice went from gay to straight.

"Oh hell no!" Connie said.

"Hey lady, here's your food," De'marco said upon entering the shop. She held up her finger to signal, just a minute.

"Come here Jerome," Connie said and headed towards her office in the back. All was looking.

Jerome lost it and broke the silence with, *"What the hell y'all looking at!?"*

As the office door closed behind them, a lady sitting in a waiting chair supposedly reading a magazine broke out with, *"He's guilty!"*

Everybody broke out with, *"Yep, sho is. Damn, that's fucked up!"*

De'marco who was at a lost looked towards the only familiar face, Nicole, and asked, *"What's going on?"*

She just shook her head, *"Poor boy,"* she mumbled, *"Nothing, De'marco baby, nothing."*

Connie turned and looked at Jerome, *"Well..."* She could tell Jerome was lying because his voice went from feminine to manly.

"Well, what?"

Connie knew what that meant. His straight voice came out when he knew he had fucked up.

"You did it Jerome, didn't you? You went up there while that poor boy was sleeping, and sucked his dick, didn't you! How you gonna take advantage of him like that!? And in my damn house!"

Jerome lost control of his mouth apparently, because the next thing he said set the stage.

He looked at Connie and asked her, *"How you figure I took advantage of that little shit, after all, you done did his daddy, then you had the nerve to prostitute the..."*

Before he could finish, Connie caught him across the face with an electric pencil sharpener. But it didn't stop there. She began throwing a combination of punches. Jerome only had time to grab her and when he did, he used all his manly strength and slammed her on her back, right on her desk. She screamed. That brought Jerome back to reality, because he was about to punch her in the face. He had her by the neck and his fist drawn back, when the office door bust open with Nicole running in, and De'marco on her tail.

"What the hell you doing!?" Nicole yelled.

De'marco snatched Jerome by the neck and slung him up against the wall. He was ready to deck Jerome until Connie called out to him.

"De'marco! No baby, let it ride." She slid off the desk to her feet with Nicole's help, holding her back.

She looked at Jerome, *"You got that baby. But note this, you're fired. Get your belongings and don't look back. You done here."*

Jerome turned back gay, and threw his hand up, *"Please, I'm outta here."*

"Yes, you are..." Connie added.

Jerome turned to the door everyone in the shop was standing there watching.

"Excuse me, excuse me," Jerome said as he walked through switching his hips, *"Let the queen through!"* He threw all his things in a little plastic basket. He and Connie had been cool for a long time. He knew he was wrong and it hurt him deep down inside, but the evil in him would not let him be out done. So as he headed for the door, he looked over at his friend and in a silly voice that cracked, he blurted out, *"You lucky I like you."*

"Whatever, Jerome!" Connie yelled.

Then he looked at De'marco, *"Call me, little Hercules."*

Although, he went out the door clapping, saying, *"Hercules, Hercules,"* he was embarrassed.

"What in the hell is going on?" De'marco asked.

Connie looked at Nicole, *"Girl, you should call the police and have him arrested."*

Connie shook her head, *"I hit him first."*

She then pointed at the busted pencil sharpener.

"Damn!" Nicole said, *"Well, what now?"*

Connie motioned Nicole to the door, *"Let me holler at De'marco."*

Nicole walked off, *"Okay, girl. Everybody back!"* Nicole said, walking through the door, *"Back, nosey people, back, shew, shew."* She shut the door behind her.

"Sit down De'marco. I need to talk to you," Connie slowly trying to sit down, holding her back.

"Please don't tell me you was sleeping with that guy!" De'marco blurted out.

Connie smirked, *"I wish it was that simple,"* she said.

As they sat in the office and talked, the gossip on the other side of the door was in full bloom.

"Tyson vs Holyfield, KO!" They were cracking jokes and laughing, when a female in her early twenties walked in.

She spoke, *"Hey, everyone!"* She sat by a lady sitting in the waiting area. She noticed everyone was in an uproar, *"Man, what's going on?"* she asked.

"It's going down in the House of Beauty!" One lady yelled out.

"Fo sho," another one added.

She looked at the lady next to her, *"What's the deal?"*

"Well," the lady started, *"Some fag got into it with some chick about her man."* Everybody busted out laughing once again.

"Stop it!" Nicole said, *"That's how stuff get started."*

Then a lady yelled out, *"Look,"* holding up a magazine, *"It's an article about men in Atlanta on the down low, called the DL Brothers."*

Everybody started saying, *"Let me see,"* and carrying on. Then, the office door swung open and out walked De'marco, with anger all on his face. Everyone became silent, as he walked by.

Then suddenly, *"De'marco, what's up?"*

He looked over, it was Michelle, Jennifer's old friend from school, who just walked in the door. De'marco barely waved as he left from the shop. He was furious. He vowed never to talk to Connie again.

"It's always something with her. And it's always something I don't need," he thought, as he jumped in his car and sped off.

The thought of a man touching him was disgusting and the thought of a man's mouth on his privates made him contemplate suicide. He began to dry heave while he was driving. A tear trickled down his cheek. He was devastated.

When Jennifer got out of class, she just drove straight home. She knew something was terribly wrong.

De'marco had called about 7 times while she was in class and he never called that much, ever. After talking for some time, Jennifer tried to console him. It was very touchy, and she knew he wanted to keep it secret. However, she made a mental note to bring it back up once all this blew over. There was really nothing Jennifer could do, but tell him things would be okay. She couldn't help but think it was partially his fault for getting so drunk.

"Man," she thought, *"I had some news of my own."*

She wasn't sure if it was good or bad, but whatever the case she figured it could wait a couple days until this situation subsided. Columbus, Ohio is a rather small place where everybody knows everybody and news travels fast, good or bad. Although for some reason, the good news traveled a bit slower.

In any event, because of that, and the fact that there are only a few black beauty shops, Jerome couldn't find a place to make a buck. None of the shops was trying to mess with him like that. He was mad at himself and at Connie. He figured he could have got at De'marco if he really tried, instead of the move he pulled at the party. He also felt Connie was on some bullshit too. She set out to turn the boy out and get her little groove on. But, when someone else wants a piece, she trying to sell the dick or blocking.

"That's what I say, fish ain't shit, but a once a month bleeding headache. Let me see that De'marco again, I'm gonna make him my man and really turn him out." Jerome turned evil in his thoughts, *"Yeah, make him my man, that's what I'll do. Let me get on the internet. I'll fix their ass."*

The days passed and De'marco and Jennifer still spoke on the incident. Jennifer tried to explain to De'marco that it would all blow over in time. Plus he wasn't known like that around town, at least she didn't think so.

But, little did they know, her old friend Michelle was doing her part, gossiping and spreading the word on a situation she had caught only the ass end of and truly knew nothing about. But that didn't stop her. She was from the eastside, Eighteenth and Mound, where some shit was always jumping off. So, that in itself gave her a license to gossip and stick her nose in folks business.

Jennifer was laid back at the house, when she got the call from Michelle.

"Hey girl," Michelle said, *"What's going on?"*

Jennifer was surprised to hear from Michelle, they didn't call each other like that since school days. Usually they just ran into each other. Jennifer used to wonder how Michelle's ghetto butt got into St. Francis De Sales. Come to find out, although her and her mama was ghetto fabulous, her dad was a pretty well-to-do man. He thought having her come live with him for a while, and her going to a private school would help better her but he was wrong. Soon as she graduated, she walked straight from the stage, out to a car with four guys in it smoking weed. They headed straight to the east side where she has been running around ever since.

"What's up Michelle? How you be? Long time no hear from you."

"Yeah, I know girl. I just been chillin' trying to get this job with the state, but I got to pass a drug test."

Jennifer interrupted, *"So what you doing right now?"*

"Oh, I'm about to put fire to this blunt.

Jennifer laughed, *"But, what about the job?"*

"I'm straight, plus this weed be having me think on some deep shit I could be doing."

"Oh really?" Jennifer asked, *"Like what?"*

"Alotta shit! I was thinking on how I could start my own business yesterday and the day before that I was like, I should go to school for nursing or medical assistant or something. I mean you know it's so much I can do. I got so much talent, plus you know all these ballin' ass nigga's be wanting of take care of me. But, I ain't trying to play wifey to nobody. Not to mention..."

"Hey, hey, hey," Jennifer cut in, *"I'ma, I'ma, I'ma. I know girl you gonna be rich."*

"Excuse me!" Michelle said, as she hit the blunt, *"So what you been doing since school? Where you work?"*

"Well, I did follow up on my goal to study medicine. I start grad school in the fall and I have a lab waiting at O.S.U. Hospital. But that's not what you called for," Jennifer said sarcastically.

"No, it sure ain't," Michelle said, *"I'm trying to remember, this weed be making me forget shit."*

"Check that out!" Jennifer said, *"So, who's your man this month?"*

Michelle remembered why she called and catching Jennifer's attempt to down play her, she said, *"Baby I'm a player. I don't have no one man. But, now that we on men... I hear De'marco on the down low? Say it ain't so."*

"The what?" Jennifer said.

"People saying your De'marco had some lovers spat with a guy. Is he bi, Jennifer or do you know?!? I mean, I heard he was held behind closed doors, now what that means, I don't know."

She was trying to hurt Jennifer's feelings and it worked.

Jennifer calmly said, *"Hey Michelle."*

"Yes."

Jennifer continued, *"I don't know what it was that was taking place when your parents conceived you, but you need to take them to court for that shit, 'cuz you so far gone, all you do each day is take up space with your retarded ass!"*

Michelle was nice and high by now and down for a juicy catfight.

"Nice try girl," she said, *"But, is De'marco gay or not?!"*

Jennifer was heated, *"No she didn't call me after all this time with some silly shit!"* She thought. *"Look you*

deprived child, ain't you suppose to be out on the corner, helping your mom get the rent money up!?"
That hurt Michelle because her mom was on drugs and had been seen doing some of the foulest stuff.

"You can have that."

"I know I can." Jennifer said, *"You calling my house with some silly shit."*

"You right," Michelle said, *"And I'ma let you go, but, let me ask you, did you know he was in the ATL with the down low brothers? You know the ones, who got a woman but sex men?!?"*

Jennifer had enough, *"Hey bitch, later for you, and please, lose the number!"* She slammed the phone down.

De'marco was halfway watching T.V. and catching pieces of Jennifer's conversation.

"Who was that baby?" He said looking over at her.

Jennifer was rubbing her stomach. She began feeling nauseated.

"Nobody she said," she was thinking about the conversation she just had on the phone. *"De'marco, what were you doing in Atlanta?"* Why she asked, she wasn't sure because she knew Michelle was good for some simple crap. She looked at De'marco, *"Hey!"* She called out. He looked over at her, but was listening to the television.

"What's up?"

"I said, what were you doing in Atlanta?" She figured she was causing unnecessary friction. Just as she started to say nothing, forget it, De'marco came out his mouth, *"Just chillin', kickin' it."*

At that moment he realized he messed up because he had gone to Atlanta with Connie on one of their many sex adventures.

Jennifer played it off, *"Oh."* She got up to go in the bedroom.

De'marco tried to see what the deal was, *"Hey baby, we having some fun tonight or what?!?"* Then he came off the couch and put his arms around her.

"So, are we?"

Then he kissed her.

"No," she said, *"Not tonight."*

He was surprised, but he didn't know what was up and she wasn't talking, so he left it alone for the moment.

"I'll talk to her tonight," he thought. *"Okay,"* he said returning back to the couch.

Jennifer went and laid on the bed feeling like she was going to throw up.

"This is too much," she thought. *"I love De'marco, God knows I do. But I know I'm not laying here pregnant by no damn bisexual man!"*

Jennifer woke up the next morning, got dressed, told De'marco who had fallen asleep on the couch, she had to get a move on, and she'd speak with him this evening. As she left, he realized he had screwed up by falling to sleep on the couch.

Jennifer went to the Poitier's house, she needed to speak the De'marco's mother. She had spoken with her on other occasions, not like this, but all the same. She knew Mr. Poitier was already gone to work.

As she pulled up, Mrs. Poitier was standing in the door as if waiting for her. She walked up to her. The pain and confusion must have been written all on her face, because as soon as De'shawntu hugged her, she said, *"It'll all be okay. Come on in."* They went to the dinning room.

"Sit down," Mrs. Poitier said pouring hot water into two cups already sitting on saucers for tea.

Jennifer couldn't help but ask, *"Were you waiting on me?"*

De'shawntu studied Jennifer as she raised the cup to her mouth and made a face.

"Yes, I was waiting for you," De'shawntu replied.

Jennifer looked at her as to say, *"How'd you know I was coming?"*

De'shawntu smiled and slowly said, *"Never underestimate a woman's intuition."* She then asked, *"How far along are you?"*

Jennifer frowned, *"Excuse me?"*

De'shawntu leaned forward and said, *"You're pregnant. How far along are you?"*

Jennifer couldn't help but smile. It wasn't like she was ashamed or anything, not yet anyway. Once she'd gotten to the bottom of this gay stuff would determine that.

"A couple of weeks to a month? Your intuition told you that?"

"Nooo," De'shawntu said. *"The fact that you picked up a cup of hot water and frowned. Then, not only did you put it down, you pushed it away from you. It couldn't be that you thought the tea was nasty, because not only did you not taste it, you never opened the tea bag on the saucer to put it in the water. You see, it was the thought of tea that turned your stomach. Pregnancy does that to you, it makes everything seem nasty."*

She made a face and stuck her tongue out at Jennifer. They both started to laugh. With that in mind, Jennifer went ahead and explained why she had come. She apologized for bringing such foolishness, but didn't know where to turn.

De'shawntu assured her it was okay, and told her she did the right thing. She also assured her that De'marco was not gay.

"We don't breed such a creature amongst the "Mandingo". She also comforted her about the baby.

"Continue school," she said, *"Have the baby. We will take care of it for you. And whatever the two of you can't afford we will take care of it. Now listen closely,"* she told Jennifer, *"Me and my husband have made it this far because we are a team, and we hold nothing from each other, we put it all on the table. For instance,*

when he gets in this evening, I will fix his dinner and tell him of our talk. It's what people do who really love each other. They share their feelings, thoughts, problems and concerns. Do you overstand?"

"*Yes.*" Jennifer answered in a humble voice.

"*So if you love De'marco and this is the man you want, then you need to have a heart to heart with him. Ask him to be a man and please be honest. Yet, you must be able to handle whatever it is he may tell you. And after it's over, if you stay with him, you leave the past things in the past and move forward. It's the only way it will work. Again, do you overstand?"*

Once again, in a humble voice, Jennifer said, *"Yes."* For some reason she felt joy, as if everything was going to be okay. A tear rolled down her face and she smiled a big smile.

"*Wow,*" De'shawntu said, "*Is there anything else you would like or need to talk about?"*

Jennifer shook her head, "*No. At least I don't think so,*" she said.

"*Well then,*" De'shawntu said, "*What are we going to name this baby?"*

They laughed and talked until Jennifer had to leave so she could catch her afternoon classes. She really felt good about things afterwards.

Once Jennifer returned home for the evening, she prepared another one of De'marco's favorite meals, baked chicken, green beans, baked macaroni and cheese with sweet yellow cornbread, with fresh squeezed homemade lemonade. They ate until they were stuffed. And talked about everything on each of their minds. Jennifer was shocked by some of the things that De'marco told her. But she remained calm and accepted it. This was a moment of honesty in order to make things better between their relationship and make it stronger.

But, when she told him she had lunch with a guy at work who liked her, De'marco flipped his lid, and told

her he was going to jack the dude up! And that she had
to quit the job. She had to fill him in on the fact that the
guy didn't work there anymore. It took her an hour to
convince him of that. All in all, they got things out front
and agreed to work together as a team. She wasn't sure
how he would react once she told him she was pregnant.
So, when she did, she was surprised to find him to be as
happy and excited as she was. He started saying, when
he was born, this and that, as if he just knew it would be
a boy. She also fessed up and told him about the visit
with his mother. He didn't care for it much, but said it
wasn't a bad thing. Everything went well, however,
there was a mood change when the phone rang. For
some reason, they both knew it was De'marco's dad. He
picked up and they began the conversation that covered
a bit of everything and lasted two and a half-hours. By
the time they got off the phone, Jennifer was sleeping.

   De'marco's dad spoke a lot about the baby, school,
life, he covered a lot of issues. He let it be known he
would help as much as they needed him to with the
baby. However, he didn't fail to stress how
disappointed he was in De'marco for not being more
careful with himself and the life he lived. He felt
De'marco was equally to blame for what happened to
him at Connie's. He was unable to understand how
anyone could get so intoxicated they would not only
have to go lay down at someone else's house, but also
not feel someone touching you while sleeping. He got
so upset about it he asked De'marco was he sure he
wasn't gay? That hurt De'marco's feelings and Martzu
meant to do this to his son, so he would know the shame
he himself felt having to hear such foolishness about his
son.

   De'marco realized the mistakes he made, and was
aware of how important it was to get right and redeem
himself. Besides he had a baby on the way. And a kid
was no joke. Plus, he and Jennifer had to get through
school. He gave his father his word he would get it

together. Still upset, his father offered no words of encouragement as he usually did.

He simply told him, *"Time will show if you've learned anything."*

That made De'marco feel real small. Out of all his years he had done nothing but make his father proud of him and why not? His father did all he could to take care and provide for him, never missing a beat. So to become an adult and start getting caught up in foolish things wasn't cool at all, and he knew it.

11
"STALKED"

*N*ow that everything was what it was, De'marco and Jennifer stepped their game up. She began to work as many hours as she could throughout the week instead of just on the weekend. De'marco went and got a job as a paralegal at one of the largest law firms in Ohio, Simon and Smit.

He was one of many on the floor. They all had their own cubicle and a phone. They had to hustle for the many clients that called in. They did this by knowing the law and being familiar with many cases. De'marco was new and the others had a leg up on him, but he worked hard and made sure he knew the law at best. He stayed busy.

Oftentimes, he was so busy, Jennifer would call and say, *"Let's do lunch."* And although he was starving, many a day he would have to refuse.

He would tell her, *"I love you and would love to do lunch, but I got to get this money."*

She would tell him, *"Sounds good, but you'll starve to death."*

"No I won't," he would say, *"Your love keeps me on a full stomach."*

That made her feel wonderful and loved, and she needed it, being in her third month of pregnancy made her feel as though she was ugly. Her already wide hips had gotten wider. Her hands and feet were getting swollen, and her face was getting fat. De'marco would tell her she looked good pregnant and for some reason he believed it made the sex better. She couldn't see how, because she sure didn't feel sexy. Plus, she couldn't figure out how he enjoyed it, seeing that many times she wouldn't let him penetrate her too deep, because she felt he would hit the baby.

De'marco hung in there though. He dealt with it like a champ.

Even the times he would wake up with her standing beside the bed butt naked with her hands on her stomach looking down at him and say, *"Look what you done to me."*

No matter how sleepy he was, he would collect his thoughts and play the roll by grabbing her and saying, *"My God! I did this? Come here maybe I can fix it."* He would lay her on the bed and kiss and rub her stomach and tell her, *"Don't worry, I see what the problem is. I need to suck the juice out."* At that point, he would go down and orally gratify her, easing her discomfort, until next time.

Yep, De'marco was rolling with the punches, stepping up to redeem himself from the foolish mistakes he'd made. Errors were allowed, being human and all, he would tell himself. But too many will cost you, and that's a price he could not afford to pay. These are thoughts De'marco entertained on his way home from work. It was payday and he realized that since he started the job he hadn't really done that much. He was fine with that, but he knew it would be a good idea to take Jennifer out somewhere nice. She had been working hard herself lately and coming home to cook.

So he called his house, *"Hey my sweet,"* he said when Jennifer picked up the phone, *"What you doing?"*

"Well," she said, *"I was trying to figure what to prepare you for dinner."*

"Awww, ain't that cute?!?" He said.

She began laughing, *"It won't be cute if I don't find something."*

De'marco laughed, *"I'll just eat you and be straight,"* he told her.

"Oh yeah! You eat me, eat me all you want."

They both laughed, *"You'd like that wouldn't you?"* De'marco asked. He was pleased to hear her laugh. He knew the whole thing of being pregnant was a challenge for her.

"Listen baby, get yourself cleaned up. Put on something nice. We're going out for dinner and if you feel up to it, we'll do a movie afterwards."

"Hooray! Hooray! Where we going to eat?" Jennifer asked.

"How about we eat where we had dinner together for the first time?!? Do you remember where that was?" He asked her.

"How could I forget, McDonalds?"

"What!?" De'marco said in shock.

"I'm just kidding, I remember," she said before he freaked out.

"Before we hang up, let me ask you, did you call a couple of times and hang up?"

"No. Why?" He asked curiously.

"Someone called a couple times and didn't say anything. I thought it might have been you clowning around."

"No, it wasn't me, sweetheart. Go ahead and get dressed. I'll be home in a minute."

He figured it would take her a minute to get dressed. So he decided to stop off and grab her some flowers and a card. He thought about what she told him. It wouldn't have been a big deal but as he thought about it, as long as they'd been living together no such thing ever happened before. Not that he could recall anyway. Maybe it was a wrong number or two, but even then, they would usually say something.

"Connie!" He thought. He hadn't talked to her in a while. *"She's probably horny and desperate, hoping I will pick up the phone and come break her off. Sorry for her,"* he said as he pulled into the flower shop.

De'marco bought a dozen roses, half yellow and half red for Jennifer. He bought her a large card that read, "Just because." When he left out, just before he opened his car door, a horn blew. He looked to see who it was.

A pair of eyes was peeking over a partially rolled down tinted window.

"Who is that?" He questioned, speaking to no one in particular. He jumped in his car and headed home.

Jennifer was happy to go out and eat. However, she wasn't in the mood for the large crowds at Easton. So, they went to Max and Erma's on 161.

As they exited the car and headed for the entrance of the restaurant, a horn blew. They both turned to see the same car that De'marco had seen earlier.

"What the hell!?" He exclaimed.

"You know them?" Jennifer asked.

"I don't think I know them," he said, *"But I did see that car earlier today."*

Dinner was good. They really pigged out! They enjoyed each other's conversation. They had been focused on work, saving money, and preparing for the baby. An outing was needed. It was a break away from the norm and greatly appreciated by them both.

Jennifer looked at De'marco with eyes that showed she had the deepest love and passion for one man a woman can have, and rightfully so, he was her high school sweetheart. The first and only man she had been intimate with, and father of her child.

"De'marco," she said, *"I want to thank you for everything. Our relationship has had its moments, but, we are still together, and I am very happy. Thank you,"* she said as her eyes watered up. She took her napkin and dabbed the corner of one eye, catching a teardrop that attempted to run down her face.

"I love you too," De'marco said as he stood up abruptly. *"I'll be back,"* he walked off so suddenly, Jennifer figured it was something she said.

"Yeah, that was it," she thought, *"With me being pregnant my emotions are out of whack, and I was probably a little too mushy for him."*

When De'marco returned to the table he just stood there with a blank look in his eyes. Jennifer didn't know what to think.

"What? What is it?" She asked De'marco. *"Why are you just standing there?"* She questioned him. *"Look, okay maybe I was too mushy but..."*

Before she could finish, De'marco had dropped to one knee, then a bright flash. The light blinded her for a brief second, then she felt De'marco grab her hand and as the light flashed again, she heard him ask, *"Will you marry me?"*

It was like a dream in slow motion. De'marco was on his knee asking her to marry him, as he slid a ring on her finger. A flash happy waiter took pictures of the moment. Afterwards, her whole body went numb. She couldn't hear the people around her clapping, *"Am I dreaming?"* She asked herself.

Then De'marco asked again, *"Will you? Will you marry me Jennifer?"*

At that point, she knew it was real!

"Yes! Yes! Yes!" She yelled at the top of her voice. The entire restaurant heard her and began clapping as De'marco stood up and she threw her arms around him and hugged him so tight he thought he'd lose his breath. As they kiss, the waiter went crazy with the camera.

Jennifer thought, *"If he continues, I'll be blind."*

So, as soon as she released, De'marco's lips, she turned to the waiter, *"Give me that!"* She said snatching the camera out of his hand.

"I'm sorry. It's just such a joyful moment. I wanted to catch it all on film." He said walking off looking as if he were going to cry. Jennifer and De'marco looked at each other and laughed.

"Here baby," Jennifer said, *"Let me sit on this side with you."* She was happy. She held her hand out and looked at the ring. *"I'll be damn,"* she said as it sparkled under the light.

A lady sitting at another table spoke up, *"Ain't it a beaut!?"* She yelled, *"He sure loves you!"* She added.

"It's a lovely ring," another lady said while passing their table.

Indeed it was, it had a large purplish diamond in the center with two diamonds half it's size on each side with several smaller diamonds circling around the three. They all set up off the fat gold band with what appeared to be silver out line. It looked as if the diamonds were exploding out of each other. She just broke down and started crying. The people still staring felt touched by the whole scene. De'marco put his arm around his wife to be.

"Are you okay, my Queen?" He asked Jennifer.

"Yes," she said sobbing, *"I'm just so happy."*

"Good," he told her, *"That's what I wanted to hear."*

"So are we ready to go home?" He asked.

"Yes, give me a second to pull myself together. Is everyone still looking?"

De'marco looked around. *"Nah,"* he told her.

Before they could stand up, the camera happy waiter came walking over with a dish in one hand and a bottle of champagne.

"Whoa!" Jennifer said.

"Yeah, whoa!" De'marco said, *"We didn't order this,"* he spoke up quickly when he saw the golden bottle of "Cristal" being placed on the table. He knew it cost every bit of two hundred dollars.

"It's okay," the waiter said, *"Your friend paid the bill,"* he pointed to someone leaving, allowing them to only catch the back of the person.

"Let me see who that is," De'marco said rising from the table.

As he walked to the door, Jennifer raised her hand to stop the waiter from pouring champagne in one of the glasses.

"Hey," she said, *"I'm pregnant."*

"Sorry," the waiter said as he placed the bottle down.

Jennifer looked at him, *"You know I could sue you?!?"*

"For what, Ma'am?" The waiter asked.

"Well, first you nearly blinded me! Then, you try to give me, a pregnant woman, alcohol."

The waiter rolled his eyes and walked off. By the time De'marco returned, Jennifer was well into the red velvet cake the waiter brought over.

"So, who was it?" She asked, *"Did you thank them?"*

De'marco sat down, *"I didn't catch them before they pulled off. It was the same car from earlier."*

"Oh, maybe it's one of the guys from your job," she suggested.

"Yeah, maybe so," De'marco agreed as he reached for the glass of champagne. He looked at Jennifer, *"To us,"* he said.

"To us," she returned.

He turned up his glass, she decided to be silly and acted as if she too were drinking champagne, though nothing was in her hand. She then let out a loud burp that was real.

"What the...?" De'marco said.

"Sorry," she said placing her hand over her mouth, *"I didn't think it would be that loud."*

A couple across from them tried muffling their laughter. Jennifer and De'marco saw them and began laughing themselves. They continued their joyful evening. Jennifer couldn't drink, so she ate all the cake. De'marco had no problem at all with two hundred dollars worth of champagne. They talked. He explained to her that the ring was a four-carat diamond ring with a fourteen-carat gold band trimmed with platinum. Jennifer was extremely happy.

"I would have been happy if it were a piece of diamond on a shoestring," she thought. The ring was beautiful, she was very aware of that. But it couldn't compare to the excitement of the simple thought of knowing De'marco was willing to spend the rest of his

life with her. That in itself was worth more than a billion diamonds.

As they left the restaurant and drove home De'marco couldn't help but wonder whom the mysterious driver of the red Saab with tinted windows was? He really doubted it was somebody from work, although he did share with them that he was going to propose to Jennifer. He doubted very seriously that anyone of them would pull off such a stunt at the restaurant and not come over and speak. No, they wouldn't do that. That he was sure of, and if by chance they would have, what was the deal at the flower shop?

"Oh well, it'll come out," he thought. However, he was sure it was Connie's doings.

As they returned home, they weren't in the door two minutes before Jennifer attacked him, showing him how appreciative she was for everything and boy did she ever. She kissed and hugged him, loved him, sucked him, drank him, tasted him, bit him, you name it, she did it. They used every part of their little apartment. But what put the icing on the cake for De'marco was when she rolled off him onto her hands and knees. She gave him a bottle that read, "Easy Slip Anal Lube".

She then said to him, *"What you gonna do?"* As she wiggled her rump from side to side with the look of a lioness in her eyes. De'marco jumped up quickly. He had seen many rumps and wanted them. Some he had, but none quite as round and firm as Jennifer's, or as beautiful. He looked at her and pointed at himself then her rump.

"Me? That?" He said with eyes wide.

She nodded her head and said, *"Yes,"* at the same time. She made her butt cheeks constrict in and out causing her anal hole to move in and out as if it were puckering up to kiss. She then makes a loud meowing sound as she crawled towards the bedroom.

De'marco grabbed the bottle of lube and roared loudly like a lion as he quickly crawled towards the bedroom.

He was so excited. He stopped, raised up and began beating on his chest like an ape, then back on his hands and knees he made a snorting noise and scratched his feet in the carpet as if he was a bull. Hell, which one he wanted to be, he wasn't sure. But an animal he was about to become, that was for sure.

"Love and life," he thought.

* * * * * * * * * * * * * * * * * *

Monday morning, and De'marco felt great! It was a wonderful weekend. Friday set the stage for the whole weekend. The dinner, the engagement, Jennifer was so pleased. They laughed, talked and shared the whole weekend being close to one another. De'marco remembered asking would she like to go show the ring to her friends and family?

"Yeah," she said but, because of the back door action, she felt it probably would be best to stay at home until things closed up.

De'marco was surprised to hear that response. He asked her was everything OK?

She told him, *"Let's just say, it's difficult to keep it all in. When it comes out, it just falls out."*

He fought hard to keep from laughing at her. Yet and still, all was well. As he pulled up at work, he knew the guys would be questioning him about his proposal. They would kid him about being married, 'The old ball and chain!' 'Another one bites the dust!' 'You'll be a full fledge drinker now', were just a few things he knew they would say. He had no problem with the wisecracks, he knew he was doing the right thing. As soon as he reached his cubicle, a couple of the guys came up.

"Well, Mr. Poitier, giving up poker on Wednesday nights or what?"

He never played poker before in his life, but he knew what they meant.

He smiled, *"It's all good. I'll be having me a Mrs.,"* he told them.

"Yeaaa! Hooray!" They all said in unison, as they began singing, *"For he's a jolly good fellow..."*

After the handshakes, pats on the back and plenty of congratulations, he sat back in his chair, happy and proud. No one said anything about the champagne and dessert that was sent over to him and Jennifer at the restaurant. So he figured it was Connie. He decided to give her a call. He thought about her and imagined her and her sexual appetite.

"It might not be a bad idea to hit that again," he told himself, *"One last time wouldn't hurt."*

He then thought against it, *"You're about to be a married man. Practice some restraint. Yeah, practice some restraint,"* he repeated to himself as he listened to the phone ring.

"Well, if she talks like she got some sense..." He then said quickly, *"Hello."* Connie's voice brought back instant memories, *"Hi Connie. How are you?"*

"Fine. Is this Mr. De'marco?"

"Yes, it is."

"Wow! What gives me the privilege of this phone call? Stranger!" She added.

"Well, Connie, I hate to call with silliness...,"

She interrupted him immediately once she realized it wasn't a pleasant phone call.

She replied, *"Well don't. 'Cuz I have business to tend to and it don't consist of you."*

"I see you still have a jazzy mouth," De'marco told her.

"De'marco what do you want?"

"Well, I had been getting a couple of hang up calls at the house, and was wondering if you may have been trying to contact me? That's all."

"First to answer your question, NO! Secondly, when have I EVER dialed the number to your house? We were a secret, like hush, hush, remember?!? I called on

the cell phone only. Sorry, must be one of your other Breezzies."

De'marco smacked his lips, *"Sorry to bother you Connie."*

"It's cool," she said, *"You just need to find the right people, 'cuz it's not me you're looking for."*

Figuring it was okay, he told Connie, *"You know Jennifer and I are getting married?!?"*

She paused, *"Oh really, that's wonderful."*

"I would like for you to attend the wedding," he was trying her.

"Oh would you," she said.

He turned sweet on her, *"Look baby, what we had was sweet and wonderful and no matter what, you'll always be my sweetheart."*

Connie was aware of what he was doing, but she couldn't lie to herself, she liked it. She couldn't tell De'marco, but she hoped he would call. She missed him and hadn't got involved with anyone, not that she thought she could have him. He was just enough, and had been enough. He was her last roll in the hay. If she got with anyone else, it would have to be something serious. Too many memories began to cloud her mind. She even began to get moist between the legs.

"Send me an invitation De'marco," she said abruptly, then hung up.

De'marco knew he had gotten to her in an emotional way. He laughed to himself, *"Serves her right,"* he thought. As he hung up the phone, he observed Calvin walking towards him with a silly smirk on his face. He didn't particularly care for Calvin. There was always something with him.

"What's up De'marco?" Calvin said looking overly anxious to talk.

"Nothing much," De'marco replied.

"What's the latest? Sooo, did he, I mean, she say yes?"

Noticing he said "he", De'marco snapped, *"What did you say!?"*

"Nothing. Here, this came in after you left work Friday," Calvin said, as he dropped an envelope on De'marco's desk and walked off. De'marco sat there looking at it for a moment.

"What is this?" He thought, as he picked up the envelope that had purplish pink letters on it that read "The Flex".

"What's The Flex?" He wondered as he opened the envelope. It read, *"You are proudly invited to join us for a full evening of fun and this card gives you V.I.P. privileges, free admission, drinks and private party rooms."*

De'marco was trying to figure out, firstly, who would send an invitation to his job. Secondly, he had not at this point in his life ever been to a club. He had no idea of where or what "The Flex" was. So he spun around in his chair and stood up with the card in his hand and asked, *"Does anyone here know what "The Flex" is?"* Immediately laughter broke out.

"What?"

"Are you serious?" Is what some of the guys were saying.

One of the female interns came over to him and placed her hand on him, as she said, *"I know all that ain't going to waste?!?"* Laughter broke out once more.

De'marco then heard Calvin say, *"I told you."*

A white guy hollered over to him, *"The Flex is a gay club that caters to its clients. If you know what I mean?"*

De'marco was shocked, *"What!?"* He turned and threw the invitation in the wastebasket. *"Why would someone send me an invite to such a place?"* He thought. *"Then again, there is more than one De'marco in the world, and it didn't have my last name on it. Plus, who knows where I work?"*

So De'marco dismissed it as being sent to the wrong person. Work was work, and Mondays were always hectic and long. Because of "The Flex" invite it made the day even longer. He looked forward to getting home so he could rest and put this day behind him. He decided not to tell Jennifer about the invite. He didn't want to have her worrying about anything. Sure didn't, he wanted her pregnancy to go as smoothly as possible. So, they could have a healthy baby with no complications. That's the Mandingo way.

* * * * * * * * * * * * * * * * *

Connie didn't care for De'marco calling her with some telephone harassment silliness, but she would attend the wedding and cater to De'marco and Jennifer.

She kept thinking, *"I gotta get him back in my life, back in my bed. Call me what you want, but all the ladies know a good piece of meat is hard to come by. So, I'ma go ahead and get this here piece back. This time I'll be a good girl,"* she thought to herself. Connie figured married life and a new baby would surely become a difficult task for a young man and at some point he would need an out. Someone to do it like he wanted with no complaints, and she would be right there for him. But this time, she would use all her womanly skills the right way to keep him. As a matter of fact, she would even offer to pay for some of the wedding. That would allow her to be around and be able to show De'marco she was and would continue to be a good girl. She leaned her head back and scrunched her face up, then let out a laugh like the wicked witch on the "Wizard of Oz," *"Aaah hanh, ha, haanh!"*

* * * * * * * * * * * * * * * * *

The week was dragging on as slow as it possibly could for De'marco. It was only Thursday, each day this week seemed to have forty-five hours in it instead of twenty-four. And out of all of days, Jennifer wanted to go shop for things for the baby. Why she couldn't wait till this weekend and go with his mother was beyond him. All the walking in and out of stores was murder on his feet. He still had on his loafers he'd worn to work. He just kept walking with her and pulling out his checkbook.

"Here," he told her, handing her his checkbook, *"You keep it."*

"Why?" She asked. *"It's yours."*

"Oh really!?" He said sarcastically, *"I ain't wrote nern check. You writing all the checks, you keep it."*

She smiled, *"Well, if you insist,"* she said grabbing the checkbook out of his hand.

De'marco laughed, *"Yeah, I did everything short of putting a gun to your head."*

"Anyway," she said, *"Let's leave here and go next door to Babies-R-Us."*

As they exited the store, De'marco remembered the conversation he had with his dad earlier, when he told him they were going shopping for the baby.

"Oh boy!" His dad said, *"This is where you get to learn patience my son. Good luck!"*

"Look," Jennifer said pointing.

De'marco looked up just in time to see that same red Saab passing by with a hand sticking out from behind the tinted window, waving.

"Who in the hell is that?" De'marco wondered. He began to get a little pissed off. He had to find out who this person was that was practically stalking him while he was with his pregnant fiancée. He grabbed his cell phone and called none other than "Mr. Get Around Town", Leroy. As he spoke with Leroy and informed him on what has been taking place. Leroy told him next time get the license plate number. With that he could find out who it was within minutes. Although Leroy had been a straight up hustler in school, selling any and everything, he managed to never be caught up in any

illegal situations. Yep, his record was spotless. That allowed him to land a job as a dispatcher at the police department, and the fact that he was a clean cut looking white guy. Boy, if they only knew!

Jennifer looked at De'marco as he placed his cell phone back on his belt. *"Is everything Ok?"* she asked.

"Yes," De'marco told her, *"Everything is fine."*

"Would you tell me if something was wrong?" She questioned.

"Yes, I would. Now, if you don't mind, I'd like to continue shopping for junior," he told her as he winked his eye.

"Oh, we can keep shopping as long as you know it's going to be a girl."

"Is not," De'marco teased.

"Is too," she said smacking him on the butt.

"Okay now," he told her, *"Keep it up, I'ma have you bent over in one of these bathrooms."*

"You freak!" She called him, then started walking fast with the cart as if trying to get away from him.

"Oh no you don't," he said as he ran up behind her and stuck his middle finger between her butt cheeks. She screamed, causing people to look over at them. They both turned silly and started looking through clothes racks acting as if they weren't together. The evening finished off well with the shopping and all. On the way home, Jennifer couldn't help but to bring up the car incident again. De'marco was a little bothered by that, seeing that he'd already assured her it was okay. She was glad she had gotten things she wanted for the baby, for now anyway. The two of them were so exhausted when they got home. They shared a bath and went straight to bed.

Jennifer had begun kissing and rubbing him.

"You gonna give me some?" She asked.

He didn't answer. And if he did, she wouldn't have heard it, as they both snored away.

* * * * * * * * * * * * * * * * *

They both were so tired, they forgot to set the alarm clock and over slept. De'marco just threw on his clothes and brushed his teeth on the way out the door. Jennifer wasn't with that one, she called in and told them she'd be an hour late. She had gotten real bold with her job, especially since her fiancée told her she could quit anytime she wanted and that he was able to provide for them. She figured with that being the case she wasn't going to wear herself out or endanger her and the baby's life trying to rush on the expressway to a job. As a matter of fact, she was going to have to leave early, because her baby shower was tomorrow. She wondered if De'marco remembered. So she called him up on the cell phone.

"Yes baby?" He said upon answering the phone.

"Hey sweetie," she whined, *"You haven't forgotten what tomorrow is have you?"*

"Saturday," he said quickly, *"The day after Friday, which is today. Which is good because it's payday, which makes it even better. Do you know why that is?"* He asked. Before she could answer, he continued, *"Because, it allows me to put some of the money you spent yesterday back into the bank. And why haven't you left for work yet?"* He asked.

"I'm going. I'm just going to be about an hour late."

"Again!?" He exclaimed, *"You might as well quit. That's five times in the last two weeks."*

"No it's not," she said, *"It's only been about five times in the last two weeks,"* she started laughing.

"Okay, you keep fooling with them folks, they gonna fire you."

As De'marco pulled into work, he noticed the red Saab. Instead of parking, he headed towards it. The car took off. De'marco followed. He threw the phone on the passenger seat and grabbed a pen as he trailed behind the car. He jotted down the license plate,

432NIN. He began slowing down as the Saab shot through a red light, almost causing a wreck.

"Whoever it is, must be crazy," he mumbled as he picked the phone up out the seat. Jennifer was still rambling.

"How you gonna say I'm crazy?!?" Jennifer asked, hearing the words he mumbled.

"Not you baby," he said. *"Hey love, let me get into work and I'll talk to you later."*

"Did you hear anything I said De'marco?"

"Yes baby, every word. Tomorrow's the baby shower. I know, gotta go, smooches." He hung up.

"That little meat head," Jennifer said.

De'marco quickly called Leroy. His voice mail came on, he left a message along with the license plate number. He went on into work, glad it was once again Friday, the last work day.

He received a call from his father around lunchtime reminding him of the baby shower. He told him, *"You can't forget things like that, especially since it's your first baby."*

De'marco told him he thought it was a thing for the females. Martzu told him that was correct, but since Jennifer's family wasn't that large and most of their family weren't in the country and the ones that are here, live in other states. De'shawntu and Jennifer figured it'd be better if everyone that was available would come.

"And how did we end up at Ryan's restaurant?" De'marco asked.

Martzu laughed, *"You have to ask you wife to be. That one was all her idea."*

De'marco thought about calling Connie and letting her come to the baby shower, then thought against it. *"The wedding is enough,"* he thought.

He watched the clock waiting to get out of there. For some reason the phones didn't ring much. Crime must not be America's favorite pass-time anymore. He felt his cell phone vibrating. He picked it up. It was Leroy.

"Hey man, what's up?" De'marco said.

"Not much," Leroy told him, *"Glad it's Friday."*

"Tell me bout it," De'marco agreed.

"Well I did a check on that license plate, and it comes back to a Jerome R. Freeman, with an address of 603 Whittier Street. That's in the German village area. So I take it this person has a little cash. Now that you have their address you can do one of two things."

"What's that?" De'marco asked.

"You can call the police and report them or stalk their ass back!"

De'marco thought for a second. *"You're right,"* he told Leroy, *"Maybe I'll do both. Thanks a lot man. I greatly appreciate it."*

"Yeah, no problem bro. Hey, while I got you on the phone, I got some brand new microwaves I'm selling for the low, low, and because you're an old friend..."

"No thanks man," De'marco said interrupting him. *Microwaves cause cancer tissue in the body."*

"So do cell phones," Leroy said, *"But I don't see you having a problem with that."*

"Hey Leroy, thanks for the info. I'll holla at you later."

Leroy determined to make a sale, *"Well, look man, I got some house shoes."*

"No thanks."

"Car battery?"

"No thanks."

"Sunglasses?"

"No thanks."

"Ok, ok, look for you, and I just got it yesterday, its brand new, a bobcat!"

"A what!?" De'marco asked.

"A bobcat man. You know one of those construction tractors with the..."

De'marco hung up.

"A construction tractor!? And I bet he was serious too."

MANDINGO LOVE

It was five o'clock. Time to go home.

12
"ENOUGH IS ENOUGH"

The week was long, but somehow De'marco made it.
Today is the baby shower. Jennifer wanted to leave out
early to get things prepared. De'marco told her to go
ahead, he'd be there. What she had to get prepared at
Ryan's Restaurant was a mystery to him.

"My woman, the wanna be ghetto chick," he thought.

In any case, he figured her going on ahead would
allow him time to run and peep out the address he'd
gotten from Leroy's license plate check. He went by
there after work the day before and saw nothing but a
few nice brick homes and duplexes. German Village
looked like a well-to-do area, somewhat historical.
More importantly he had to get to the bottom of this
stalker situation. First, a car blew at him while leaving
the flower shop a week ago, then the same car blows at
him and Jennifer while entering the restaurant. A half of
Red Velvet cake is sent over to them along with a
$200.00 bottle of champagne, and to top that off, he gets
to work to receive a VIP invitation to a well-known gay
club that causes him to be literally persecuted all week
long. And not to forget, the brief high speed chase
yesterday morning.

The invitation situation, he was able to handle, until
Mr. Calvin made the mistake of asking him if his wife
was a hermaphrodite. That made him blow his top. The
things he said to Calvin could have cost him his job.
Luckily, his supervisor heard and agreed Calvin was
way out of line. Yes, it was very necessary to find out
just who this was stalking him. Although he and Connie
had their moments and fair share of outlandish dealings,
he felt now, that this really wasn't her doing. He could
tell it in her voice, she wanted him back in her life. He
had even been thinking about giving her another shot.

Her bedroom skills were worth it. Not to mention, still to this day, he hadn't seen lips like she had on her love muffin, nowhere! They were so large, even in her jeans, it looked as if she had on not one, but two pads!

"Later for that," he told himself realizing the thought of her was causing him to become aroused. His cell phone rang. He picked it up on the first ring, *"Hello."*

"Hey De'marco, this is Leroy."

"I don't want a construction tractor," De'marco said quickly.

"No, no, no, that's not why I called."

"Then what?" De'marco asked.

"I got the phone number to that address if you want it?!?"

"Oh, that's cool," De'marco grabbed a pen, *"Go ahead, what is it?"*

"2-4-4-7-8-7-7"

"Is that a Columbus number?" De'marco asked surprised at the display of numbers.

"Yeah," Leroy said, *"And check this out. A detective friend of mines plays with numbers and the order they fall in he said it spells 'B-I-G-P-U-S-S'! So, there's a good chance this person asked specifically for this number from the phone company."*

"Oookay, 'BIG PUSS'" De'marco said as he looked at the number pad on his phone and realized it was true.

"Well, thanks man, I appreciate it."

"No problem," Leroy told him.

"And look, I know with you about to get married and have a newborn baby and all, your money is probably tighter than a frogs cunt, and that's waterproof. But, just so you know man, I got baby stuff and I do layaway."

Once again, De'marco hung up on Leroy.

"Let me get outta here and head across town to check this address. BIG PUSS, hunh?"

* * * * * * * * * * * * * * * * * *

As De'marco found the street, he picked up his phone and dialed the number, no answer. Just the answering machine with the sound of an angry female's voice, *"Leave a message!"* It said, then a series of beeps followed by a long one. He wasn't sure if he should leave a message, but figured, why not?!? He would do what he could to stop this person from stalking him before he put the police on them.

"This is De'marco Poitier. Somebody at this number is stalking me, and whoever it is needs to quit before we have some problems."

"So, its some female. But who?" He thought. *"But why do the plates come back in a mans name? Unless, yeah, unless it's one of the married women Connie was selling him to."*

More than likely that's what it was. He would find out a little later when he called Connie. Right now, he had to get to the baby shower. And if the woman gets in trouble with her man from him leaving a message on the phone, oh well, she should have kept it real instead of playing some stalking game, causing unnecessary problems and inconvenience.

De'marco arrived just as everyone else did with the exception of Jennifer, of course. As he entered the restaurant, he met his dad coming out of the restroom.

"Hey, Dad!"

"De'marco!" Martzu said, *"Will you ever learn son?"* He asked De'marco.

"What'd I do now?" De'marco asked with a concerning look on his face.

"Well son," Martzu started to speak, slowly and calmly, *"Your wife to be is having a baby shower and yes, it is a thing more so for the women, but because of the small size of our available family members, the few men were asked to join too. Now, we could have declined, but we didn't. For that reason, and because*

it's your baby, means you could have been here on time."

"I'm not late!" De'marco protested. *"Look, people are just getting here. They're still getting out of their cars."*

Martzu laughed, *"Oh, I'm sorry son. I didn't know that's how things worked."*

"What does that mean?" De'marco said as they approached the ladies.

"Hi everybody! Hi mom!" De'marco said.

"Hi son!"

De'marco leaned over to kiss Jennifer, she turned her head away.

"Glad you decided to come," she said. *"It wasn't like I needed your help with things."*

De'marco looked over at his father who had a silly grin on his face.

Jennifer continued, *"Instead, you want to come late and have me do everything myself."*

Then De'marco made a mistake that would never be forgotten. He came out his mouth and said, *"Help you with what stuff? It's a restaurant with a self -serve buffet. Not to mention, sweetheart, this is for you, not me."*

Martzu just dropped his head. De'shawntu not only put one, but two hands over her mouth. As you look around it appeared as though everyone was preparing for impact.

Before he could realize what he'd done, Jennifer jumped up and screamed, *"No! Wrong! It's not for me. It's for OUR baby! I'm sorry you were too busy to realize that. I'm sorry you were too busy to help me decorate things, so OUR family and friends could see and feel a part of something nice! But, in order to know any of that, you would have had to arrive with me! But, you were too busy for that. And where were you anyway!?"*

She stormed off crying. De'marco stood there, looking like a white mouth mule. He began to glance around. In doing so, he noticed the light pink and baby blue ribbons hanging throughout the room along with the many balloons. Several of them read, *"Congratulations"*, a few others said, *"It's Your First Baby!"* On the table, were plates and napkins with the same color scheme as the balloons and ribbons.

"Damn," he thought to himself, *"She told me she was leaving out early to get things together. I told her to go ahead. All this, and here I come with nothing."*

He heard someone clear their throat. He looked out the corner of his eye to see Jennifer's mom sitting there with her arms crossed over her chest.

"You see me young man! Everyone's here but my daughter."

He looked over at his dad, it was like a slow motion picture with no sound. He saw his dad's lips moving but heard nothing. His lips read, *"Go – get- your – fiancée."*

De'shawntu stood up to go and assist her son by going after Jennifer who had stormed into the ladies restroom. Martzu grabbed her arm and motioned for her to sit back down.

Martzu stood up and looked at De'marco with piercing eyes. *"Son,"* he said, *"You need to snap out of your daze, take your foot out of your mouth and go get your woman."*

De'marco began to speak, *"Sh, sh, she's in the women's restroom."*

"Go, get your woman!" Martzu demanded.

De'marco hurried off, realizing he had screwed up big time.

When he got to the restroom, he knocked on the door, *"Excuse me, excuse me,"* he sounded pitifully as he walked in.

Two women were standing with Jennifer handing her tissues to wipe her face. They looked up at him, *"Is this the person that hurt you?"* One of them said to Jennifer.

"The person that hurt you?" De'marco thought to himself, and even more surprised, when Jennifer said, *"Yes."*

One lady said, *"Well, I think he's here to talk with you. Is it okay for us to leave you alone with him?"*

"What!?" De'marco said.

Both ladies looked at him with mean stares. That made him quickly apologize. Jennifer told them it was okay.

As they passed him heading for the door, one of the ladies hit him and said, *"Bad doggy!"*

De'marco placed his arms around Jennifer, and wasted no time apologizing.

"Baby," he said, *"I'm sorry. Very, very sorry. You must forgive me. All this is still new to me and I'm learning as I go. If you can forgive me, I promise it won't ever happen again. You and the baby will always and forever be first in my life."*

Jennifer was glad he was quickly apologizing, she wanted to get back out and see what people brought for the baby.

She looked at him with puffy eyes, *"You promise?"*

"Yes, baby, I promise."

"With all your heart?" She asked.

"Yes, with all my heart."

"With sugar on top?" She added.

"What?" De'marco said. She acted like she was going to cry again.

"Okay, okay, with sugar on top. Now, can we go?" He asked. *"People are waiting on us."*

"Like I was you, hunh?" She said.

De'marco just put his hands up in surrender.

"Take your time," he said.

"Let me clean myself up before we go back out there."

"Okay," De'marco said, then asked, *"What the devil is that smell?"*

Jennifer giggled, *"Welcome to the ladies room,"* she said.

As she finished up, she looked at De'marco and told him, *"I know you didn't mean any harm. But you have to learn to be considerate."*

"You're right," he said, *"Baby, can we get out of here? The smell is killing me."*

"Come on cry baby," Jennifer said grabbing his hand heading for the door.

"Excuse me," a voice said from one of the stalls, *"Would one of you mind grabbing a roll of toilet tissue from one of the other stalls and hand it to me from under the door?"*

De'marco and Jennifer looked at each other and started laughing as they ran out of the restroom. Everyone applauded them as they returned. The ladies all hugged Jennifer, and told her don't worry.

One lady spoke loudly and told her, *"Because he's a man, you have to expect dumb stuff."*

For nearly ten minutes, it was a relentless assault on men.

One of De'marco's work buddies that showed up, said to him, *"Don't worry Marco. That's just one of the many mistakes you'll make before you get it right. But, you'll get it, or become a deaf mute."*

All the men started laughing.

Martzu came over and put his arm around De'marco, *"Well son, welcome to the starting gate of becoming a man."* He patted him on the back and laughed hard. Then he looked at De'marco and said to him, *"I can't believe you told her this wasn't for you, it was for her..."*

The crowd of men laughed. One guy said, *"Yeah, you didn't look too bloody when you came out the restroom. So, you got off lucky."*

"Yeah, yeah, that's true!" They all agreed.

One guy pulled out a box of cigars and handed them to De'marco.

"Congrats!" He said.

"Thanks," De'marco responded. They all began chatting.

Then he heard Jennifer call out, *"De'marco, come see!"*

De'marco wasted no time, *"I gotta go,"* he said, and then took off.

Martzu looked at the other gentlemen, *"I think he's getting the hang of it."* They all laughed, only to be interrupted by their wives calling each of them. And best believe they all hurried over to see what their wives wanted. They all gathered around to watch Jennifer open gifts and take pictures. The evening carried on well. Everyone had eaten until they were stuffed. They laughed and shared conversation mostly about Martzu's heritage and the legend of the well-known Mandingo. De'shawntu was proud they found so much interest in her husband. Yes, all was going well. It appeared that everyone had forgotten about De'marco's blunder. All except Jennifer, of course. She reminded him from time to time of how he was in trouble when they got home, *"Don't think I forgot."* She warned. De'marco was standing in front of her looking at her playing with one of the toys that had been bought for the baby.

"Oh, my God!" De'shawntu said suddenly, *"What is that?"*

De'marco heard her, but kept playing with Jennifer. He realized everyone had gotten silent, then he heard a voice say, *"Hey everybody!"* He turned around, and was blown away as he looked at what could only be described as a nightmare.

Standing there, plain as day was Jerome, the gay guy from Connie's shop that she had fallen out with. Jerome, the guy who had taken advantage of him in the most evil way while he was sleeping at Connie's' party. He stood there staring at De'marco with his hands on his hips as if he had the right to lay claim. Everyone just looked at Jerome. De'marco couldn't figure out what the joke was. *"It had to be one,"* he thought. He didn't know Jerome and he surely didn't like him because of what little he did know about him. Yet, here he stood, with his hair slicked back, eyeliner with blush on his cheeks, with bright red lipstick. Maybe that could have been overlooked. But, the extremely loud purplish pink, skin tight, form fitting mini dress was just too much. The spaghetti straps really did look like spaghetti on his manly shoulders. He somehow had what looked to be breast, although hair was sticking out on his chest. The dress was so tight, not only could you see the lines from his panties in the front of his dress, you also could see the print of his whole penis, balls, and all. At the end of his hairy legs on his gorilla looking feet, he had the nerve to have on a pair of pink open toe shoes that had his feet hanging over the sides.

"Hi De'marco!" He said.

Jennifer pushed De'marco to the side, he'd been blocking her view. She was so blown back by what she saw she just yelled out, *"What the fuck!?"*

"Hey girl!" Jerome said.

"Do I know you?" Jennifer asked.

At that point Jerome turned evil, *"You didn't ask that when you ate up the cake I sent you and De'marco drank up the champagne."* He continued with his antics, *"And De'marco, how you gonna leave that silly message on my answering machine, seeing that you was right in front of the house, why didn't you just come knock on the door? The car was parked in back. I was in the tub. You could have knocked, you wasn't in a hurry to get here anyway."*

Jennifer looked at De'marco along with everyone else, but she had fire in her eyes.

Jennifer's mom fell backwards holding her chest where her heart is, *"Lord, say I ain't so!"* She said before she hit the floor.

Realizing he had done enough damage, Jerome spun around to walk off. The dress had the back out and it was cut so low, you could see the top of the pink thong he had on.

As he walked off, he looked over his shoulder and said, *"Call me De'marco, since you couldn't invite me to this little shindig. I invited you to "The Flex", VIP at that."* He snapped his fingers in the air and walked away switching what little piece of narrow ass he had. It was a sight to see!

The entire restaurant saw it. Martzu was holding De'shawntu who covered her eyes in disbelief. Everyone was so caught up in the spectacle that they didn't even notice Jennifer's mom flat on her back with her legs sticking straight up in the air. Jennifer called out to her mom. A couple of people rushed over to help her. As they lifted her up, she was praying and deep into it. Her head jerked back and forth and she kept saying, *"Yes Jesus, Amen!"*

Jennifer looked over at De'marco and asked him, *"What was that all about?"*

She was so embarrassed and hurt, she wanted him to feel the same, *"I know this ain't more of that faggot crap again!?"* She yelled.

Martzu stood up with his wife who still had her head buried in his chest.

"Ladies, gentlemen," he said as he nodded his head, *"It's been an evening, until next time,"* and they began to walk off. Others began to excuse themselves. They waived goodbye to Jennifer, to her mother. They hoped she felt better. De'marco sat down, his mind was racing a hundred miles an hour.

"Why?" He kept asking himself

Jennifer's mother stood up, *"Are you going home with me, or are you going with him?"* She didn't even look De'marco's way.

"Mom, what!?" Jennifer said. She snapped, *"I'll give you a call in the morning. Be careful driving home. I love you."*

Jennifer was embarrassed, ashamed and confused, but she loved her man and she was going to hang in there with him.

"De'marco!" She said with a fierce look in her eyes, *"Let's get this stuff to the car so we can go home!"* He got up and began to slowly gather up the gifts. He thought of everything that had just happened.

"As soon as I get the chance, I'm calling Connie and getting the 4-1-1 on this dude. I can't let him get away with that. Hell to the nah!" De'marco thought.

Once they arrived home and gotten things unloaded from the cars, and after a few moments, Jennifer couldn't hold it in any more.

"De'marco," she said calmly, trying to be mindful of how he may be feeling. *"I need you to share with me what's going on, so things will be clear in my mind. You have to realize this is not the first time something like this has happened."*

De'marco felt hurt that she would even question his sexuality. He looked at her in anger, *"So, you think I'm gay?"*

Shocked at his response, she let out a laugh, but not because she found things to be funny.

"Look, I said I needed you to make things clear so I'll know what to believe."

De'marco knew she had every right to question him on today's events.

"Okay, Jennifer," he said, *"Give me a second."* He went to the bathroom to wash his face. Upon returning to the living room, he noticed Jennifer hadn't moved one inch. He grabbed a glass and some ice, fixed himself a drink and sat down beside her. In all honesty, he didn't know what the hell was going on and why this fag was stalking him. However, he would share all he could think of with his fiancée, and why not? He had nothing to hide.

De'marco and Jennifer spoke for a couple hours. He filled her in on all he knew and where he'd known

Jerome. Albeit, he hadn't *known* him, he'd only seen him at Connie's shop.

Jennifer didn't hold back, she asked De'marco many questions from every angle. She had even went as far as to ask him had he ever thought or fantasized about being with a man?

De'marco didn't care for that form of questioning but answered honestly all the same. She even asked him about his desire and fascination behind having anal sex with her.

She was very blunt about it, *"De'marco seeing that you're not gay, and don't have homosexual tendency, why do you enjoy fucking me in the ass so much?"* She said looking very eager for a response.

He did not want to answer that, but sadly enough he had to reveal one of a man's dark secrets. *"It's more so an ego thing for a man,"* he told her. *"To see not only how much he's loved by his woman, but also how far she'll go for him and to what measure. Not to mention, the moan you get from a woman during anal sex is more intense than vaginal which adds to the excitement. However, like I told you, it's mostly all an ego thang. Like when you all perform oral and we want you to swallow, it does nothing for us, its just ego."*

Once the conversation was over, she let him know she believed him.

"What do we do now?" She asked, *"Call the police? What?"*

"Well, first I'm going to call Connie and see what's this guys hang up. Then we'll go from there."

De'marco seemed to be relatively calm on the outside, but deep inside he felt pure rage, and he planned to unleash it on Jerome. He had never felt this way before. His thoughts of anger even scared himself. But as a man, he refused to allow some gay guy to disrespect, embarrass, and degrade him. Nah, he couldn't have that.

"Let's go to bed baby," he said winking at Jennifer.

"Let's," she said as she ran in the room and jumped in the bed. He walked into the room, seeing her already in bed asked, *"Is it on or what?"*

"Yeah, right," she told him. *"Was it on when you let me get things together for the baby shower by myself,"* she said as she pulled the cover over her head and started making a deliberate snoring sound. She stopped for a second, *"And don't forget to turn the light out,"* she told him, then returned to her snoring.

"Oh, well," De'marco thought to himself as he hit the light switch.

* * * * * * * * * * * * * * * * * *

The night seemed to carry on, as De'marco tossed and turned. He would fade in and out of sleep. He rolled over and looked at the digital clock on the nightstand. They had only been in bed 3 hours. It was eating at him too much. He couldn't let things go down this way. His family and friends saw what was the most embarrassing moment in his life. He pulled the cover back and rolled out of bed.

Jennifer moaned, *"Baby, it's cold,"* she said in a whiny voice. He pulled the cover back over her and walked out the room, but not before hearing Jennifer say, *"Thank you,"* and return back to sleep. He headed for the kitchen. He grabbed his cell phone off the coffee table as he passed. He pulled out a chair from the dinning room table. He dialed Connie's number. The phone rang four times. He was about to hang up figuring she was out on a mission. He looked at the time on the phone it was twelve thirty a.m. Connie answered sounding sleepy.

"Hello?"

"Whaaat! You at home?!?" De'marco said being sarcastic.

"De'marco?" She asked.

"Yes, it's me. Who were you expecting? And why you not out at the club somewhere?"

"De'marco, I cut all that extra stuff out awhile back."

"What!? Say it ain't so. Why?" De'marco teased.

Connie paused for a second, *"Well, I was trying to figure how to get you back in my life and that seemed to be a good start."*

She was serious, De'marco could hear it in her voice, but he tried her anyway.

"Yeah right," he said, *"So you waiting around to see if we can mix things up again, knowing I have a baby on the way and about to get married?"*

"Exactly," she said just as calm.

"Why!?" De'marco asked with an attitude.

"It's worth it," she said, *"But look, I know that's not why you called. What's up?"*

"You're right," De'marco took a deep breath and continued. *"There seems to be a problem with a friend of yours…"*

"Who's that?" Connie asked, figuring it had something to do with one of her female associates.

"Faggot ass Jerome," De'marco said as the once subsided rage built up in him again.

"Jerome Freeman?" Connie asked

"That's him," De'marco said.

"Hold up," Connie said, as she sat up in bed and turned the light on. De'marco now had her full attention.

"What do you mean a problem?"

She listened closely as De'marco told her of the chain of events that had taken place over the past few weeks. She couldn't believe what she was hearing! But, she knew De'marco wouldn't make up such foolishness. She also knew Jerome was capable of some crazy crap, but up until now, she had only heard rumors. When De'marco finished, Connie apologized over and over again. She knew there was no chance for her and

De'marco now. Jerome had entered De'marco's life by way of her.

"De'marco," she said feeling lower than low, *"If there is anything you want me to do, just tell me. Anything!"*

"I hear you," De'marco said. *"Right now, I want you to fill me in on the guy. What's his problem? Is he normal? Tripped out? What?"*

"Okay," Connie said, *"I can do that."*

She proceeded to tell De'marco how she met Jerome and what she knew about him. How he used to have his own salon and was doing well at one time, but he kept getting caught up in situations until he lost everything. She gave him a job at the shop because he could do hair and he had the clientele. She knew he was capable of some bullshit, but she never would have guessed this, and not with an associate of hers.

As she finished, she told him, *"Like I said before, if you need me for anything, I'm here. But, it wouldn't be a bad idea to put the police on him. He's stalking you and you have witnesses. To hell with him! If he's down for some silliness like that, then let the 'folks' handle him."*

"Yeah, maybe you're right," he said. *"Well, it's late, I'll holler at you another time."*

Connie couldn't help but ask, *"De'marco, where does this leave us?"*

De'marco let out a small laugh. He felt Jerome was a direct result of him dealing with her, but he also knew she wasn't responsible for this man's actions.

"Good question," he told her.

Having no idea where it came from, Connie blurted out, *"I love you."*

"Bye Connie," De'marco said hanging up the phone.

As he placed the phone on the table, he stood to head back to the bedroom.

"So, is everything okay?" Jennifer asked.

De'marco hadn't noticed her sitting on the couch.

"How long she had been sitting there!?" He wondered. *"Everything is fine."*

She stood up and grabbed his hand in the dark, *"So, we can return to bed?"*

"Yes, we can," De'marco told her leading the way. As they snuggled back under the covers, she sighed.

"What's wrong with you?" De'marco asked her.

"When are you going to tell me the truth about you and Connie?" she said.

"I've told you," he said, *"There's nothing else to tell. Now, let's go to sleep. It's late."*

"It was late when you dialed her number," she told him, *"But, I'll go to sleep."*

De'marco hadn't realized the volume on his cell was up loud enough that in the quiet of the apartment while Jennifer sat on the couch listening, she not only heard Connie ask where does that leave us, she also heard the woman say, 'I love you'. De'marco fell asleep first, and it was Jennifer's turn to toss and turn in bed, only she had no one to get up and call.

* * * * * * * * * * * * * * * * *

Sunday went by quickly, with the exception of De'marco speaking to Leroy and his father. He and Jennifer slept most the day away. They slept so much Sunday, they woke up at four a.m. Monday. De'marco cooked them breakfast while they talked and he told Jennifer he wasn't going into work today because he was going to the police department to place a report on Jerome. That was partially true. He also hoped that by not going in today, it would allow the gossip of Saturday's incident to die down. He helped Jennifer bathe and get dressed. As he saw her off, he told her to call him at noon and if he was done at the police station they would do lunch. Jennifer kissed him and told him that would be fine, and off to work she went, on time.

De'marco decided he would lie back down for an hour before getting dressed.

* * * * * * * * * * * * * * * * *

It was Monday morning and Jerome sat on his couch looking through the want ads. Ever since Connie fired him and people got wind of what happened, it had been hard for him to get back in a salon. Hair had been his bread and butter. It was all he knew, the only job he'd ever had and now that was ruined because of Connie and some young big sweet penis fling she was having.

"That's okay though," Jerome thought, *"I'll fix both of them."*

He'd done his research on the internet and had what information he needed to keep up with De'marco. He was content with the thought of getting De'marco to become his lover. He had even pulled up over De'marco's parents house at one time, with the intention of causing havoc there. When he arrived and saw Martzu walking from the mailbox and the size of him, he decided against it. The thought of revenge and what he saw in De'marco's pants that night didn't compare with the evil Jerome had inside of him. He was so determined to get back at Connie through De'marco. He knew she was in love with him, and planned on hurting her by becoming his lover. He was young and inexperienced when it comes to true game. These were just a few of the foolish thoughts he entertained as he sat on his couch looking at all the bills piled in front of him.

"Let me get this ball rolling," he thought as he reached over for the phone to call De'marco.

* * * * * * * * * * * * * * * * *

De'marco rolled over, not really sleeping, more so deep in thought. He had called in to work. His supervisor overstood and told him to take as long as he needed to get things worked out. He called Leroy to ask him where he needed to go, and to whom he needed to talk to. Leroy gave him the information he needed and told him he had a gun he would sell to him in the event he decided to take things into his own hands.

"Thanks, but no thanks," De'marco told him, even though he honestly felt that wasn't a bad idea. It was eleven a.m. He knew he wouldn't be able to meet Jennifer for lunch, so he figured he'd better call her. The battery in his cell phone began to die down, so he placed it on the charger and used the house phone.

"Hi baby!" Jennifer answered happily. *"So what's up? Is it on? Where we eating at?"*

"I'm sorry baby," De'marco said, *"I'm just getting ready to leave out. I had to make some calls and things took longer than I expected."*

"Oh well," she said, *"I wasn't hungry anyway. So where you headed now?"* She asked.

De'marco's phone began vibrating on the charger.

"Hold on baby," he said.

He snatched the phone up, *"Hello!"*

"Hey, De'marco baby!" Jerome said trying to sound like a female.

"Who is this?" De'marco asked.

"It's me baby, Jerome."

De'marco lost it, *"What the hell you calling my phone for? And what is the problem with you? Where's all this foolishness coming from?"*

Jerome had expected this and his evilness had gone into overdrive.

"Look baby, I'm sorry for what has taken place. Maybe we can talk about it. Yeah, that's what we should do, get together and talk about it. Want me to come over?"

"What!" De'marco said, *"Are you crazy!? You mean to tell me you know where I live?"*

Jerome told him his address and then added, *"I would have been come over, but you got the little piece of fish over there."*

"Fish? What!?" De'marco said.

"You know?!? Jennifer." Jerome said.

To hear this crazed fool say the name of the person he loved must have sent him over the top. He himself became evil.

"You know what Jerome…?!?"

"What baby?"

"I know where you live too." De'marco told him, *"And I'm on my way there."*

"Okay, I'll be here."

De'marco hung up and went to put the rest of his clothes on. He was determined to hurt Jerome. He called Leroy and made plans to meet him so he could get the gun. He hung up and left out in a rage. He had something for Jerome. He thought, *"Sure do."*

* * * * * * * * * * * * * * * * *

Jennifer heard every word of the conversation between De'marco and Jerome, in fear of something terrible happening, she left work. Headed after De'marco, she called the house phone and got no answer. She called his cell phone and it kept going to voice mail. She was unaware that De'marco left it at the apartment and the battery was dead. She had no idea how to reach Leroy, and wasn't sure if she should call De'marco's mother and alarm her. So she did the next best thing. She called the other woman. Yep, she called Connie.

She had been aware that De'marco was dealing with someone else for awhile, especially when he stayed out late and didn't return home until the next day. Regardless of what De'marco's excuse was, she was no fool. When her and Connie talked during the party at her house it was all put on front street between them.

They exchanged numbers and had been in touch periodically ever since.

The thought of sharing her man was crazy and unheard of, until she spoke with De'marco's mother one time about what she should do concerning his being out until the next morning. De'shawntu told her, for many years the men of the Mandingo have had more than one woman. Many of them had their women live in the same house. She told Jennifer of the several occasions she'd shared Martzu.

She looked Jennifer in the eye and didn't blink when she told her De'marco is no different. It's in his blood. *"He will have other women,"* she told her. *"And although it may calm down a great deal, it will be that way into his old age."*

De'shawntu also informed her if she was unable to handle it or refused to put up with it, she should pull out now before it's too late and her feelings got too far gone. Then she would drive herself and him crazy trying to cope with it.

Jennifer remembered crying when she asked, *"De'shawntu, how do you go about dealing with it. Once your feelings are already deeply caught up?"*

De'shawntu told her, *"As crazy as it sounds, find out who the other woman is and become friends with her."* Jennifer eyes got big when she said that.

"What!? Are you serious?"

"Yes," De'shawntu told her. *"The reason why is, it allows you to know who he's with and where he's at when he's not with you. As well as, you know who your competition is. That also allows the two of you to work together in keeping him from branching out with his desire to have a harem of women. As crazy as it may sound, fight it if you so choose, but you'll lose in the end. For it is not a matter of his mind state, but a condition of his nature, and every man on this god given planet shall live out their nature. That's the one thing you can rest assure of and in closing, know this, the*

more of a man's nature you acknowledge and are aware of, the easier it is for you to exist in peace and harmony with this man. Hold tightly to these words my child and overstand them in order that you do not become foolish like the many women of American society who live to grow old having had many, many men. Yet, have none by their side when they die, because they spent their life fighting a losing battle to change a man's nature, something that was never meant to be changed. If it was, God would not have given it to them that way. And many women know this to be true but, yet fail to accept and deal with its reality until they've grown too old to be desired."

Those words hit Jennifer like a ton of bricks. Her grandmother had plenty of money, but had been married three times. She would always say, *"I ain't dealing with no cheating man."* She died alone. Her mother had money, and dealt with several men and was growing older. This was the reason she accepted Connie. When they spoke, there was a mutual agreement although they had not told De'marco. They decided if he requested it, they would have put up no fight.

"Hello! Hello!" Connie yelled into the phone.

"Connie listen, this is Jennifer."

Jennifer began telling Connie what had taken place on the phone between De'marco and Jerome. Connie told Jennifer to come by the shop and they would ride together to Jerome's place. They both agreed that De'marco, though he was angry, more than likely wouldn't take things too far, as neither of them had ever seen him truly violent.

* * * * * * * * * * * * * * * * * *

De'marco wasted no time meeting with Leroy, who sold him the gun. Yet and still, he told him he was only kidding about taking matters into his own hands.

"Yeah," De'marco said, *"I hear you. I'm just gonna scare him a little. If that don't work, I'll put the police on him."*

He pulled off before Leroy could say anything else. Leroy called his cell phone, no answer. He wanted to tell De'marco there weren't any bullets in the gun and he could have sold him a couple for twenty-five cents each.

De'marco pulled up at Jerome's place with the thought of blood on his mind. Jerome's blood at that. He pulled the gun out and approached Jerome's door. He was angry and afraid. He had never hurt anyone and really didn't want to now. He knocked, then rang the doorbell. He knocked again. He heard a voice say, *"Hold your horses,"* and started fumbling with the locks on the other side of the door.

De'marco asked himself, *"What am I doing?"* As he put the 22 automatic in his pocket. Jerome snatched open the door wearing a woman's sleep shirt. He knew De'marco was mad, and if for no other reason, he knew he would come. So, Jerome was ready. He started running his game.

"Oh, oh, De'marco I know you're mad."

"Damn right!" De'marco said as Jerome unlocked and opened the screen door.

"Listen," Jerome said, *"Let me tell you why I did those silly things. It was all because of Connie."*

* * * * * * * * * * * * * * * * * *

Jennifer arrived at the shop in no time. She knew where it was because she had taken her mother there on many occasions. When she came in the door, Connie was on somebody's head. Jennifer was pissed.

"Look Connie, what you gonna do?"

"I'm coming," Connie said, *"I'm almost finished. I had already started when you called. Not to mention, you got here so fast."*

217

Jennifer would have left her, but she had no idea of where Jerome lived. Connie finished within twenty minutes.

"Come on girl. We'll take my truck."

Jennifer looked over at her and said, *"I thought hair salons weren't open on Mondays."*

"They're not," Connie said, *"That's what happens when you owe somebody a favor. They want you to go out of your way to repay them. Put your seatbelt on."* She then looked at Jennifer's pregnant belly and said, *"That's if you can. Cause I'ma be driving fast. Jerome lives a little ways from here."*

"Oh great!" Jennifer said, *"I should have just called the police."*

"It'll be okay," Connie said, *"Now tell me what happened again?"*

* * * * * * * * * * * * * * * * * *

Jerome concocted some outrageous story about Connie and her plan to hook him and De'marco up. But first, she planned to turn him out. He fixed De'marco a drink and handed it to him. De'marco had no intentions of drinking with this fool, who was even crazier in person. He couldn't believe, when he looked down into the glass, he saw what looked like a pill dissolving. He pretended to be drinking it as Jerome kept on with this story.

"Man, this is a strong drink," De'marco said, *"What is it?"*

"Oh it's Henny," Jerome said, *"Let me go get you a chaser."*

As he went in the kitchen, he pulled the knife out the back of the thongs he had on.

"Won't be needing this," he told himself.

He poured a glass of Pepsi, *"Pretty soon, that X will kick in and I'll have him."*

He ran back into the living room and handed De'marco the glass of soda, noticing De'marco's glass of Hennesy was empty.

"I see you finished your drink, you want another one?"

"Sure," De'marco said.

To the contrary, De'marco had lifted up the cushion on the couch and poured the drink out. Jerome handed him another drink and sat down, purposely putting his feet up on the couch so his night shirt rose up, showing his nuts sticking out the sides of the thong, that was made for a woman, no doubt. De'marco turned his head away in disgust, feeling his anger rekindle inside him.

Jerome had the nerve to try him by saying, *"Don't worry, we won't use that unless you say so. You'll learn, I'm very submissive."*

That blew De'marco's top. He began replaying all the things Jerome had done, from Connie's party, to the fight at the shop, the stalking, the invitation at his job, to how he crashed the baby shower and said those embarrassing things to make him look bad. He then remembered his father calling Sunday afternoon telling him he didn't know what that was all about and he had never been so embarrassed. And for the first time in his life, he heard his father say he was ashamed and disappointed in the steps he had taken in his life that lead to this.

At that point, he just cocked back as far as he could. Jerome was so caught up in telling more of his lie he never saw it coming. De'marco slapped him upside his head so hard, Jerome saw a white light and his ears started ringing.

Before he could move, De'marco snatched his puny body up off the couch. When Jerome came back to his senses, De'marco had him bent over and heard him say, *"You want to be fucked by a man?"*

Jerome didn't care for the smack upside the head and had he had time, he would have returned the blow with the half-empty liquor bottle. But since De'marco had him bent over, tearing his thong off. He was thinking, *"Okay, he likes it rough. Bring it on."* Jerome's evil had gotten the best of him at that moment. He didn't notice De'marco snapped from the pressure.

"You want a man to fuck you so bad you are willing to ruin his life? Destroy his family…" As he spoke, he spat on his hand and stroked his manhood.

"Bring that mo….,"

Before Jerome could finish, De'marco rammed his meat in Jerome's rectum.

"Oh my God!" Jerome yelled. *"Hold up baby boy."*

But De'marco heard nothing, as he dug into Jerome. Everything kept flashing through his mind, of how the psychotic fool of a man had set out to ruin his life behind some shit with him and Connie. All De'marco saw was visions of the baby shower, the car chase, Jennifer questioning him, doubting him, his father's words, people at work laughing at him. De'marco snapped, his grip was so fierce on Jerome he didn't feel Jerome clawing at his hands, nor did he hear Jerome telling him to stop. De'marco just pumped and pumped as hard as he could. He lifted Jerome off the floor. He was stroking him so violently. Jerome looked like a rag doll in De'marco's hands. De'marco pumped and pumped until he came back to his senses and he felt a burst of wetness on his penis.

"I know he didn't cum out his ass," he thought. It made him pump Jerome's already limp body several more times. Then he heard Jennifer's voice.

"De'marco!" What have you done!?" She yelled.

He looked over his shoulder to see Jennifer and Connie standing there. Connie had her hands over her mouth as if she was in shock. Jennifer grabbed her stomach and started crying. De'marco just looked at them.

He then said, *"What's wrong with y'all?"*

He looked down to see himself holding Jerome's lifeless body in his hands with blood coming out of his rectum, where his penis was also inserted. As he slowly loosened his grip, Jerome's body slid from his hands to the floor, face down with his butt sticking up.

To be continued…

A DION JONES NOVEL

Thanks...
To the Creator for giving me the ability to write
and have such a vivid imagination☺. To my A-
Team, Wylena & Vonetta, get'em girls!

I'd love to say thanks to all who have supported
me by purchasing Mandingo Love. And to all my
people in Columbus, Ohio. What's up?! Family
and friends. Much love to all of you.

Shout outs to:
Jennifer Keaton, "lil" Dion, Derrick, Mrs. Keaton,
Ira. My cousins, Baby Harry, Kim, Tiffany, Bear,
Ray, Peanut. Greg, Rufus, Lisa, Debbie, David,
Donny a.k.a. D Dub, Derrick Lipsy a.k.a. Lipo,
and all the Easley and Watkins side, Calvin, Scott,
Connie, Larry a.k.a. Lynch, Cindy, Monica,
David, Mario, Aunt Brenda, Aunt Ann, HA!☺
Aunt Linda, Marshawn. The entire Jones side—
friends and associates, James E. Freeman Ha,Ha!
Leroy, Albert, WHAT?! Michelle Dyson, Mike,
Ant, Chill Will, Kelly Mabra, Tiffany, Debbie
Summers and Nicole Gregs, Tangie Ponder
(white), Juanita Harris, Lauren Lovell (L.L. Lady
Love), The Grove, Shelby, Monique Freeman,
Sharlon Howard (Detroit), Tammy Oliver,
Davonte, Eugene Vaughn, Ernest Day, Yo! Sister
Nicole, Debbie, Joe, Jeff Smith, Dee Miller,
Yolonda, George Brown (Tink), Missy Finny,
Karen Clark (Northside), Caren Murphy. The
Coats, all y'all, Tom, Nikki, Lesleda, Etta, Angie

*McClendon, Tyreik, Leslie Fuqua, Mark
AnthonyII (Mic). Tonia Moore, Brian Gregs,
Victor Latimore, Samiko Whiteside (So Sexy, So
Fine), Anesfia (Niecy) South Carolina, Ozzy ATL
baby, Andre, Lamont (Texas). To my brother and
sister, Skeat, and Desiree, Love y'all! Much love
to Columbus, Ohio from your undercover (hint)
bad boy.
If I didn't mention you, nothing personal, my
editors weren't feeling all the shout outs☺.*

*It's simple, pen in one hand, pad in the other, I'm
the literary world's champ!*

Love, Dion Jones

*For Comments Or What Have You, Hit Me At
djnovelist@aol.com*

<u>Coming Soon!</u>

Turned Out (A Mandingo Love Sequel)

Player, Cheater, Or Damn Fool

The Madam

For Ordering Information Call 770-897-9990, Or Order Your Book Online At:
    www.penhousepublishing.com